The Longer Road Home

A Modern Day Self-Help Tale

by Cat Cohen

Published by Cat Cohen Unltd

OTHER BOOKS by CAT COHEN

Road Horizon Division
MY DESERT BLOG CABIN (2009/2013)
How the author came to build his home in a rural settlement twenty miles north of Palm Springs.

TALES OF A CENSUS WORKER (2011)
A journal of the author's experiences while canvassing for the 2010 census in the high desert areas of Southern California.

ROAD STORIES SOUTHWEST (2010/2013)
Off-the-beaten-path travel adventures from three journeys in New Mexico, Arizona, Southern Colorado and Northeastern Baja California.

ROAD POEMS U.S.A. [Snapshots in Verse] (2010)
Insightful observations and photos from the author's coast-to-coast journeys from southwest to northeast and points in between.

Savory Publications Division
CHICKEN SOUPS FROM AROUND THE WORLD (2011)
Chicken soup recipes from 39 countries covering techniques and ingredients from equatorial Africa to arctic Alaska and very many temperate zones.

WHINE CONNOISSEUR'S GUIDE (2009/2013)
co-author Avry Budka   A tongue-in-cheek guide to the history of whines, whinemaker's art, whining and dining, whines for every occasion.

DIVING OUT IN LA (1984/1986)
co-author Avry Budka   A nostalgic and witty cult classic guide to the best low-cost eateries in the Greater Los Angeles area during the 1980s.

Koan Music Division
WRITING AND MARKETING SONGS FOR AN ORIGINAL ACT (2013)
An informative discussion of important songwriting issues questions such as performance, message, audience, genre, style, and industry format.

THE LONGER ROAD HOME

Written by Cat Cohen
Edited by Avry Budka
Cover Design by Gwyn Kennedy Snider

C 2015 [David] Cat Cohen

ISBN # 978-0-9899390-3-4

Library of Congress Control Number 2015913314
Published by Cat Cohen Unltd, Morongo Valley, CA 92256

Printed in the United States of America

Cat Cohen Unltd
ROAD HORIZONS DIVISION
PO Box 275   Morongo Valley, CA 92256
cat@catcohen.com   www.catcohen.com

First Edition – August, 2015

Disclaimer

The Longer Road Home is a fictional work. Though most events are based on real life stories, the names, locations, and details have been changed to protect innocent and guilty alike, both living and deceased. The focus here is on the lessons learned in Sam's struggle to overcome a multitude of inherited and self-afflicted wounds on his long and winding path to self-realization.

There is an eagle in me that wants to soar,
and there is a hippopotamus in me
that wants to wallow in the mud

Carl Sandburg, American Poet

ACKNOWLEDGEMENTS

I want to pay tribute to many of my fellow night owls, musicians, recovering addicts, and AIDS patients whose trials, tribulations and valiant efforts to rise above the obstacles in their paths helped give me the impetus to create this book.

I want to thank my friends Norma Fain Pratt, Karen Robinson Stark, Liz Howard, and my cousin Madi Lake for encouraging me to write down this story. Much appreciation goes to Avry Budka, my self-titled editrix, for ironing out countless kinks in this text and guiding me though the challenging transition from narrative journalist to fiction writer.

In addition, I am grateful to have received valuable feedback from Linda Barnett, Harold Piascik, Frank Amos, Steve Fuji, Stina Jacobson, Igor Koruluk, Bruce Singer, Desda Zuckerman, Jo Anne Kurman, and Geoff Forward, who took the time to read early drafts of this text and give me valued constructive criticism.

While getting this work ready for publication, I received helpful ideas and support from fellow Palm Springs Writers Guild members Ed Lopatin, Bob Hurlbert, Melody Fleming, John Fraim, and Arlene Morgan, among others. I've also been a grateful recipient of encouragement and sage professional advice from book distributor Amy Collins and my book cover illustrator Gwyn Kennedy Snider.

Finally, I'd like to express my gratitude to 12-step buddies Connie B., Rufus B., Allene P., and Lowell S. for some of their tasty quotations that I've incorporated here.

The eagle flies on Friday, Saturday I go out to play.
Sunday I go to church and get down on my knees and pray

Lyric from "Stormy Monday Blues"

FOREWORD

This book is a work of fiction, a chronicle of Sam Freberg's life. Sam's narrative is based on the tales of people in the pop music, gay, New Age, Native American, HIV, and 12-step communities that I've had the privilege to be part of. It covers a span of recent American history as seen through my reluctant hero's eyes, and I've tried to encapsulate several social and liberation movements through the lens of his personal and spiritual evolution.

I hope Sam's efforts to grow from doubt to confidence, weakness to strength, and self-deception to the discovery of his unique truth serves as an inspiration for others who have traveled or entertain embarking on similar journeys. No matter how far down life leads you, or how dark the traps you fall into, draw on your inner fortitude, keep the faith, and don't stop believing in yourself.

Love and enlightenment to all,

Cat Cohen

TABLE OF CONTENTS

<u>INTRODUCTION</u>

Featured Speaker

I awoke one fall morning with a knot in my stomach. The first thing I saw was my labor of love, the house I'd recently built on my desert acreage. On some days I wanted to pinch myself to make sure that this refuge was not a figment of my imagination. But on this day there was no urge to pinch; I was overcome with fear. As much as I wanted to retreat to the sanctuary of sleep, I got out of my sofabed, gathered the covers, and put the frame back into couch form. Walking into my living room, I couldn't help but see the photo on the fireplace mantel of me as a hippie with long hair performing at the keyboard where I'd once scrawled *[SEX - Cool! DRUGS - Cool! ROCK 'N ROLL - Forever!]*.

Trying to overcome my anxiety, I prepared my usual brew of dark roast, glanced out the kitchen window to the colorful flowerpots outside, and raised a cup of joe in a gesture of celebration to the day. Starting to feel better, I turned on the radio hoping to catch the weather report on the local rural station. Instead, I heard Amy Winehouse's smoky cigarette-affected voice singing that she didn't want to go to rehab. The ache in my gut came back. I wasn't looking forward to my 12-step meeting that day.

Ordinarily, this was a source of support and fellowship I enjoyed. However, I was to be the featured speaker telling my story of descent into addiction, rebirth through the program, and recovery from a lifetime of sick behavior. I'd suffered through so many desperate all-nighters trying to camouflage the emptiness I felt after a string of disappointing romantic relationships. These failures were products of a history of low self-esteem, having been the punching bag of a dysfunctional family and growing up as a gay man in a disapproving straight world.

I was haunted by how I'd fallen into such an abysmal lifestyle and how much work I'd had to do to climb out of it. This took years of spiritual study, therapy sessions, and participating in recovery groups like my current one. As I got dressed, I wondered how I could synopsize six decades in only thirty minutes. I slipped on a pair of new running shoes, a sharp contrast to the weather-beaten pairs I used to slink around in, my earlier days having been filled with so much guilt and shame.

I knew the group wanted me to be an inspiration to the new arrivals with their freshly revealed wounds, a testimonial of encouragement to those with short-time sobriety, and a validation of steadfastness to the longtime abstainers like me. Some of these veterans had been there to help me get back on my feet when I used to fall off the wagon repeatedly. "Sam, this was only a slip." "We've all been there." "Stay on the path." "Don't use this as an excuse to act out again." And so on.

I prayed to my Higher Power to find a balance between my admissions of wrongdoing and story of redemption. My nerves were so rattled one would have thought I was going to address an arena full of people, not a modest gathering of fellow addicts. I remembered my high school mentor Mrs. B, the woman who'd launched me on a path to self-discovery in my teens, hoping her spirit would guide me as I spoke.

While preparing breakfast, I whistled for my affectionate pit bull Reyna and filled her doggie bowl with kibble. After we each finished our meals, I leaned over to allow her, as misunderstood by society as I'd been, to give me a tongue bath. She licked my face with the appreciation I needed. Ever since I plucked her away from a life of abuse in a neighboring hamlet, we'd bonded in a mutual co-existence of comfort. "Good girl. I love you too. Stay here and be a good dog. We'll play fetch when I get back. I promise."

Reyna went over to her doggie bed, sat down, and started licking her paws. I wished that I possessed the wellspring of happiness she exhibited, a constant source of amazement to me. As I looked over to see her Buddha-like face, I reminded myself that I was getting there in my own way. Grabbing the keys to my pickup truck, I repeated the Serenity Prayer attached to the keychain to remind me of this.

I glanced down at my watch, relieved there was time to spare. Yet this cushion was just more space to ruminate about what I was going to say to the group. As I drove down the hill, my life seemed to flash before my eyes. How could I live up to everyone's expectations?

While winding around a curve in the road, I heard a thumping sound. *Oh no*, I thought, *not a flat tire*. When I pulled over to the side of the asphalt, my right front tire had deflated to the rim. "Damn," I cursed. This truck had a jack, but I'd never learned how to use it properly. I got out my cell phone and hurriedly called AAA. Upset at my bad luck, I yelled impatiently to the dispatcher, "Hurry, I need help right away." After giving her the location, I added, "I'm late to a meeting."

She replied, "Sorry, there's one person before you. Our driver will get there as soon as he can. It should take about 30 to 45 minutes."

I hung up and called my sponsor. "Darryl, wouldn't you know, I've got a flat tire and have to wait for assistance. I'll probably be late. With my luck, I won't even be able to make the meeting."

"Sam, what are you talking about?" he responded. "I bet you forgot about Daylight Savings. There's two hours before we start."

I cringed, feeling like an idiot. "Gosh, I did forget. Boy, did I leave early. Maybe I can still get there on time."

"If you can't make it, we can always reschedule your presentation."

"But I'm so psyched up for it." I didn't want to reschedule now that there was a chance for me to attend. "This was supposed to be my big day. Why do things like this always happen to me? I'm sick of…"

"Hey, you're talking like a victim again. You've been in recovery long enough to know that shit happens to all of us. Don't worry. It'll work out. Keep me posted and I'll share it with the group."

"Right. I'll try to chill. I'll call you as soon as I'm back on the road."

After hanging up, I realized I'd been flying off the handle like my rageaholic parents. I was raised in a family where every molehill was turned into a mountain and every mountain a transcontinental range. I started reliving these formative years, examining how my life was set in motion even before I was born. I remembered what my mom had told me about how she'd met my dad, and went on from there.

PART 1
AS TWIGS WERE BENT

CHAPTER 1
TROUBLED CHILD

Irv and Sheila

My turbulent history started the way most of ours do with the coming together of two adults of opposing genders during their reproductive years. My parents, Irv and Sheila, were working-class Jews who moved to California from the crowded streets of Brooklyn and Queens. In their late twenties, they were drawn to each other for differing reasons.

As my mom approached thirty she hadn't found a partner, much to her parents' chagrin. Her younger sister Ellen had married an ambitious fellow named Jack who was off to a promising start in the costume jewelry business. Gertie, their mother, warned Sheila, "No prospects, mine daughter? I didn't raise you to be an old maid. If a gentleman asks you to dinner, don't play hard to get."

One day, Jack brought Irv Freberg, a buddy of his, over to meet my mom, hoping to interest them in each other. Irv was attracted to her curvaceous body, even as he was put off by her strong personality. Her sights were set on a well-to-do gentleman who'd court her with flowers and charm. Blue-collar Irv had a romantic repertoire as limited as his pocketbook. Yet he had a quality that promised, if not affluence, a sense of security. After dating for a while they began a passionate affair.

The 1930s were winding down. Europe was on the brink of war and finding jobs during the Great Depression was challenging. Tired of not working, Irv visited L.A. where his interest in engineering led him to try airplane maintenance, a growing source of employment there. It also might keep him out of the army in case war broke out. He got a position at a hangar in a hamlet in the desert and begged Sheila to join him there.

Reluctant to leave the nest of family and friends, she held out. But her parents kept after her to get hitched and she gave in, riding the Southern Pacific to California to be with him. The couple drove to Las Vegas as the 1940s began and got married in a civil ceremony without any friends or well-wishers present. There was no catering for Mr. & Mrs. Freberg, just a nice meal, some gambling, and onto their honeymoon suite.

They lived in a tiny rented house with a view of the nearby pine-covered mountains. Like her heroine Rosie the Riveter, my mom got a job on an assembly line making munitions. When the fighting ended, their positions were terminated. The pair moved to Los Angeles where they lived in a one-room apartment near downtown. They were so poor, their motto was "if we had ham, we'd have ham 'n eggs, if we had eggs."

Not long after the atomic bombs were dropped on Hiroshima and Nagasaki, I was conceived. A much smaller explosion took place in my mom's uterus when a Jewish sperm from my dad said "How do you do?" to one of her unfertilized eggs. Toward the end of the gestation period, he wondered if he'd married the wrong woman. As long as their love life had been heated, he overlooked her demands. Her honey-do's and don'ts grew as her discomfort increased. Sex became less frequent; his doubts festered.

In those days people rarely divorced. Though Irv wasn't relishing becoming a father, he accepted the duty of becoming the family provider. At a job with a firm manufacturing radios he learned how to produce them, a feat for someone with little education. He disliked following a fixed schedule and anticipated opening his own business.

Meanwhile, Sheila fantasized about a child who had important missions in life. Perhaps this was to make up for her not having had the opportunity to do anything special with her own. This focus on the new arrival came at the expense of her spouse, sowing the seeds of hostility between my father and me. Irv had mixed feelings. The thought of sharing his wife's decreasing amount of affection with the baby filled him with foreboding. But I was to be someone to pass on his lineage and, in a way, make him immortal. He was pragmatic. Her daydreams were an ongoing concern. How could any child live up to them?

My Early Arrival

Almost a month before my expected arrival Sheila started getting labor pains. As they increased in frequency, she asked Irv to take her to the hospital. I entered the world three weeks ahead of schedule. At five pounds, I was small for a newborn and would stay below average in stature until my teens.

My mom's Scottish doctor predicted that I'd have broad shoulders and grow up to become a champion swimmer. He probably told this to all the mothers of boys in the maternity ward. Mark Spitz, however, I was not meant to be. If I could have spoken then I might have wisecracked, "Doc, don't give my mom any crazy ideas. I'll be lucky if I can swim ten feet with an inner tube."

She had other plans for me, perhaps another Matisse, maybe another Picasso. Irv wanted me to pursue a career as a nuclear scientist, like the ones who'd recently developed the bomb at Los Alamos that had ended the war. That was a respectable field of work, not a sissified one like an artist.

Soon after I was born, my father opened his own radio shop. He spent long hours there, leaving early and coming home as late as possible. His employees said he was a kind and compassionate boss. Yet at home he was a tyrant, and my parents fought repeatedly.

He'd yell, "Did that brat spill his cereal again? He should know better."

She'd protest, "But he's only a toddler."

"You're too soft. If you don't stop him, he'll walk all over you."

Hearing them argue, I cried loudly. My dad yelled, "Aren't you going to do something? Give him a *clop on the cup*! That'll shut him up!" Instead of silencing me, it only made me cry even more. He exited the front door shouting, "I can't take any more of this. I'm going back to the shop. That boy better be quiet when I return."

My father fell into a pattern of chastising me for every little mistake, real or imagined, while my mom protested in vain. Having no say in this, I grew up feeling guilty for my most basic needs, let alone my wants.

When I was two years old, we moved to a tiny one-bedroom house off Venice Boulevard with a large lemon tree in the backyard. I liked to climb down the wooden stairs into the grassy area surrounding the tree and delighted in scooping up blossoms and smelling their fragrance.

I enjoyed riding with my mother downtown on the Red Car rail line to the Grand Central Market where she shopped for produce at the European-like stalls. Buying the freshest merchandise at the lowest price, she'd exclaim, "These strawberries are only 10 cents a pound. What a bargain! I'll cut up some for you as soon as we get home."

"Mommy, I don't want any berries. Can't we stop at the candy booth where you buy me some licorice? Please? Please?"

Judy & Leslie

When I was five, my father transported his business into a larger shop, and our family moved to a modern apartment complex in nearby Glendale. At the end of the '40s, my sister Judy was born. I was intrigued by her arrival. At first, I liked helping to care for her. But sometimes I was jealous for not getting the attention I was used to. Her tantrums soon spoiled any peace left in the family. I retreated into my own private world to block out the dark emotions that erupted in the household. I'd come up with sinister plans to shut her up such as *The next time I get a tootsie pop, I'm going to stuff it in her mouth.*

A couple of years later, when my mom became pregnant again, we moved to Hollywood to be closer to my dad's shop. The nondescript stucco apartment building was near where, thanks to Eisenhower's national highway system, a new freeway was being constructed. I liked to scamper off to the site, play in the construction zone, and enjoy staring at the workmen as they built the scaffolding. Neither of my parents noticed anything queer about me at the time. They might have had suspicions if they'd heard me sighing, "I wish I had muscles like that. What a man."

We lived close to the famous Capitol Records building with its distinctive circular architecture. Not far away were celebrity names inlaid in gold letters below stars on the pavement starting at Hollywood and Vine. While watching the same TV shows as the rest of America, we had no more connection to Tinseltown than someone living in Iowa.

One day when my mom was walking me down this famous thoroughfare, I whined, "Why don't I get a star?"

She replied, "Honey, you're a star to me. That's all that matters."

By the time I was seven years old, we still lived an insular existence, not going out to the colorful movie theaters nearby or dining in any famous local restaurants like Musso and Frank's. If we'd done so, I would have begged for a bowl of Musso's French onion soup with a layer of Gruyere cheese on top. Instead, my wish list was more modest - a Swanson TV dinner of meat loaf and mashed potatoes.

When Leslie, the youngest member of the family, was born, I was excited to have another sister. Judy resented her new sibling and made life uncomfortable for her. I was a sensitive child and felt their pain, cracking corny jokes to dispel the tension and often escaping to a safety net I built deep inside myself. Sometimes I'd go on a long bike ride and leave my sisters at home to duke it out.

Judy had light brown hair and blue eyes while Leslie was as dark as my dad. I was in between with his dark hair and my mom's blue eyes. One day, Leslie fell down the back porch stairs. Hearing her cries, my mom screamed hysterically and summoned my father. "Come home quick. Leslie hurt herself. She needs you 'til the ambulance gets here."

"Ambulance? I'll be right there. Did Sam push her again?

"What do you mean?"

"That instigator son of yours drives those girls nuts. I'll give him what he deserves when I get home."

"No you won't. He had nothing to do with this."

"Stop coddling that little bastard."

"He's your son, too. Just because he doesn't have your brown eyes doesn't mean that…"

"Enough already. I'll be right over."

As Leslie was rushed to the hospital, my father was sure that I was at fault. In his eyes, Judy could do no wrong and I could do no good. Although it was an accident, there was enough guilt in my family to go around. Being the oldest child, I bore the effects of most of it.

On my eighth birthday, while playing by the unfinished freeway, I pierced my hand on a long nail. My mom rushed me to an emergency room. It was painful and scary. When the doctor gave me a tetanus shot, her hysteria only added to my discomfort.

During my convalescence, Judy felt compassion for my discomfort. I tried to put on a stoic act like my father, but I played the event for sympathy instead. "It's only a mild case of gangrene. Hopefully, they won't have to amputate the whole arm."

My dad was proud of my active mind and talent for mathematics. I'd memorized the calendar and could tell the day of the week anyone's birthday would fall on any given year. He'd show off my mental prowess, bragging that I was a chip off the old block. I also loved maps, spending hours reading the L.A. Thomas Guide, following the main roads from one side of the city to the other.

But other facets of my personality deeply disturbed him. When he tried to take me to join a few buddies on a man's night out at a wrestling match, I refused to go and made a fuss until I got left at home. I preferred to stay with my mom and listen to her friends talk recipes and complain about their husbands' behaviors. I mimicked their gestures in such a way that I became a laughing stock.

One night, a friend of hers asked, "Where's my purse? I need to freshen my makeup. Oh, isn't that cute? Sam is carrying it like it was his own."

She tried to coax me, "C'mon Sammy, give it to your mother."

I whined, "Do I have to?"

My mom responded, "Yes. Be a good boy."

My father often said that I should have been born a girl. In contrast, Judy showed such loud aggressive behavior he'd joke that we should exchange gender. Clearly preferring his little girls, he was affectionate with them in ways he never showed to me. Instead, I suffered from his short fuse. It was not unusual after some violent corporal punishment for me to have horrible nightmares afterwards.

Nathan, my dad's father, had been born in Warsaw to very religious parents. As a boy, he rebelled and became a Communist. He and his wife Rachel ran a teahouse that became a meeting place for Marxists in the early 1900s. After the couple was arrested during a raid on the tearoom, they escaped from jail and fled to America, settling in a leftist community in Brooklyn. When my dad and his sisters Rebecca and Zelda were born, Nathan created excuses to go off on escapades with his Red cronies. He was a rolling stone who rarely stayed put.

To my father, Nathan was a source of shame. Worried that I would also never amount to anything, my dad became a harsh taskmaster in an attempt to thwart this. "We're raising a social misfit. He's got his grandpa's genes."

My mom protested, "How can that be? You like to complain he was the iceman's boy. You can't have it both ways."

"They say traits often skip a generation. Just wait until he grows up like Nathan, spouting Commie propaganda, wanting something for nothing."

"So instead you give him nothing, even when he does something right. He's got a good heart. You just refuse to see it."

This was the era of television's *Leave It To Beaver* and *Father Knows Best*. There was little resemblance between the Freberg family and the Cleavers. The politeness, obedience, and paternal wisdom of mythical TV was nowhere to be seen. We were in each other's faces, all talking at once. Nobody was ever listening. It was no wonder I grew up to be so disturbed.

Uncle Jack & Aunt Ellen

Meanwhile, Uncle Jack, Aunt Ellen, and their two daughters lived a luxurious life provided by his successful jewelry business. When they came to visit, they took us to swanky restaurants. I admired this side of the family. Once, when I tried to order an expensive dish off a menu at a plush eatery in Beverly Hills, my father chastised, "What do you want now?"

"Everyone else got to order escargot, why can't I?"

"You're too young for such a fancy dish."

"But I really want to try it. And veal cacciatore too."

"You're getting a hamburger plate and that's it."

When I protested, he smacked me on the face in front of everyone. Though aghast at this display of temper, no one called him out on it. I felt I wasn't even worth chopped liver, a dish I identified with. When the family got home after such events, I'd cry myself to sleep.

In the late '50s, we moved to a Jewish neighborhood so we children could learn about our heritage. Despite this, there was no mention of religion at home. Instead, my father reigned like the Almighty, as vengeful as the Old Testament deity. Deep inside, I believed there was a merciful God somewhere in the universe. He just didn't reside nearby.

My parents raged constantly, dinnertime a daily tirade. Indigestion was so prevalent that Tums were passed around like after-dinner mints. Sometimes in the middle of the night my dad would burst into my room to unleash his temper, cursing and hitting me until the anger was spent.

I compensated for these dark environs by pedaling my bicycle to travel agencies on Wilshire Boulevard, pretending I was planning a vacation abroad. I'd ask for brochures. One day, I took an elevator up to the top floor of a modern office building to tell the receptionist I was going to France. She escorted me into the office. As I stood in front of an agent sitting behind his desk, the man asked, "Son, can I help you?"

I started out in an authoritative voice, but had trouble keeping up the charade. "My mom sent me to find accommodations in France. We're planning a two-week vacation there, visiting Paris for several days."

The agent replied, "Which parts of the city will you be visiting?"

"Do you think we could stay at the Eiffel Tower?"

"Wait a minute, kid. Did your mother tell you that?"

"No. I don't know anything about Paris. But I really want to go there."

"Look, I've got a lot of customers to take care of and I don't have much time. Here's a pamphlet about what to see in Paris. Come back when you're serious about making arrangements."

I took the brochure and ran to a bus bench where I read through it. While I was excitedly going over the information, an older, well-dressed lady wearing a large formal hat sat down near me to wait for the next bus to Beverly Hills. I spoke to her with enthusiasm as I pointed to some images in my brochure. "Ma'am, I'm going to Paris. See, there's the Eiffel Tower and the Notre Dame cathedral."

The woman answered, "Really? My brother lives in the Latin Quarter."

"That sounds exciting. Do they speak Latin there? I know Pig Latin."

She took a pen and paper out of her purse, scribbling something and handed it to me. "When you get to Paris, look up my brother, Monsieur Alban. Tell him his sister Giselle said to show you around." When the bus arrived, she boarded and waved, "*Au revoir, mon cherie.*"

I was smitten with this woman's invitation. I rushed home to tell my mom. After listening intently, she gently tried to talk me out of this fantasy. Despite the fact she also wanted to visit Paris someday, she warned, "Don't share this with your father. He won't understand."

I continued my pursuit of travel itineraries, assuring agents that I'd be back to make reservations. Occasionally, I bragged about this to my dad who scolded me for being out of touch with reality. "If you mention one more trip to Europe, I'm going to pop you one. That's for rich people. Know your place. It isn't on a plane to France."

He tried to teach me to achieve my goals gradually, but I wanted everything right away. He predicted failure for every idea I came up with, every dream I got excited about. This caused me to live out his prophecy, reaching for the stars only to fall short again and again. After a while I stopped confiding anything important to him. Instead, I reached out to others, especially strangers who wouldn't confront me with the foolishness of my desires.

Uncle Ernie and Aunt Zelda

Relations from the other side of the family also came to visit. My dad's sister Zelda had married an easygoing man named Ernie. When these working class New Yorkers and their two vivacious daughters stayed with us, sleeping on sofas and rollaway beds, the quarters were cramped but everyone got along well. Unlike Uncle Jack and Aunt Ellen, they took time to relate to us. When I'd share one of my wild schemes, Zelda enjoyed playing along, making them even larger.

"Aunt Zelda, when I go to London, after seeing Big Ben, do you think they'd let me visit the Royal Palace?"

"I'm sure the Queen would want to meet a fine young man like you."

"Is there anything you want me to say to her?"

"Tell her that Zelda Bruckman from Long Island sends her best wishes and so does her husband Ernie."

"I can't wait to give her your message. Do I have to curtsey or bow?"

"Sammele, just be yourself. She'll understand."

Just as the two of us burst into laughter, my dad sent me to my room while he chewed out Zelda, "Don't indulge him like that."

She replied, "We're only playing. You take this too seriously."

Overhearing them, Ernie joined in, "The boy's ten years old. Let him enjoy being a child. He'll be an adult soon enough."

Zelda backed up her husband, "Ernie's right. Just because you had a rotten childhood doesn't mean you have to make his rotten as well."

My dad responded, "Stop telling me how to do my job. No boy of mine is going to grow up to become a fool."

I was grateful to have Ernie and Zelda in my life. I wished that I could have them for parents instead of mine.

A few years earlier, Sheila had told my father she'd heard that children with mathematical ability like me often had musical talent. He thought math was better off used in science, but she convinced him to let me have some piano lessons. They found a local music teacher.

Miss Brady lived in an old craftsman style house nearby. Taking to her instruction immediately, I also picked up notation skills from her. At home, I'd make up my own pieces. One day, I wrote down a composition and showed it to her. After the lesson, the usually staunch middle-aged lady ran outside to my mother and shouted, "You have a talented child. He could go far in music."

My mom couldn't wait to tell my father, "Miss Brady says Sam's got talent. Who knows? Maybe we've got another Mozart for a son."

"Don't get any ideas. She probably says that to all the parents, like that *cockamamie* doctor who told you he'd be a champion swimmer."

"We should start saving up to send him to Julliard."

"You're as bad as Zelda. Next thing you'll say is he's going to be the next Paderewski. It's enough you want me to pay for those lousy piano lessons. I'll not have my son grow up to become a starving musician."

I really enjoyed my sessions with Miss Brady, but when I went through a period when I didn't practice, my dad put a stop to the piano lessons. Though miffed, I found a new focus for my creativity at the public library where I checked out several books at a time. To keep me intellectually stimulated, as well as my sisters, he bought us the World Book Encyclopedia. I read volume after volume, sometimes pouring through every page savoring all things beginning with the letter "m" from cover to cover. In a typical afternoon I'd pour through malaria, mambo, Marshall Plan, marshmallows, and Martians.

I liked to quote facts about history, geography, and my favorite subject, diseases and their symptoms. After reading about an illness, I'd pretend to catch it. One summer, I fell ill with typhoid, the plague, dysentery, smallpox, and whooping cough, conditions that required nurse Judy's assistance. I whined, "I'm getting a tropical fever."

She replied, "Mommy's not home. What can I do?"

"Get me a damp washcloth and some aspirin."

"But I can't reach the medicine chest."

"Some good you are. Now I've got the chills."

"Mommy will be home soon."

"I just hope I'm still alive when she gets here."

When my mom returned, I broke out in a case of the sillies and cried out dramatically, "I've come down with Rocky Mountain Spotted Fever. You need to call an ambulance right away."

She did not think illness was a laughing matter. Having survived tuberculosis in her teens, she worried that her children would get deathly sick and took us to the doctor at the slightest symptom, which only made the whole family paranoid about our health. Despite all of this concern, she indulged us often in unhealthy treats. Every week saw a sweet tooth fed and glutted. The family fell into a daily sugar rush followed by a crash, an argument, and everyone off to bed without issues resolved.

At many a mealtime she'd bark, "Eat your broccoli."

"But I don't want broccoli, I want ice cream."

"Finish your vegetables or no one's getting dessert."

This tension was relieved by the arrival of Ernie and his family. I sat down at the piano and entertained everyone by playing one of my own compositions. Everyone applauded with much gusto, especially Ernie's daughters who were creative souls that appreciated the arts. My dad often bragged about my ability and then launch into a tirade that I refused to practice. Ernie protested that he expected too much from me.

After we children left the room, I overheard the adults arguing.

"Sam is so talented."

"The boy is too sensitive for his own good."

"What do you want from him, perfection? He plays beautifully."

"He's a *faigele*, going to bring us *tsuris* someday."

I had no idea what the word *faigele* meant, but I knew it wasn't good. I wished they'd stop arguing and leave me alone. But this was all chump change compared to the abuse I'd receive in my teen years.

CHAPTER 2
TEEN TRAUMA

Miss Stewart and Coach Stone

I was a quick learner in school and knew most of the answers. Hogging much of the discussion, I must have driven many of my instructors crazy. One day, when a teacher asked our class, "Can anyone tell me who was the first European to travel on the Mississippi River?" I shouted, "Hernando De Soto."

"Very good, Sam. Now does someone know in what year he did this?"

When no one else responded, I blurted out, "1541."

She snapped, "Let someone else answer the question. Raise your hand and I'll call on you when I'm ready."

One teacher, Miss Stewart, was especially alarmed at my type A personality. She tried assigning me extra work to keep me occupied and out of the other students' way. The more she threw at me, the more I rushed to finish it. Like the addict I was to become later in life, too much was never enough. "Miss Stewart, did you know that in 1950, Argentina had 23 provinces, a population of 17 million, a GDP per capita of $5,000, and its peso lost 70% of its value from 1948 to 1950?"

This woman suggested that I skip a year to be with students more at my mental level. Perhaps this might slow me down. She scheduled a conference with my parents and they agreed. I was bumped up a grade to the one just before secondary school. Though now I wasn't as ahead of my class, I was socially dislocated by not being with my friends. This was a hefty price for my advancement.

By the time I entered junior high, most kids were going through puberty. Already behind on my biological clock, I was further disadvantaged. This was a problem in gym class when the other boys started developing manly features and their penises started growing. I was ashamed of my undeveloped genitals. In the showers, I'd stare at the other boys' privates, then dart my eyes away before anyone would notice.

Coach Stone drove his students to do more calisthenics, run faster, and compete harder. I was a physical guy, but my body was so small I could barely keep up with the others. I also began daydreaming about some of the handsome athletes in my class. When the coach called any slacker a sissy or a faggot for falling behind, I kept my mouth shut.

One would think an issue like this would be something a boy could ask his father about, but there was a lack of communication between us. When it came to sexual matters, he was strangely mum. His only reference about sex was well after it became known that I'd already been told which body parts joined together to produce offspring.

He tried to dampen my curiosity. "Your mother told me you were bothering her about the birds and the bees again."

"I wanted to know why boys have penises and girls have vaginas."

"Don't use such vulgar language in our house."

"Are penises and vaginas bad things? My friend Michael talks about them all the time."

"You're too young to talk about sex."

Sheepishly, I asked, "Is sex a bad thing?"

"Sex is only for making babies. Otherwise, it's dirty and immoral."

"But Michael says…."

"I want you to stay away from Michael. If you mention any more sex talk around me, I'll clobber you."

My mom also never discussed sex with me, but became an influence by accident. She liked to read racy novels with graphic descriptions, sometimes leaving them lying around the house. When I was in my early teens, I found a copy of a salacious paperback on the living room coffee table and was captivated by the main character's first sexual experiences. Thinking no one else was home I fantasized about my role model's actions and started masturbating. My father suddenly walked into the living room and caught me in the act.

Instead of saying, 'Why don't you do that in your bedroom in private?" or "Masturbation isn't good for you." he raged, "I always thought you were a pervert. Now I know you are. You disgust me!"

I ran into my room before he could beat the crap out of me. When I recovered from the humiliation, I resorted to the hair of the dog that had bitten me. A compulsively sexual being was born.

There was nobody I could turn to for advice. This embarrassment stunted my sense of masculinity. My same-sex attraction only added to this negative image of myself as I grew to adulthood.

Reggie & Charlie

Down the block lived my friend Reggie, a boy I'd hung out with since the third grade. We'd ride our bikes together in the neighborhood. A few months older than me, Reggie was like the brother I'd always wanted. Whatever he did, I copied. When Reggie got a new flannel shirt, I wore one like it. When Reggie worked a paper route delivering the afternoon news, I got a similar one. After Reggie's mother served us spaghetti and meatballs, I begged my mom to do the same.

We played in the playground after school together. On the weekends, we'd take the bus and go fishing off the Santa Monica pier or go out on the half-day boats. We used similar fishing rods with the same reels, identical tackle boxes, and brought home bonita, sculpin, and bottom fish for our mothers to cook. Members of the same scout troops, we had a Mutt and Jeff quality about us, Reggie the taller Jeff, and me, the shorter, squatter Mutt. We shared a lot of fun times.

But when we entered our teens, this closeness disappeared. Reggie shot up several inches in height while I hardly grew at all. He began hanging out with girls instead of me. I didn't share this desire. "Hey, Reg, you wanna go fishing off the pier this weekend?"

He responded, "No, I'm busy."

"You're always busy these days."

"I'm seeing this girl, Dolores. She's absolutely wild about me. And she knows how to put out, too."

"That's good for you, but where does it leave me?"

"Go find your own chick."

"I'd rather hook me a bonita than chase a cheesy senorita."

"Not me, what I've got on the line is a lot more fun."

My hormones had not yet started motivating me. When they did, I found my male playmates more intriguing. The thought of snuggling up to a girl gave me the willies. I tried it once and found it very awkward. I missed hanging out with Reggie and was envious of his good looks and dirty blonde hair trained in a greaser-like pompadour with an Elvis Presley curl cascading from his forehead.

One day when I was hanging out in Reggie's house with Charlie, a mutual friend of ours, Reggie led us into a back room where he'd stashed some porn magazines. Tossing one to each of us, he opened a copy for himself. As he stared at the images of the big-breasted models inside, he opened the zipper to his levis and began playing with himself. Charlie and I did likewise. Reggie and Charlie were soon lost in fantasizing about these busty women.

Reggie exulted, "Miss June's big tits are gonna make me come."

Charlie shouted, "Miss July is getting me hot. How about you, Sam?"

I'd put my copy down and was busy staring at my friends' erections. They were much larger than mine. Reggie noticed this and called me out on it. "What are you looking at? You got our own magazine."

Charlie added, "What's the matter with you? Are you queer?"

Embarrassed, I ran home and locked myself in my room. Turned on by what I'd just witnessed, I finished what we'd started in solitary. Not able to get the images of my friends in their aroused states out of my mind, I repeated this activity often. Attracted to, yet afraid of what happened, I avoided Reggie and Charlie for several weeks. Our damaged friendships were never repaired after that.

Not only had I lost a fishing partner, I was threatened by the girls who'd taken him away from me. These were the ones who teased and peroxided their hair, doing their best to look seductive. After my dad's warning about the sinfulness of sex, I found them repulsive. The only girls I wanted to spend time with were nice ones with brains, not those who showed off their figures.

I made an overture to a homely girl named Jayne, "Hey, I know some interesting facts about Argentina. Would you like to split a hot fudge sundae while I tell you? I've got some brochures in my backpack."

"Sure, as long as it's a double scoop. But honestly, I'm not really interested in Argentina. OK?"

"Oh, all right."

At the age of fourteen I was one of the only kids in my class under five feet tall, male or female. I pretended that this didn't bother me and put on a clown act behind a mask that intensified with time.

I didn't have to grieve over the loss of my friendship with Reggie for long. My father had his sights set on a more modern home and began taking us to the San Fernando Valley to search for a new place to live. This happened when I was about to enter high school. Ready for a change, I had a new target on which to focus my energy. I thought *Oh boy, maybe I'll meet a nice girl there who wants to talk about Buenos Aires.*

Hard Landing In Redneck Suburbia

Every Sunday we explored housing developments, visiting a series of open houses. Searching for the largest home within our budget, my dad expressed this deep-seated desire to my mom. "Honey, can't you just see us in one of these huge houses? They're a far cry from those little shacks in Brighton Beach."

She answered in a dreamy voice. "I just love the large kitchens with all their push button appliances. O'Keefe & Merritt, Gaffers & Sattler, Amana, Whirlpool, I wouldn't know which one to press first."

Seductively, he teased, "In our swanky master bedroom with that tiled Roman Tub in the master bath, I'll give you a button you can press."

I became consumed in the family's quest for a new residence, pouring over the floor plans on the brochures of the model homes. I was more attracted to the design of these structures than their appliances and decor. I'd delight in penciling out residential designs of my own. Sometimes, I'd work past my bedtime and my folks would order me to stop and retire for the night.

After several months of house hunting we found a house we liked. We had stars in our eyes; a rebirth in a new neighborhood was approaching. Papers were signed, monies transferred, construction was finished, and escrow closed. We were launched into a new life. Though nowhere as luxurious as what Ellen and Jack were living in, this was a far cry from the one-room apartment where I was born.

It can be said that the best-laid plans of mice, men, and transplanted Jews in the suburbs turn to rubble and dust. Before long, my parents, who'd been on the best of terms during this transition, resumed their daily sniping. My dad had overlooked that these structures were built cheaply. The walls were paper-thin and acted like a microphone, exaggerating every domestic squabble. Many of our neighbors had similar conflicts, having tried to buy grandeur on a dime. Though a few were down-to-earth souls, most acted self-importantly in their oversized cardboard mansions.

Artificial Puberty & One Eyebrow

Shortly after I enrolled at my new high school, my father deluged me with advice. "Son, you need to find yourself some Jewish friends."

"Jewish friends? There's not many of us out here."

"You just can't trust Gentiles."

"But Dad, you don't trust anybody, Jew or Gentile."

"The cashier at Safeway called your mother a dirty Jew for making him check some prices he rang up against the ones on the shelves."

"So was he right or wrong?"

"You have to watch out in this neighborhood. One never knows when somebody will draw a swastika or something."

"If you're so paranoid, why did you move us here out to the sticks?"

"Where else could we afford a four bedroom house? Sometimes you have to make sacrifices."

"That sounds Christian. Didn't Jesus sacrifice his life for…"

"Don't you utter that name in our house. One more mention and I'll…"

"You're the one who's always saying for Christ's sake."

"I can say it, I'm older than you."

"That's not fair."

He always had the last word. "Who said life is fair?"

My mom also nagged, "Join a club, get elected to office, find yourself a girlfriend! Your nose is stuck in a book. You've got to be popular."

Adolescence was awkward for me. I was gun-shy about meeting new people, still short for my age, and very insecure. As if I didn't feel self-conscious enough during these developing years, my mom obsessed about my short stature. She took me to one specialist after another to test my vitals and see if anything was wrong.

My father protested. "Besides being such a waste of money, you're giving the boy an inferiority complex."

She replied, "You think he enjoys being called a shrimp at school."

"I didn't reach my full height 'til I was seventeen. Give him time."

"If we wait until then, he'll become neurotic."

"The problem with you is that you never let nature take its course."

"Nature has never been my friend."

My mom pursued a medical solution and her persistence paid off. I was shown to have a thyroid deficiency. A specialist told her, "We can solve this problem by giving your son some hormone shots to induce puberty. This might also help correct his hypothyroid condition."

"Whatever you say, doctor. I just want my boy to be normal."

After a course of hormone injections, I shot up several inches by my sixteenth birthday. My voice deepened, I developed a mustache like my dad, and my penis grew out of its undeveloped state into a respectable size. Finally I could shower after gym class without shielding my privates from the curious eyes of the other guys comparing themselves to the group to see if they were adequately endowed.

My mother nagged me about another physical shortcoming, the merging of bushy arches over my blue eyes. This "unibrow" seemed so unsightly to her, she took me for regular visits to an electrologist inside a beauty parlor. My dad was outraged at this activity and needless expense. "You're turning him into a faggot."

"You're such a good role model? You never play football with Sam. You've never even taken him to a Dodger game."

"You know how much my back hurts."

"And my ulcers don't act up when I look at my Neanderthal son?"

The fact that the electrologist was an overweight woman with bad breath and a gruff manner only added to my unease. If any of my school buddies had seen me there, I'd have been laughed off the campus.

One evening after eating too many of my mother's home baked cookies I came down with indigestion. Later, I had a nightmare in which I was on a cruise to Europe sitting at an opulent dining room with white linen tablecloths and vases of fresh flowers. I was reading some brochures about places I was going to visit while the waiters kept bringing me one pastry tray after another. I chose several items, savoring each.

Then I got so sick I had to be taken to the boat's infirmary to have my stomach pumped. A nurse entered my room looking like a cross between my mom and the electrolysis lady. She examined me, "Let me take your pulse. *Oy vey*, it's so weak. As soon as we arrive in Europe, we've got to fly you back to the mainland."

"Wait! I want to go to London and Paris."

"Meanwhile, I'm putting you on a diet of green Jello to clean you out."

"But I ordered escargot, filet mignon, and abalone, not that crap."

She brought in a doctor who looked like my dad. The man tackled me, forcing my belly down in the bed. As a needle was inserted into my ass, I awoke screaming, "Don't make me eat any more Jello. I'll puke."

My folks ran in to see what the yelling was about. Mom cried, "You thought I was kidding when I said our boy was insane?"

Dad added, "I told you we need to send him to military school to straighten him up."

"He needs more than straightening. He needs a straitjacket."

"All he needs is a good drill sergeant. That'll get him into shape."

The Key Club, The Buick, & Linda Kleinman

It was challenging for me in my new neighborhood. High school was filled with surfers, bikers, greasers, and bible bangers, and I didn't fit in with any of these groups. Schoolwork was easy, so I went to the local library and checked out novels by Dostoevsky and plays by Chekov. I couldn't discuss these dramatic works with my fellow students who read Teen Beat Magazine and listened to recordings like Leslie Gore.

At night, I'd turn on the AM-FM radio my dad had given me and tune into KNOB-FM, the jazz station. I especially liked the funky keyboard stylings of Herbie Hancock's *Watermelon Man* and cuts from Miles Davis and John Coltrane albums. My mother kept on nagging me to be popular, a quality low on my list. She advised, "We weren't meant to live by our brains alone. You should be more well-rounded."

"Ma, I'm just getting to the good part of *War and Peace*."

Finally, I gave in to her requests and joined a club. The only organization that fit me was the Key Club, a branch of the local Kiwanis. Within a short time, possibly because of my ethnic last name, I was made treasurer. Being good at math, I excelled at this. However, there was no one in the group with whom I wanted to be friends.

During this period, an announcement came over the high school loudspeaker. President Kennedy had been assassinated. The red, white, and blue U.S. flag sat above the California state flag with its large brown bear as they were flown at half-staff in front of the school entrance. These banners rippled as the winds unfurling them shifted direction.

Back on the East Coast, a prophetic songwriter named Bob Dylan had just finished recording the songs for his *The Times, They Are A-Changing* album. Not politically aware at the time, I had no idea that this national tragedy, like a foreshock of an earthquake, would become a catalyst for so much chaos in the world around me. A few of my teachers made some mention of the event, but class discussions and life in general went on as usual.

Occasionally, my club sponsored a social outing. I was uneasy at these, arriving late and leaving early. When my classmates were going out with girls and breaking into pairs in the bedrooms and backyards of their suburban homes, I didn't participate. It wasn't because I didn't have any hormones raging. After all, I did receive those shots.

My reluctance to integrate into any campus group disturbed my mom. She nagged, "When are you going to find some friends? "

"But all the other kids do is hang out and listen to songs by the Shirelles. They don't like jazz records."

"And you haven't found a nice Jewish girl to ask out?"

"If I meet one from Buenos Aires, I'll date her. I can talk about Argentina for hours."

"Most people don't care about Argentina."

"I'm not like most people."

"You'll never get a second date that way."

"I don't want a second date. I don't even want a first one."

"Dolly, do you know what a wallflower is?"

"No."

"That's what I was at your age. It gets very lonely being stuck in your own little world. I want my little boy to be popular, to be happy."

"I'm not your little boy."

"So, if you're not mine, whose are you?"

I was able to get my comeuppance on this matter. Just before my seventeenth birthday, my dad bought himself yet another new Buick sedan. We Frebergs should have owned stock in GM, since we were such loyal customers. Instead of trading his old car in, Irv gave me the 1956 Century. It had a white body, a black top with metallic scoops carved into sides of the chassis, and lots of chrome in the front. This was a surprise, since he was not one of my biggest fans. Perhaps, he thought car ownership might help me learn to become a man. I did get a 100% score on my DMV test and parallel parked to perfection.

Overjoyed to have my own wheels, I loved to cruise the neighborhood. So proud of this car, I vacuumed and washed it often. The fact that my father had given this to me made me feel redeemed in his eyes. Maybe he wasn't as much of an asshole as I thought.

Then one day, Mom set her foot down. To retain the keys to the car, I had to go out with a girl, hopefully Jewish, to prove I was grown up. I'd never dated a girl before and was apprehensive about fulfilling her demand. But I really wanted to keep driving the Buick around town, so despite my adolescent shyness, I started searching for a prospective date.

One of my classmates was a lively girl named Linda Kleinman. She had a Jewish surname, her father being one of our tribe. But he'd married a dark-skinned Afro-American woman. Linda looked more like her mother than her dad, except for the large nose. She and I shared an interest in books, especially ones by American authors.

"Linda, what's that book you're reading?"

"*Catcher in The Rye.*"

"Didn't they ban it from the library?"

"Right. It's too controversial for some people, but not for me. I had trouble finding it and had to borrow a copy from my aunt."

"What's it about?"

"A mental case that rebels against his phony prep school friends."

"I can relate. I feel like a fish out of water in this school. Is there a chance I could read it when you're finished?"

"Only if you promise to take good care of it. The book isn't mine."

"I'll be very careful."

I had no interest in being physical with Linda, but she was the only girl in school I knew well enough to ask out for a date, even if there might be some repercussions in doing so. The possibility of ruffling a few feathers appealed to my passive-aggressive nature. Little did I foresee the disruption this would cause.

One day, to my parents' great delight, I told them I was going out with Linda. At the mention of her last name, they smiled at each other with a great sense of relief. My mom took me aside to tell me how proud she was. "At last, you're going to have a girlfriend."

I deflected, "We're just going out. Don't be so pushy."

"Me, pushy?"

"The next thing, you'll be pestering me to go steady with her."

"God forbid, a steady girlfriend wouldn't make you happy? It would make me very happy."

"You can't force happiness."

"But you can nudge it a little. I can't wait to meet your Linda."

"She's not mine."

"Not yet."

The date was a stop for burgers and a drive-in movie. As I was leaving, my dad slipped me an extra ten bucks for the occasion and winked. Mom told me to bring the girl home afterwards. I knew this confrontation was bound to occur sooner or later. Because I could never say no to her, that night was the night.

Linda and I had a fun evening. At the burger place, she played the Motown song "Heat Wave" by Martha and the Vandellas on the jukebox. While the passionate lyrics didn't ignite in me any feeling for my date, I was struck by the lively music and the sound of the vocal arrangements. Maybe pop songs weren't so bad after all.

After our meal, we laughed our way through *"The Pink Panther."* Both of us were in a good mood when I drove her over to my house. I brought my folks to the car, feeling this would be safer than inviting her inside. What they saw made their jaws drop. After some small talk, I excused myself as politely as I could and drove off quickly.

I knew I'd have to pay for this when I got home. When I opened the front door and slinked inside, my father exploded. "I thought you said her name was Kleinman, a nice Jewish girl. It's bad enough you went out with a *shikse*, but a *schvartse* on top of that. You're grounded. That car is to stay in the garage."

"But she's Jewish, half Jewish on her father's side. She has a brain and she's funny."

He lost it. "But she's a Negro. I'll not have anyone in my family associating themselves with a nigger, even if she's part Jew." Then he sauntered into the master bedroom, slamming the door behind him.

My mom remained in the living room with tears running down her cheeks. Not bigoted like my father, she had affection for colored people. At one point, she'd hired a black woman when she was helping my dad grow the family business. This maid was treated like one of the family. But that night, this affection was nowhere to be seen.

"You've insulted Irving. He'll never trust you again. I wouldn't be surprised if he takes your car back." Then she gave me another jab. "I don't care if your girlfriend is black, but one only is a Jew if their mother is one of us. You went out with a *shikse*, even if her name is Kleinman." She joined my dad, also slamming the door.

The two of them argued so loudly, their voices must have been heard over at Linda's house a mile away.

My dad started the commotion, "It's all your fault."

"No, it's yours."

"I told you that child would turn out to be no good."

"He brought a girl over. You want he should bring us a boy?"

I also broke out in tears and rushed into my room. My sisters quaked in their beds, having heard the whole thing. The gods above must've been laughing hysterically at the melodrama below.

Gracie & The Chocolate Greasy Baby

After a couple of weeks, my father came down from his judgmental pedestal. Not that he forgave me for dating a member of the black race. Instead, he was preoccupied with moving his radio manufacturing business to a new larger location. This left him little time to think about my transgression. During this period, his back started bothering him. Overmedicating this condition, he got hooked on pain pills. They tended to exaggerate his already dark personality.

He didn't have to worry about the possibility of miscegenation in the family for two reasons. My relationship with Linda was strictly platonic. Then as it turned out, it was short-lived. A couple of months later, her family moved back to the city near downtown. A mixed-race family in those days was out of place in the suburbs.

I missed her, but a replacement soon came into my life. I met a cheerful plump girl at a local deli, the only Jewish establishment in the area. When I went inside to buy a dill pickle to snack on, she got in the line next to me to purchase some *mandel* bread, a biscotti-like pastry. This vivacious young woman let her dark brown eyes overrule her stomach and had ordered a dozen pieces from the girl behind the counter. Seeing me buy so little, she inquired, "Are you out of money, or just not that hungry?"

"Thanks for asking. I've blown my budget for the week."

As we each paid our cashiers and were leaving the establishment, she observed me eyeing her pastry and asked, "I could use a little help with these. Want to join me at a table out in front?"

I responded eagerly, "I'd be glad to."

Both ethnic types, though from different backgrounds, we soon became fast friends. She said her name was Gracie, and she revealed that she'd moved to the Valley from Detroit with her immigrant family. Her father had opened up a large snack bar that sold American and Greek food. A year older than me, Gracie worked in the family business and developed a habit of helping herself to leftovers there.

We both were foodies and could talk cheap restaurants and holiday recipes until the cows came home. Meeting after school and on the weekends, we'd order take-out food from local hangouts to bring to a nearby park. Our favorite was Chinese. Outfitted with several white containers with red pagodas printed on them, we opened them regularly at our usual picnic table, eating and laughing hysterically.

When I playfully teased, "I'll trade you a spare rib for a butterfly shrimp," she joked, "But you already finished all the ribs."

"So how about one of my egg rolls?"

"It's a deal."

Sometimes Gracie told me she thought I was handsome. I'd blush and disagree, pointing out guys I'd rather look like, usually taller, blond, and more athletic. She thought my choices didn't have as much character as I did. Whenever she made an advance toward me, I backed away. I'd chosen an overweight girl to spend time with because on some level I thought she'd be safe. I wasn't interested in pursuing anything further. Gracie soon realized that friendship was all she was going to get from me. Once she gave up her romantic desires, we settled into a supportive buddy relationship.

One day, she extended an appealing invitation, "How would you like to come with me to Greek Orthodox Easter services? My family always has a midnight feast afterwards complete with *avgolemeno* soup, *spanikopita* triangles, and *baklava*. You'll really love it."

Taken aback, I answered, "But I'm Jewish."

Not put off by my reluctance, she replied, "So what?"

"What about your family? They wouldn't mind?"

"They're very open-minded."

"Lucky for you. Mine aren't. If I invited you over for dinner, it would be *shikse* this and *shikse* that."

Puzzled by the term, she asked, "What's a *shikse?*"

"It's a not so nice word for a non-Jewish girl."

"Oh, I get it. That's too bad. I'm sorry."

"So am I."

I enjoyed the late night Easter service where the priest wore colorful robes and spread incense around the room as he walked up and down the aisles. Even more festive was the feast afterwards.

Later that year, we went to several ethnic food and music festivals. For months, we shared many dreams and commiserated about the frequent troubles at our homes.

One afternoon, she confided that she wanted to have lots of chocolate-smeared greasy kids. I liked children, but besides not wanting to be tied down, I couldn't even imagine doing what was needed to produce one. I worried that something must be wrong with me to have no interest in crossing this bridge. *Was I as worthless as my dad kept telling me?*

A few weeks later, Gracie disappeared. She stopped contacting me and didn't answer her phone. Then it was disconnected. I was crestfallen. I went to her father's food stand, but it was closed down. I heard nothing for several months. Since she was no longer in school, I had no way of checking her records. This seemed to be a dead end.

Then one day I saw a mutual friend who told me she knew where Gracie was. I begged her to take me there. She agreed, but warned me not to get my hopes up. I followed her in my Buick as we caravanned to the Sawtelle district of West L.A. where, in a one-room unit in an old courtyard full of tiny Spanish style cabins, Gracie was hiding out. When we knocked on the front door, she opened it carrying a crying infant in swaddling clothes.

The emotions were mixed for both of us. My former confidante smiled proudly as she exclaimed, "Isn't he beautiful?"

I joked in response, "If I had known, I would have brought some chocolate for you to smear his face with."

We laughed like nothing had changed. Yet so much had. Our friend left us together to catch up and drove off. Gracie told me she was seeing a Mexican laborer living in the courtyard. The guy was possessive, so I couldn't stay. "It's great to see you, but you must never visit me like this again. If my boyfriend knew you were here..."

Incredulous, I interrupted, "What do you mean?"

"In fact, you better leave right away. If he catches us together, it could get very ugly. If you value either of our lives you must..."

"What? I can't believe this."

She stammered, "I'm sorry."

I hugged Gracie, wishing her well. "I really miss you."

With tears welling in her dark eyes, she uttered softly so as not to be heard easily, "I love you, Sam. I always will. Goodbye."

When Gracie closed the door, there was nothing I could say. I drove back to the Valley in a state of despair. But I didn't have much time to grieve the loss. I'd just graduated high school and had a lot on my plate. Ironically, the university I was going to attend was only a few miles from where she was staying. I'd be so close to her, yet so far away.

Mrs. Jensen, Mr. Kirschbaum, & The Musical

In my second year in high school, I discovered that a music theory class was taught there. When I signed up, I was far ahead of the other students. My instructor, Mrs. Jensen, was so enthused about my progress she set up a meeting with my folks, encouraging them to let me study music at the university level. Although my father wanted me to go to college, he insisted that I major in engineering. He thought music was for hobbyists, not a serious career. Mrs. Jensen begged him to consider otherwise. My mom voiced her support for the teacher.

This became a lively source of debate when they got home where they shouted angrily. "Engineering!" "Music!" "Engineering! "Music!" Seeing she was dealing with such stubbornness, my mom pleaded, "Let Sam study accounting and he'll do music on the side."

I quickly mastered every exercise in my harmony books. At the end of the semester, Mrs. Jensen arranged for me to take the course again, saving a few minutes each day to assign me customized projects. Meanwhile, I studied keyboard with a private teacher in the area. To pay for these lessons, I began teaching piano to children in the neighborhood. This pleased my parents greatly. They encouraged me to save my earnings, not blow it on impulse shopping like my classmates.

Not only did I have the good fortune to study with Mrs. Jensen, I had an English teacher, Mr. Kirschbaum, who taught a special course for advanced students. These instructors were friends and noticed that their pupils had unique talents. They decided to have us collaborate on a school project, a musical.

From our first meeting, this group of budding geniuses coalesced. I enjoyed being with fellow creative souls that, like me, did not fit into any of the cliques on campus. We came up with a story about a mythical high school with a goofy anti-hero. Lewis, one of the writers, suggested, "Let's make our main character a real nerd."

Another writer asked, "Like us? What's interesting about that?"

Lewis continued, "We'll turn him into a campus hero."

A writer named Winston commented dryly, "That could never happen here. In our school, they only idolize football players."

Another member suggested, "What if he has a crush on a cheerleader who thinks he's a real jerk. Our nerd buys her a malted at the school cafeteria and almost spills it on her. But he does a cool step to avoid this disaster. Someone nearby imitates his move. This catches the eye of one of the football players who copies it and it becomes the latest rage."

Lewis agreed, "That sounds bitchen. Then what?"

"Everyone wants to know where it came from and the cheerleader points to the 'nerd.' The dance craze takes over and our hero gets the girl."

Winston remarked, "Sam, can you write a song about this?"

I was thrilled to get this chance to participate. "Sure thing. I'll do a spinoff of "Since I Fell For You" but make it a lot more uptempo."

Lewis let out a yell, "Even more bitchen."

The musical took two months to write and a month for the Theater Arts department to stage. It was well received. My folks came to a performance. Although my dad bragged about the show, he was reluctant to praise me directly, determined that I wouldn't go into music.

To celebrate the musical's success, a member of our group hosted a party, inviting the writers and our parents. Spirits were high. Everyone boasted how great the show went over. I'd never been acknowledged publicly for my creativity before. I got to share these accolades with my new best friends. Most parents attended, including mine, sharing drinks while getting to know each other. Some of the excited mothers and fathers made toasts to their children's accomplishments.

"Lewis came up with much of the plot. I'm so proud of him."

"My daughter Eileen wrote a lot of the dialogue and some of the clever lyrics. Here's to her health and future success."

"Winston wrote some really great jokes. Good work, son."

After each toast, the room resounded with loud roars of cheerful affirmation. When it came to my dad's turn to speak, he took a different tack. "Sam has such a swelled head he thinks he's ready for Broadway. This is as far as he's gonna get. It's all downhill from here."

The room became eerily silent. No one could believe someone would say something so cruel. I left the room at once. It was not new for my father to pop one of my bubbles, but this was his most damaging effort to date. On my way home I was so upset I almost drove my Buick into a lamppost. We hardly spoke to each other for weeks.

The musical took place that May. Graduation ceremonies were held the following month. What should have been a source of pride for me became painful instead. Though I received compliments from fellow students, I felt worthless inside. I tried to put my father's words out of my thoughts and prepare myself for college. After much bitter argument, my parents agreed that I could try my hand at music, but in return I had to live at home and commute to campus. So I set up a carpool situation with a few students from my graduating class for September. I could hardly wait for my new studies to begin.

CHAPTER 3
COLLEGE GLORY

Triple A

This reminiscing was interrupted by the sound of my cell phone ringing. It was all I could do to get my mind collected enough to answer it. I barely clicked on before the phone went into message mode.

A voice said, "Am I speaking to Sam Freberg?"

I muttered, "Yes."

"Mr. Freberg, I'm sorry to tell you that your driver had to answer an emergency call on the way to your car."

"Like I don't get emergency status?"

Patiently, the dispatch person went on, "Are you injured?"

"No."

"Then I hope you understand. It'll be another 30 minutes or so before he can get there to help you. He'll give you a ring just before he arrives."

After I hung up, I called Darryl right away. "It's me again. Triple A had to answer another call before me. They said that it's some sort of emergency."

My sponsor tried to be supportive. "Sorry to hear that. I'll tell the group you might be late."

I complained, "Why does this always happen to me?"

"It'll work out one way or another."

"I'll try to look at it that way."

After putting down the phone, I tried to calm my shaky nerves. I'd been enjoying revisiting my early years. Before long, my mind resumed its journey to the past, this time recalling the glory of my college days when I'd experienced some of my best times.

Lewis & Winston

During the summer before starting college, I spent time with two of my writing group buddies, Lewis and Winston. We listened to music, played games, and experimented with weird recipes like one Winston had invented, a beer milkshake. Take a glass of beer and a scoop of ice cream and whip it up in blender. It sounded gross. We poured the mixture into glasses and tasted it.

Winston quizzed, "Well, Sam, what do you think?"

"It's not half bad."

"C'mon, you haven't finished it."

"The shake starts off well, but I can do without the aftertaste."

"You get used to it. Anyone want seconds?" There weren't any takers.

We did other fun things that summer such as having a wine tasting party. I had little experience with wine except for the token glass I was allowed to consume at the Freberg Passover meals every year. Although my family wasn't religious, my Mom served traditional holiday foods. I ate heartily, but with alcohol I was a lightweight.

A dozen kinds of wine were served at the party. Being inexperienced, I thought I was supposed to drink a glass of each and gulped down one tumbler after another. Midway through the evening, I got so sick I had to make several trips to the bathroom to upchuck. My buddies laughed, "You're supposed to sip an ounce, swirl it around in your glass, and then determine which ones you like and which you don't."

"Now you tell me," I moaned.

I switched to soda. This was so unpleasant, I swore I'd never consume that many drinks again. And I never did. With the other addictions that were to plague me through the years, alcohol was never one of them.

Mrs. B. & The Two Roads

Another activity we shared that summer was hanging out with a former teacher, Mrs. Beachum. We all had studied mathematics with this amazing woman, the only black instructor at our high school. Mrs. B., as we called her, was a non-conformist with a very high IQ. A divorcee living in an ultra-modern home on the outskirts of town, she entertained some of her ex-students with dinners featuring gourmet meals she cooked herself. Intellectual conversations and debates invariably followed.

Preaching a philosophy of being oneself despite what anybody else thinks, she was an advocate for individualism and personal liberty. "Follow your instincts and see where they lead you. Life is full of surprising adventures when you keep an open mind."

Hearing this, I protested, "I love adventures, but my dad advises me to put my nose to the grindstone instead. He says that lofty goals are a waste of time. I'll only fail if I take on too much."

Smiling like the proverbial Cheshire Cat, she responded, "If the great minds of history had listened to naysayers like him, Columbus wouldn't have discovered America. We might still be thinking the earth is flat. Sam, you're so creative. Don't be afraid to express yourself."

At one of these gatherings, I asked her, "What is the sound of one hand clapping? I read this in a Zen book, but couldn't figure it out."

"Honey, I can't give you a simple answer. Many monks sit on mountain tops for years to meditate on this."

"So what do they find?"

"I don't want to spoil it for you."

"At least, can you recommend any mountain tops nearby to visit?"

"We've only got hills around here. Don't rush it. You'll be climbing your own mountains soon enough."

"But I don't want to wait until I find the right mountain. Can you give me a hint?'

She rose and solemnly pontificated. "For the sake of argument, let's say that there are two roads to enlightenment. The first one is short with quick answers you may not fully understand when you get to the end. The longer one has many curves as it goes through a series of hills and valleys. On this path you'll need to learn many lessons. Which one do you think leads to a better outcome?"

"Obviously, the longer road. But I want to know so much right away. I hate waiting for anything."

"Sam, haven't you heard the saying that good things come to one who waits? When you're in a hurry you can miss a great deal along the way. Slow down. Be patient."

"Patience isn't easy for me."

"That doesn't mean you shouldn't practice it. Patience is nature's way. You've got your whole life ahead of you. Be more like the tortoise that slowly works through life's challenges than the hare sprinting and looking for shortcuts around them."

Like other controversial figures, Mrs. B. was revered by some and reviled by others. If my dad had known that I was attending these discussions, he would have complained to the authorities about her being a subversive needing surveillance. Even more liberal parents had their suspicions about her wayward influence. If this had been in the South instead of Southern California, she might have been run out of town.

She was ahead of her time, leading a spontaneous life, playing jazz albums on her hi-fi, spouting poetry as she danced her way around the fringes of society. For kids like us on our way to college, she was a taste of what was emerging nationwide, the social revolution of the '60s.

Probing The Outskirts

That fall, Lewis and Winston left for their schools away from home, while I began my commute to West L.A. One of the young men in my carpool was Dennis, a tall athletic guy with a blond crew cut who lived with his devout Christian family a few blocks away. Dennis had been a star on the high school football team and a campus hero.

Unlike many of the other young men in school, he wasn't interested in chasing girls or partying. A disciplined fellow, Dennis was studying to become an engineer. Except for his bible beliefs, he was exactly the kind of young man my father wanted me to be. I enjoyed sharing a ride with him, but unlike my friend Reggie from years back, we had little in common. Conversation between us was minimal.

Returning home after school, I was obsessed with Dennis. Before going to sleep, I'd fantasize about what it would be like to hold him in my arms and have sex with him. I wasn't sure how men experienced sex with each other. My only exposure to this was the writing on the walls of a restroom stall I discovered in a bowling alley while in a league there. The obscene messages and crude drawings of erect genitalia portrayed for enticement aroused my curiosity.

During my senior year in high school, I'd drive to the bowling alley after classes to browse the latest additions, a same-sex equivalent of Reggie's porn magazines. They were accompanied by hateful references to being a pervert and a faggot. Sometimes there was a Jesus Saves message interspersed among them. These portrayals of sin and warnings about the need for salvation were a forbidden world. The fact that I was drawn to them was my deep secret.

One day while reading the postings, I started playing with myself. Lost in a fantasy of doing with Dennis what I imagined was pictured there, I didn't hear someone sit down in the stall next to me. I was startled to see a young man peer from below the divider, asking if I wanted to do one of the activities I'd read about. This stranger who'd burst into my private world made an imploring gesture and said to meet him outside in a blue car parked behind the bowling alley.

I was overcome with fear. When Reggie and Charlie had exposed their privates to me a few years before, I ran home for safety. This time, I decided to follow the invitation and see where it led. Sure enough, there was a blue Chevy parked in the back. As I approached, the young man rolled down his window and motioned for me to get inside. I complied. He was not as handsome as Dennis, yet not vulgar like the graffiti scrawled in the stall. When the invitation for sex was repeated, though I was very nervous, I nodded my head yes.

The young man tried to reassure me, "Relax, I'm not going to hurt you. I'd bring you over to my house, but my mom's there. We can't do anything in this lot, but if you let me drive you to a private place not far away, we could fool around over there. You up for it?"

Though afraid to speak, my eyes revealed an eagerness to try. The teen continued, "Don't worry, I'll bring you back here afterwards."

I managed to utter a faint "OK."

We hardly talked as the blue car made its way a few miles into the countryside. Soon, we turned down a dirt road and parked under a grove of sycamore trees. There was no one around. The only light was that of some stars twinkling through the car's windshield.

I saw the silhouette of this slender young man lean over to put his mouth on mine, then reach his hand down and undo the button and zipper to my jeans and pull them down. I did the same to him. We continued kissing and took turns going down on each other. Excited, I shot immediately. My partner kept stimulating me and I was ready for a second round in no time. Within an hour, I'd crossed the border from virginity to an experience I couldn't believe would feel so good.

On our way back, the boy said his name was Tim and revealed that he was nineteen years old. I was only seventeen, but neither of us thought about age as a criterion. What we'd just done was illegal. It was against the law on three counts. Sodomy was a felony at that time, we'd done it in a public place, and I was underage.

Tim gave me his phone number, saying, "Use this carefully. If my mom answers, hang up."

I apologized, "Sorry, I can't give you mine. My folks would go ballistic if they knew about this."

Not put off, Tim said, "I know." He reached over and clasped my hand, adding, "This was nice. I enjoyed it."

To my amazement, I admitted, "I did too."

Once we got back to our starting point, both of us were anxious to be back on our own. I arrived home much later than usual and scampered quickly into my room before anyone could ask where I'd been.

We met a few times in locations where we couldn't be seen. The excitement and pleasure we shared diminished as we became afraid of intimacy. Being queer in those days was asking for trouble. After a while, we decided to nip the affair in the bud.

With nobody to turn to for advice, I went to a nearby college library and read up on homosexuality. All I could find there were clinical sociology reports painting a grim picture of deviant behavior and a high suicide rate. On television shows, gays, as we were starting to be called, were portrayed as losers, neurotics, and criminals. What bothered me was that most of these characters were effeminate queens that turned me off. What I was attracted to in a man was maleness.

I resolved to give up this "bad habit" and retreated to my fantasy world. Like my brochures about going to Europe, I thought these itineraries were better suited to my mind than real life. I found solace in a pop song, the Everly Brothers' "All I Have To Do Is Dream."

I threw myself into my studies. As Mrs. Jensen had advised, I told the music department of my work with her, producing a letter she'd written to document this. They agreed to give me credit for a year of theory classes and enrolled me in a sophomore course. I was now in my element, no longer one of the few brainy kids.

I also loved my other classes, especially physical and cultural geography. When it came to maps, my inner cartographer was liberated. Ethnic studies and social structures also fascinated me. As I'd done in earlier years, in addition to reading all of my textbooks, I went to the library to check out countless others to pour through.

At the university, I attained a measure of self-esteem long denied me. When I returned home after school, I had as little to do with the family as possible. They were involved in their own dramas, and I tried to steer clear of the turbulence.

In my freshman year, I received all "A"s and "B"s, except for a "C" in phys ed. True to form, my father complained about anything short of an "A". "So what's this poor grade in gym class? Can't you keep up with the other kids? When I was your age, I played a lot of baseball."

Standing up to him, I said, "I'm not you, Dad. I'm not a jock. What about the other grades? I did well, huh?"

He barked, "You can do better." Once again, smarting under my father's criticism, I slinked away.

Despite this badmouthing, he did have good news. His radio business was doing so well, he volunteered to pay for me to live on campus the following year. The only stipulation was I had to take on more piano students and buy my own school supplies. It was a deal I did not refuse.

The Great Outdoors

The following summer, when Lewis and Winston got home from their first year at college, they invited me on a two-week camping trip. Not only was I a novice at drinking wine, I was a tenderfoot at camping. Up for adventure, not to mention being thrilled at the prospect of getting away from home, I agreed enthusiastically. I had no idea what I was getting into. It was to become a rite of passage, a significant transition to manhood.

Winston was an experienced camper, and Lewis had also spent some time hiking in the great outdoors. In stark contrast, I'd lived a sheltered existence. The only vacations my dad took our family on were short hops to places like Bakersfield, Oceanside, and Desert Hot Springs. One was an aggie town, the next, a working class military beach community, and the third, a dusty desert hamlet. Yet, the activities we experienced there were pretty much the same.

At the start of one family vacation, he shouted with gusto, "OK everyone, pile into the Buick, we're going to Bakersfield."

Not thrilled by this, I answered sarcastically, "Yeah, I know. We're going out for pancakes, a little swimming, and then steak."

"Son, you can always stay home."

Resigned to never getting my way, I brought my usual reading material along. Once ensconced in our home-away-from-home, we lounged around the pool and dined out on a budget. There were no fancy trappings like bellhops, bistros, or amusement parks, rarely any visits to local tourist attractions. Simple as these places were, they were welcome changes from the domestic disputes in town.

As a result of this humble style of vacationing, it wasn't much of a step down for me to do without the amenities one had to forgo on a camping trip. My buddies helped me purchase a sleeping bag and we assembled some groceries to prepare on the road. Winston brought a camping stove and lantern; Lewis's mom let us borrow the family's station wagon for our junket.

Before heading to the Rocky Mountains, we drove through the Sierra Nevadas to Lake Tahoe. The first night of the trip was a rude baptism for me. Our campground on the western shore of this huge body of water at over 6,000 feet in elevation had a blanket of snow on the ground, unusual this late in June. We set up our gear, lit a campfire, and shared a meal of canned beef stew and instant mashed potatoes. Winston strummed a few blues chords on his guitar and sang some songs. As darkness fell, we climbed into our sleeping bags.

It was fortunate we'd brought along heavy-duty gear suited to cold weather, since the temperature that night went well below freezing. My body shivered in my flannel-lined surroundings, and my teeth chattered. No matter what position I tried to sleep in, I couldn't get comfortable or warm. I was so afraid of freezing to death I longed for daylight to arrive, wishing that I were with my family at the City Center Motel and the El Rancho Coffee Shop next door.

It was summer and dawn came early. Some hot cocoa and oatmeal brought me back from what I considered a brush with a premature demise, not to mention an aching back from sleeping on a hard surface. Being more seasoned, Winston and Lewis said it was colder than they expected, but they were not traumatized like I was. For once, I had to drop my big baby act and keep complaints to myself.

As the trip progressed, the conditions became easier. I grew accustomed to the deprivations that came with camping. The scenery we visited was breathtakingly beautiful, especially the pine forests, wildflowers, ferns and vibrant flora bursting into spring growth. All this natural grandeur blended into the majesty of the Colorado mountain ranges with their boulders, glaciers, and snow-capped peaks.

The only mishap that occurred was near the Continental Divide at 10,000 feet in altitude. We were visited by a sudden thunderstorm that sent us dashing into the station wagon to sleep inside for the night. Its hard steel floor made ground cloth covered earth seem luxurious. By the time we returned home, I was a changed person. Learning to brave a few fears and discomfort was a good character builder. I discovered the joys of being in nature and the experience turned me into a dyed-in-the-wool outdoorsman.

The Dorms & The Culture Vulture

In September, I moved into the dorms, my first time living away from home. Besides that trip to Colorado, the only time I'd been away from my family was when I'd gone to a summer camp before my twelfth birthday. I felt uneasy in a roomful of strange boys. There weren't any classes other than arts and crafts, no place for me to demonstrate my intellect. I felt intimidated by the other kids.

I participated in the activities such as hiking and swimming, though far from the champion my natal doctor had predicted. On one of these hikes I ran into some poison oak, coming down with a rash and itchy skin. I had to stay at the nurse's quarters for a few days. When I returned to my bungalow, each group was busy preparing a stage presentation to culminate our time in camp. The skit for my group included having someone get dressed up as a girl. While I was away, I was chosen to play the part. Given a skirt, blouse, makeup, and told to act feminine, I had no interest in behaving that way. I walked around as butch as I could, which the other boys found entertaining.

"Sam, you're a riot."

"Yeah, you try walking in these heels. And this skirt is too tight."

"But you do it so well."

The day of the performance, I played the role, but as soon as I got offstage I ripped off my clothes. Being in drag was not for me.

In contrast to camp, living in the dorms was a joy, a relief to be away from my parents' nagging. My roommate was an attractive blond surfer who made it clear from the start what a straight guy he was. I never even had the chance to fantasize about him.

Here, I met many new people. Among them was a group of Christian students living in the dorms who were very different from my upbringing. Partying, dating, and sexual conquest were not on their agenda. Not anxious to deal with my sexuality, they were a good fit. Sometimes we met off-campus with a progressive pastor for a discussion group about contemporary values and campus issues.

A member of this group named Neal had a vibrant energy, an interest in almost everything, and a theatrical manner that I found appealing. This gifted fellow could talk about any subject. One couldn't help but be impressed with his command of art, history, and culture. Knowing I could learn much from him, I sensed we'd become good friends.

We became roommates the following year. By then, we were as inseparable as I'd once been with Reggie and Gracie. We went to art exhibits, attended concerts, and dropped in on lectures by visitors to the university from around the world. Neal landed a spot on the Student Cultural Commission and got free tickets. He'd go to so many events, he was known around campus as the Culture Vulture.

I tagged along, receiving an education that often surpassed what I learned in my courses. A whirlwind day might include a Baroque ensemble concert, a Matisse showing, a lecture on the Bushmen in Angola, a German cabaret film, and a tour of the campus botanical gardens.

We enjoyed being roommates. Besides having deep discussions, we hoarded food from the dorm and student body cafeterias, a collection of snacks squirreled away in our desk drawers. When other dormies wandered into our room, they were treated to sandwiches, cheese strips, fruit, nuts, and candy. These culinary indulgences accompanied socializing well into the late evening hours, sometimes at the expense of our studies.

In my sophomore year, I enrolled in a classical composition class. At first I enjoyed this exposure to highbrow music. But as the styles got more abstract, they were difficult to share with my friends.

One night while cramming for a music test at the library, I fell asleep on a desk. I dreamed that I was on the TV show *Name That Tune*. Sitting across from me was Neal. We were competing to be the first to recognize a popular or classical melody. The first person to run across the stage, ring a bell and correctly identify the song was given a midnight snack. Three correct answers awarded the contestant a month of free campus activities.

I recognized the first song as "California Dreaming" by The Mamas and the Papas and was given a salami sandwich, which I ate right away. Neal named an aria from a Verdi opera, got a Baby Ruth candy bar, and gulped it down. I missed the next melody, which Neal identified as a theme from a Beethoven piano sonata. He got a cheddar cheese ball. I rang the bell for the fourth tune but forgot its name, forfeiting a can of nuts. Finally, Neal identified "When You Wish Upon A Star" and won the free pass. While he was showing off his prize, I got sick and had to be sent to the hospital.

The announcer apologized to the audience and admitted that the crew had thought that the salami looked a bit old, but they used it anyway. He asked everyone to pray for my health and tune in next week for another episode. I woke up sick to my stomach and had to remedy this with a strong dose of Pepto-Bismol.

I wasn't cut out for fine art music and began hanging out in the theater arts and folklore departments instead. In the 1960s, sounds of protest singers like Bob Dylan and Simon and Garfunkel blared from campus hi-fis. I joined this movement and let my hair grow long.

Jewish Student Union & The Tutorial Project

My only exposure to Jewish religion had been at friends' bar mitzvah ceremonies. As much as I was stimulated by the cultural diversity on campus, I felt a need to connect with others from my own background. So I began attending meetings of the JSU (Jewish Student Union).

This occurred during the Johnson years. Long after he succeeded Kennedy as president, we were still stuck in Vietnam. I shared many of JSU's liberal concerns about the war. Like most college students at the time, many of us believed we shouldn't have gone there and needed to bring our troops home. At a few meetings, members played recordings of Bob Dylan, an icon we proudly referred to by his real name of Bob Zimmerman, a fellow Yid. "Masters Of War" was one of my favorite songs.

I voiced the slogans of peace, love, and freedom the group espoused. With Mrs. B.'s advice ringing in my ears, I did so knowing that this was going against what my dad would advocate. His hero was Richard Nixon. My mom had voted for Kennedy and Johnson. Politics gave my parents another reason to argue.

A JSU activity that I especially enjoyed was a Tutorial Project held in the Watts neighborhood in South Central Los Angeles. It was an outreach program to help disadvantaged children in the black community that had difficulties in school. This was set up to support kids whose parents subjected them to drug addiction and abuse. I was proud to make a contribution, however modest, to improving the plight of these youngsters.

Jews had been active in the Civil Rights Movement for many years. A few of the older JSU members had marched in Mississippi and Alabama. I was impressed when they told us stories about the freedom fighters, black and white, that dared to challenge the law enforcement and legal systems that went to great lengths to keep the races segregated. This local program was a good example of one minority group helping out another.

Every week, a bus transported my group of campus volunteers to Watts. I was assigned to a nine-year-old boy to help him with his reading and spelling, using flashcards and other visual aids. In addition, I took it upon myself to build the child a planter box to encourage an interest in gardening. We planted some radish seeds together, since I knew that they only took a month to be ready for harvest and children need immediate gratification. He delighted in watching the plants sprout from the soil and got excited seeing the weekly growth of green leaves. We thinned the plants and harvested a few edible red and white globes. He proudly showed them off to his mother and his friends.

Another activity we volunteers did was to help a local church with cleanup and light construction. This day of manual labor was rewarded by a homemade dinner of fried chicken and soul food. After digging trenches and putting up wallboard, a meal like this was welcome. The socializing afterwards was an effective bonding experience.

A few students got out guitars and sang folk songs. Some of the churchgoers joined in, singing some hymns and blues as well. There was lot of jamming, but since there was no access to a piano keyboard, I could not participate. This motivated me to learn to play guitar.

I enjoyed this group of young Jews, but when discussions turned to marriage and family, I was uncomfortable. My same-sex desires persisted, and the views of many members made me nervous. Though not everyone's point of view, the official stance was that homosexuality was a sin. By extension, that made me a bad person. I didn't feel evil, just wanting the touch of another man. I believed strongly that God, if there was one, created me this way.

I kept my opinions to myself, knowing I could be a pariah if I revealed too much. There were other outdated abominations in Jewish scripture like not eating pork or crabmeat. I thought *What is so bad about wanting to kiss another man on the lips? On an overpopulated planet, gay sex could be a good thing.*

That year, I experienced a few hit-and-run sexual encounters on campus with young men whose cruising eyes met mine. These were furtive experiments in empty dorm rooms or remote stairwells. Once I even crawled into the back seat of a car in a dark corner of a parking structure late at night to share a quick touch and go. Afterwards, we pretended we'd never met when we ran into each other.

Carol & The Bluegrass Wedding

At a JSU meeting I met a girl who lived in my dorm. Her name was Carol. She played a style of old-time country music on the guitar called bluegrass, picking, strumming, and singing songs about piney woods, hound dogs, and coal miners. Shy and reserved, she was a refreshing contrast to the high-strung females in my family. When I expressed an interest in learning to play some of these songs, she volunteered to teach me.

On one occasion I asked her, "Could you show me the G chord again? Damn, these strings hurt my fingers."

She had the patience of a saint. "You'll get used to it."

"I hope so."

I found a used guitar in the student classifieds. Soon I was strumming with the throng of campus folkies as we sang, "How many roads must a man walk down before you can call him a man?"

Carol and I started playing together regularly at nearby parks. She'd fix us a picnic lunch and we spent many afternoons practicing traditional songs and singing country harmonies. She developed a crush on me, which needless to say was unrequited.

One day, she invited me to her parents' house. Her mom served us a home-cooked meal that included one of my favorite dishes, chicken matzo ball soup. Afterwards, we sang songs to entertain her folks. It wasn't long before I became aware Carol's mother was talking up her daughter's attributes, especially domestic skills. Her husband echoed short phrases of agreement. I was being courted, not by Carol, but by her parents. Though flattered, I had reservations. I'd signed up for guitar strums and some matzo balls. This was getting in too deep.

I met Carol while moving in a traditional direction. Yet, as much as I'd try to fantasize about a bluegrass wedding with a band playing mountain music and Jewish favorites, I just couldn't see this vision to completion. After the ceremony, the rabbinical blessings, the vows, and breaking of glasses, I'd have to face the honeymoon suite afterwards. Try as I might, the only sounds of romance I could hear were the sorrowful tones of an Appalachian fiddle echoing my self-pitying cries of unfulfilled love. I knew I had to continue on my lonesome path of the wayfaring stranger.

Cherie & Lust In The Chaparral

During the summer before my senior year, I reconnected with Lewis and Winston. Where there'd once been a group of three, five people now sat around the table of shared camaraderie. My buddies brought their new girlfriends, leaving me the lone single.

Though Winston came from a waspy family, his new love was an earthy Jewish girl named Barbara. I liked her down-home warmth. Lewis, hailing from a family of Jewish academics, was seeing Harriet, a fun, fair-haired Scandinavian girl. In the company of these cross-cultural pairings, I was relegated to a position I became accustomed to, a fifth wheel. I hoped there might be a tall, buff athlete in my future.

We met often, combining intense discussions and humorous banter. TV news programs like *The CBS Evening News with Walter Cronkite* launched long conversations about daily issues.

"It's awful how they beat up so many of those Chicago protestors."

"I agree. Whatever happened to our free speech rights? Those guys are every bit as patriotic as the John Birch Society extremists."

"It's an American tradition to voice your opinions."

"If Nixon gets elected, we'll all be in trouble. He might spy on us."

"Hey, do you know why a Greyhound cashier in Selma got stuck with extra bus tickets during a Civil Rights protest?"

"No, why?"

"Nobody wanted to sit in the back."

In addition, we played cards and board games. I was sorry to see the summer come to its inevitable end. Lewis and Harriet needed to go back to school a little early. Before returning to campus, Winston and Barbara decided to go on a short camping trip with a classmate of theirs named Cherie, an art major who was transferring to a school up north. Cherie was a tall, slender girl with long blonde hair, a brilliant mind, and a devilish streak. I joined the threesome on a junket to the chaparral in the foothills of the Santa Barbara Mountains.

Barbara and Cherie cooked camp dinners that were far better than the canned food we boys had once prepared. Relaxing at our campsite while downing a few beers, we voiced our concerns. Winston brought his guitar along to play some blues. This gave me the opportunity to show off my guitar skills. We jammed as the sun set in the pastel-colored western sky. After Winston and Barbara retired, Cherie and I fell into an intense discussion about modern media along the lines of Marshall McLuhan, author of a book popular with the college set at the time.

I joked, "Imagine an Andy Warhol style slow motion film of popcorn kernels popping, one every thirty seconds."

She replied, "That's so cool. The art crowd would go nuts over it."

"Yeah, this could take pop art to a whole new level."

"Popcorn art. We'll start a new trend."

When it was time for bed, there was a warm Santa Ana wind spreading an intoxicating fragrance through the sagebrush. The beers had my head swimming as well. It only seemed natural for us to crawl into a tent together. Unaware of my same-sex orientation, Cherie led me into a night of carnal pleasure. To my amazement, I responded and enjoyed the experience. In the morning, I woke up luxuriating in sensuality, yet very conflicted.

After a fun day and intense night, we returned to L.A. I was incredulous. She was female, a shock to my self-image. Despite this, in a strange way I became infatuated with her. On campus, I radiated a macho swagger I never thought myself capable of.

Obsessed with Cherie, I drove a long distance to share another intense weekend with her. I was on a real high. One night, when I got a phone call from my dad, my macho pride couldn't stop me from bragging that I was seeing a girl.

At first, he was delighted. "*Mazel tov*. Tell me, is she Jewish?"

"I don't think so. She's got long blonde hair and light blue eyes."

"If you're seeing a *shikse*, I forbid it. Have you fooled around with her? If you went past a kiss on the cheek, I'll clobber you."

"Too late, dad. I think I'm falling in love with her."

"What do you know about love at your age? Sounds like that Gentile whore has got you by the balls."

"She's not a whore. And I thought you'd be happy for me."

"Don't ever bring her home to us, not like you did with that Negro girl. Wait until I tell your mother about this. You're nothing but a scumbag."

After he slammed down the phone, I cursed myself for opening up to him. Now I had more of my life I needed to keep secret.

I was truly confused. I still had strong desires to go out and cruise men. Yet I needed to see where this new love interest might lead. Undeterred, I called Cherie and arranged to visit her the next weekend. When I arrived, instead of welcoming my advances, she rebuffed them. "I don't know how to say this. I've enjoyed being physical with you, but…"

"But what?"

"I really like you, but we can't have sex together any more."

"Why not? And why didn't you tell me earlier? I didn't drive over 300 miles just to talk about modern art."

"I couldn't say anything over the phone. You see, my ex…"

"I don't want to hear anything about him. You told me that he was your ex. We were having such a great time together."

"He wants to get back with me. I'm sorry."

I mumbled, "Not anywhere as sorry as I am."

I grabbed my things and rushed out the door. On the way back to L.A., I sank into a deep depression that took me months to get over. This seemed to have been such a hot romance I couldn't believe that it had ended. On campus, I'd occasionally run into Carol, who was still pining away for me. But after my experience with Cherie, I was no longer attracted to the straight-arrow lifestyle Carol represented. I was drawn instead to more outrageous people who, like me, had axes to grind.

PART 2
WINGS BROKEN & HEALED

CHAPTER 4
COMING OUT

Theater Arts & The Gay Ghetto

In the theater arts department, rebellion was easy to find. A rock band called The Doors had studied there a couple of years previously. Since then, they'd topped the recording charts with their song "Light My Fire." Also popular was Jimi Hendrix, a black hippie guitarist with a psychedelic rock style that was flooding the airwaves with his hit "Purple Haze," a state of mind many students like me related to.

I got a job as an accompanist for the department. One of the shows in which I played piano that year was a drama about a conflict between warring parties in Northern Ireland set in a house of ill repute in Belfast. After my disappointment with Cherie and coming from a family often battling each other, I felt comfortable in this dark setting.

A cast party with food and alcohol followed each production. I scarfed the goodies, but when it came to libations I stopped after a couple of glasses. When joints were passed around, my aversion to smoking was triggered and I declined. After witnessing my parents struggle to give up cigarettes, I resolved never to start. There were enough other questionable behaviors waiting for me to latch onto instead.

Like many theater groups, this troupe had its share of gay people, some living nearby in West Hollywood. Through them I was introduced to the gay community. Many guys were as affected as the characters in the plays I'd accompanied. Some stereotypical campy effeminate queens I found a bit irritating, yet at the same time I was attracted to their wild sense of humor and edgy attitudes.

"Blanche, your jewelry is divine. Where did you find it?"

"Thanks, dearie, I bought the bracelets at Saks Fifth Avenue, part of that fabulous Jack Goldstein line. For paste, it's not bad. You should have seen the hunk it helped me land last night."

"Lucky for you, bitch. This belle hasn't been asked to the ball in ages."

"Sweetie, you should try some of Goldstein's stuff. It might help a poor girl like you get some man appeal."

They were talking about my uncle's jewelry. Saks was one of Jack's best clients. I chuckled to myself, *What would my dad say if he knew that part of my uncle's fortune came from selling to queens like these?*

Also in the gay crowd were butch guys who wore black leather and metal chains. These macho wannabes often drove huge motorcycles. Many of them put on gruff facades and wore bright-colored handkerchiefs in the back pockets of their 501 Levis. I had no idea what these hankies meant and was afraid to ask. I'd find out soon enough.

Neither extreme appealed to me. I was attracted to more natural guys like straight athletes, campus folkies, and long-haired hippies. The West Hollywood dudes who dressed in jock attire seemed to be playacting. To my dismay, hippies weren't yet part of the gay scene.

At a gathering of gay men that I attended, it was decided to have an orgy. Before I knew it, I was given a hit of amyl nitrate, known as poppers, which sent my pulse racing and my lungs gasping for air. Then I was stripped of my clothes to find myself hooked up with two guys at once. The momentary excitement of feeling both of their erections simultaneously was quickly overshadowed by the intensity of the drug rush that made me feel like I was choking.

"Excuse me, I can't breathe in this position. Take that plastic toy out of my butt! It hurts. And I don't like my nipples pinched, either. No, I don't want any more poppers. I think I'm coming down with walking pneumonia. Anybody see where I put my jeans?"

The next morning, I woke up in my dorm room with a splitting headache. I resolved not to attend any more orgies. But the cruisy bars and streets near Decorator Row were another matter. With my hormones raging, these became outlets to explore. Availing myself of the one-night-stands that were easy to obtain, I began living out the words of the song

"Strangers in The Night," exchanging glances that led to sharing bodily fluids and not much else.

Trolling for sexual encounters was much like the life style of a gambler, rolling the dice to see who'd take me home, whose bed I'd land in, and whose shower I'd use to freshen up in the morning before going back to school. There were hardly any repeat visits. WeHo, as this gay mecca was often called, weaned me away from my campus-centered life. College classes were stimulating, but there was a new world outside of school just waiting to be experienced, not to mention a whole lot of men.

Graduation, The Beatles, & Venice Beach

My parents attended my college graduation ceremony, but hardly said a complimentary word. At a dinner afterwards in a steakhouse that my dad enjoyed, my mom tolerated, and I hated, they unleashed a mixture of faint praise and strong admonitions. My father began, "You finished school, but you didn't study engineering."

My mom followed, "Julliard this was not. How will you support a family with a measly bachelor's degree in music? We saved so you should get ahead, not fall behind."

I defended myself. "I'll be a teacher. Aren't you proud of me?"

He replied, "Teachers just get by." Then he talked past me directly to her, "Our boy is going to starve, just like I told you." I choked on my steak and felt like going to the men's room to throw it up. But I kept it inside, like so much else I didn't reveal.

Living at home, I traveled to teach piano students, staying out as late as possible. Although preferring a break from classes, I applied for and was admitted to graduate school. Having almost enough funds to rent my own place, I continued living with my folks to save up the rest. I grew tired of hearing them complain about me as a lost cause.

"With his long hair and Nehru jackets, Sam has become a hippie."

"Irving, it's just a phase."

"Next thing you know, he'll join a commune."

"He'll grow out of it."

"'When I'm in my grave that'll happen. He'll never straighten up."

Little did they know how un-straight I'd become. "Love is just a glance away," became my mantra as I hit the streets of WeHo. One day, while listening to the Beatles song "She's Leaving Home," I identified with the anti-heroine departing from her nagging parents. I gathered my savings to find my own place, even if I couldn't afford a nice one.

I'd been to a few parties in the beach towns of Santa Monica and Venice. Comfortable with the casual lifestyle there, I searched for a place removed from but still close to grad school. Many other students lived nearby, especially the liberated ones. At twenty-one, I was ready to declare my independence.

A childhood memory of Venice Beach was walking into a coffee house where bearded beatniks played bongos and recited poetry to jazz music. This was an undeveloped area of shacks at the time. My mom had advised my father to buy a parcel of land there, sensing it would increase in value over the years. He pooh-poohed her suggestion. "What do you know about real estate? We'll be pissing our money away."

"When the neighborhood doubles in value, you'll be sorry."

"Hell could freeze over before that happens."

A decade later in the 1960s, Marina del Rey area was well on its way to becoming a millionaire's playground. This was yet another missed opportunity of my shortsighted father.

Apartment hunting in Venice, I discovered a tiny bungalow, once a servant's quarters for a court of arty apartments around the corner. Its landlord was an old Jewish man whose hands shook. He didn't maintain these residences, leaving his tenants on their own in return for reasonable rates. Most of the inhabitants were bohemian types.

My mom came to visit the bungalow while I was moving in. She was outraged by the disrepair the house had fallen into as well as the dirty parking lot and littered sidewalks. When the landlord dropped in, she shouted, "How can you let my boy live in such filth?"

The man replied, "Low rent doesn't come with custodial service."

"I'm going to report you to the authorities."

"Go ahead. This city has bigger fish to fry than your little *tatele*."

I tried to stop her attack. "Leave him alone. He's not a well man. He's got Parkinson's."

"I'm not a well woman, either. My ulcers are acting up."

In disgust, I cried, "And you're not giving us all a headache?"

After the landlord exited, she left in a huff. "If you move in here, don't ever come to me for help."

An actress friend of mine who'd arrived to support me settle in there witnessed my mom's outburst. I apologized profusely, "I'm sorry you had to see this. My family is nuts."

My dramatic cohort responded, "Your mother was a goldmine. I'm auditioning for a Bette Davis part next week. Now I know exactly how to act, gestures and all. I see Oscars in my future."

Once I moved in, I studied for my seminars during the week. With not much else to do on the weekends, I discovered a local beach where gays cruised in their cars. My "bachelor pad" became a place to bring tricks over for recreational sex. I started out looking for a connection with an attractive man, perhaps seeking the approval I never got from my father. Not finding Mr. Right, I'd settle for Mr. Right For the Night. The next morning, if my "friend" wasn't there, it didn't matter. The passion was spent with no meaningful connection. This sexual addiction fed upon itself, never filling my needs. Affection had rarely been shown in my family, so I had no idea what love really felt like.

Rock Bands, Hippies, & Drugs

Cruising had some fun moments, but these fleeting pleasures followed by abandonment led me into deep states of despair. No longer having easy access to the socializing of my dormitory days, I fell into a lonely, introverted existence. Although unhappy with this solitary life, I wasn't ready to do anything to change it.

Then an unfortunate event gave me a kick in the butt. After a fruitless evening searching for a companion, I drove back alone to my sanctuary in what had become a familiar state of depression. Parking my van in the trash-filled driveway, I noticed a broken window on the side of the house. The place had been ransacked, my guitar and stereo system both gone.

Given the neighborhood and the amount of tricks I brought over, I should have expected this. While I sensed it was only a matter of time before I'd be burglarized, it still came as a shock. Why would anyone do this to me? Feeling naive and vulnerable, I took it as a sign that I needed to move to a safer, more sociable location. I found the solution in an old brownstone on the Venice boardwalk.

This old-style flat had craftsman windows, built-in bookcases, and crown molding. I could hear the waves crashing onshore from my bedroom. Here, it was easy to make friends. Anytime I felt alone, I could walk outside and find a community of artists, hippies, and beach bums like me. People often congregated on the sidewalk bringing musical instruments and jamming. In this social environment I felt much more at home.

One afternoon, my parents visited me in another new Buick. After parking in a dusty lot behind the building, they were incredulous when they walked up the three flights of stairs to my unit. As they entered, my dad uttered a complaint I repeated to my buddies afterward. "I traveled 3,000 miles to get away from brownstones and you decide to move into the only one in Los Angeles." This was the nicest thing he had to say.

My mom was even more disapproving. "Your other place was bad. This one is worse. You'd think we were still in the Bronx. You'll never get a nice girl interested in you in this rotten neighborhood. Who'd visit you here, let alone want you, even?"

I replied, "Nothing I do ever pleases you guys. You haven't said a word about the picture windows or crown molding. I think you'd better leave. I don't need anyone to come here just to put me down."

"I tried to raise a good boy. All I wanted was for you to be happy."

"Ma, I am happy here. If you can't see this, there's not much I can say."

My dad motioned to her, "Let's go." Then he sneered at me and said, "Don't worry, we won't bother you here again."

As they were leaving, I overheard her cry out melodramatically, "Irving, I tried to talk some sense into him. Where did we go wrong?"

"Honey, I kept telling you, but you wouldn't listen."

Seeing them drive away, I felt a mixture of sadness and pride. How ironic that it took a confrontation to realize how happy I was here.

I experimented with many things such as vegetarianism and fasting, even going on a diet eating nothing but fruit and nuts for two weeks. This caused me to become light-headed, and I dropped ten pounds. This was a fun kick, but hardly a regimen to stick with.

Another new experience was marijuana, something I'd delayed because of my aversion to smoking. But one night at a party, someone brought out a hookah, a gurgling water pipe. Because this was different from cigarettes, I gave it a try. From the first puff, I enjoyed the high. This developed into a fun habit. My new hero was Ray Charles, whose hit song at the time was "Let's Go Get Stoned."

I'd go on a sweet binge, eating frozen cookie dough cut up in slices that I shared with fellow potheads, then listen to long rock music jams, losing myself in the colors, patterns, and images running through my mind. At someone else's keyboard, I'd improvise riffs in various styles. Pot opened a lot of doors for me, even if it lessened my ability to follow through with my academic studies. Bob Dylan reinforced this practice with his song, "Everybody Must Get Stoned."

Meanwhile, in grad school the instructors had me write in dissonant styles I didn't care for. A friend suggested I check out a state college across town where the curriculum emphasized applied instead of academic music. When research proved this true, I transferred there.

Concentrating on folk styles, I spent a lot of time in the library researching blues, gospel, and mountain music. Inspired, I put my hedonistic habits on hold. Buying an upright piano, I practiced adding new songs to my repertoire. My technique improved greatly.

A friend of mine named Billy played guitar in a rock band in a neighboring beach town. "Sam, check us out. This club next to the pier is full of surfers, ho-dads, and groupie chicks. We play cool Chicago blues tunes like Howlin' Wolf and Muddy Waters songs."

At the club, though girls would come on to me, I was more interested in staring at the surfer dudes. One night, Billy asked if I wanted to sit in and jam. The group began a 12-bar blues and I played an impressive solo. A week later, Billy called to say the keyboard player had left. He suggested that I audition to replace him.

"Am I good enough for you guys?"

"If you play like you did the other night, I know you'll get the gig."

I soon became a band member and bought myself an electric keyboard. With a regular gig, I began living the triple life of an academic student, beach bum, and performer in a rowdy rock club. In the words of one of our blues songs, I was "rollin' and tumblin', rollin' all night long."

Sometimes our band played like gangbusters, but on other nights the music was uncoordinated. Each musician had his private jones. The flashy guitarist was a pothead, the bass player liked downers, the drummer was fond of speed, and the lead singer consumed several beers a night. My vice was apple cider, and the guys teased me for it. The lead singer being related to the bar owner kept us employed.

After one spirited night, I returned home so tired I fell asleep on my sofa before getting into bed. I dreamt that my blues group was on American Bandstand in front of Dick Clark to be rated by audience members. The judges of their first song, "High Heeled Sneakers," were Winston and Lewis. They said the music was OK but needed some tightening up. Our second number, "Got My Mojo Working," was to be evaluated by Cherie and Carol. Cherie said that my mojo didn't work very well. Carol was flustered and asked what a mojo was. "Is it a noodle pudding or what a hound dog leaves behind on the carpet?"

When Dick Clark whispered the answer, Carol turned beet red. "I have to excuse myself from judging. I've never seen Sam's mojo."

For the third song, "Evil's Going On," two policemen sat in the judges' seats. They gave the band a "thumbs down," saying they had to take me to the station for questioning. One of them slipped handcuffs on my wrists as they led me offstage. I protested, "What did I do?"

The reply was, "You were playing the blues without a permit. Wait 'til we tell this to the judge." I woke up shaking like a leaf.

With this hectic schedule, I hardly had time to cruise men. In school and onstage I was challenged, developing two different kinds of musicianship.

The Peace Corps & The Shaman

After the end of my second year of grad school it was time to start on my master's thesis. I had problems finding the right topic and focus. Even if I could define my subject matter, my interest in school was fading away.

A factor that weighed heavily on me was the draft. I'd registered with the selective service at the age of eighteen. Now twenty-two, my student deferment was about to run out. Being a peacenik, I did not want to go into the army. Though I had fantasies about being part of a group of buff guys in uniform, I was afraid of combat and hated following orders. Far worse, my attraction to men, if ever found out, could subject me to ridicule and perhaps violence.

Although my dad never served in the armed forces, he got on my case about enlisting. "Son, the army will make a man out of you."

"You weren't in the military, were you?"

"I was needed to repair airplanes."

"I'll find another way for myself, too."

He goaded me, "You're just chicken."

"You won't be happy 'til I'm killed in action and you can make matzo ball soup out of my carcass."

Whatever my father advocated, I went in the opposite direction. One day, while walking through campus, I noticed a poster promoting the Peace

Corps and decided to look into it as an alternative. I wanted to do service for my country, just not go to war.

At an interview, I answered all queries honestly except one, "Are you homosexual?" Thinking a "yes" would disqualify me, I checked "no." Another question was "Where did you want to serve?" I listed Chile because of its similarity to California. My second choice was India because of my interest in Eastern music and religion.

In a few weeks, I received a letter inviting me to a 2-week training session. If I passed I'd be assigned to a tiny island in the South Pacific. Though not one of my chosen sites, I didn't mind. It was a break from school, far from my family, and a real adventure. I'd serve my nation and keep the army off my back.

The training was held at a state college campus similar to my current school. We slept at the dorms and ate in the student cafeteria. This brought back memories of food fights, such as when I once sent cubes of Jello soaring across the room using my napkin as a launching pad.

The volunteers had been selected from all over the U.S. I found out later we were sent to serve in a rural area because most trainees in my group were from small towns. Why I, a city dweller, wasn't placed in an urban setting remained an unsolved mystery.

Besides discussing our duties, there were more interviews to weed out bad apples. One was with a psychologist who inquired about my home life. I played down the household abuse. Interrogated again about my sexual identity, I lied. I had my affair with Cherie to refer to and also a one-night-stand with a girl groupie of the rock band I'd played in. She only came onto me because she wanted to brag to her friends that she'd made it with the keyboard player. That night ended in disappointment for both of us.

I passed training with flying colors. We volunteers were given vaccinations to keep us from contracting any exotic tropical diseases. Then we were handed out duffle bags filled with generic clothing for the South Pacific. I was on pins and needles. Not since my trip to Colorado was I as thrilled about a forthcoming adventure.

We were flown to Hawaii and then to Guam. A smaller group was transported to a tiny airport town two hundred miles farther. This was near the island that was to be my home for the next two years. After countless hours of travel, we made the last leg of our journey by boat. Everyone was exhausted, but rest would not be mine right away.

When we walked onto the dock, the entire village was there to greet us. Ceremonial drums were played, flowers were strewn, and each volunteer was offered a leaf, powder and nut. All except me refused this. Always game to try something new, I was shown how to put white lime powder and the nut inside the leaf and chew on it. I did as I was told. Immediately, my mouth was full of dark purple juice and I was overcome with an intense stinging sensation. I spit out the mixture as my eyes almost burst out of their sockets.

The villagers broke into riotous applause. What I'd sampled was betel nut, a popular mild narcotic. When consumed regularly, this fruit of the areca palm tree wore away tooth enamel and many villagers had teeth missing. Though temporarily the village laughing stock, I was shown respect for having been brave enough to try it.

We interns were taken to a large room where a feast was held in our honor. After the meal, we were introduced to our host families. I was led to a corrugated tin shack woven with rope tied to thatched leaves on top. A section of a room in this modest home was reserved for me, complete with bedding and a mosquito net to be placed on top of me while sleeping.

The next morning, the woman of the household, who said to call her "mom," served me a meal of fish, taro, tapioca, and tropical fruit, their basic diet. Unlike many of the others, my "island mama" was a good cook, varying the way she prepared these ingredients. Having an adventurous palate, I took to these foods right away. In contrast, most of the other trainees complained that their meals were boring.

For several weeks, we reported to a large tent where we were instructed in training the villagers to speak and write English. Having had prior teaching experience, I was comfortable with this. My natural curiosity led me beyond my group of interns to make friends with some older volunteers who'd been on the island for years. I found them to be a fount of knowledge and a source of salvation, yet unwittingly would aid in my undoing. When I asked one of these veterans, "How long have you been here?" his reply was "I arrived when JFK was President."

I confided, "I was so upset when he was assassinated."

"We all were. When Johnson took over, Sargent Shriver supervised the Corps, and we were able to carry on his work."

"What kind of jobs did you guys do?"

"Electricity and plumbing, whatever made village life better."

Another volunteer was much more bitter in his description. "That was until Nixon became President. Now all we're supposed to teach them is how to do office work when the navy moves in."

Startled, I blurted out, "The navy?"

"Yeah. They intend to make this area a replacement for Okinawa if we get kicked out of there. These harbors are well protected for a fleet."

"You mean that P.R. about helping humanity was a bunch of bull?"

"Welcome to the real world."

This took the wind out of my idealistic sails. Although discouraged in my commitment, I was buoyed by a new discovery. When I overheard a volunteer mention that a shaman practiced on the island, I asked to be introduced. A meeting was soon arranged.

In a small hut on the outskirts of the village lived a slight, old man who wore bright-colored clothes, jewelry, and feathers unlike the simple village attire. His mannerisms made any WeHo queen seem as butch as John Wayne. This demure witch doctor sat me down on a bench, lit some incense, and repeated a few words that sounded like he was summoning magic as he chanted some haunting music. I was transported to another dimension. When the shaman was finished, he put his hands on my shoulders sending powerful energy through my body. Then it was over, and the man motioned for me to leave. I thanked him with a few native words and gestures.

Once back with the group of veterans, I was full of questions. "Do the locals know about this man? He's so effeminate."

One of them answered, "He is revered by the villagers. Gays here are considered to be special people with unique gifts. Many of them are healers who practice magic."

I gushed, "Gay people on the island? Do the trainers know this? I was told that the Corps doesn't allow homosexuals to serve."

"Many of the administrators are so homophobic we don't discuss it."

I took my volunteer friend aside and asked him, "Has anyone else had a ceremony like I did performed for him?"

"You're the first. I asked him questions, but he wasn't interested."

Curious about this, I inquired, "Why with me then?"

"He must have sensed something special about you."

I blurted out recklessly, "Maybe it's because he could tell that I'm gay."

"I thought so. He really seemed to like you."

Filled with paranoia, I begged him, "Please don't tell anyone else about my orientation. I could be asked to leave."

"Don't worry, I'll keep it secret. But you never know what gets said among the villagers."

I wondered if I had shaman potential. I'd always been interested in diseases. *Maybe I'd become a healer one day.* Then suddenly I was scared. What if word got out about my sexual preference? I'd lied to get into the Corps. Now I could be kicked out if this information was revealed.

When I returned to training, I was mum about the shaman. Outside of class, I confided to a few of the others the cynical reason we were asked to come to the island in the first place. I felt these wonderful people had as much to teach us as we had to show them.

As the training was ending, we new volunteers were nearing our first assignments. Suddenly, I was summoned to where the instructors lived and told to gather my things. I was being shipped off the island. When I asked why, there was no explanation. Panicking, I did as I was told, figuring that someone must have ratted on me.

Before I had a chance to say goodbye, I was transported to the airport town and told to stay there until the next flight departed in a few days. Then I was taken to a married couple, two older volunteers who housed me in the interim. Both were warm and welcoming. Once I settled in and had some time to relax, the husband said, "They're getting rid of you, too. You must've been hanging around the old timers."

"The older volunteers were a lot more interesting than the trainees."

His wife added, "Two other people were sent home last week. They must be clamping down."

As we shared a meal of ramen noodles, a dish handed down from the occupiers of this once Japanese settlement, the man mentioned something that put my paranoia at ease. "The new Peace Corps administrators are angry at us Kennedyites," he related. "They don't want anyone destroying the morale of the new arrivals by saying we're being used as pawns, not serving humanity as advertised."

I asked, "If that's how you feel, why are you guys still here?"

The woman's answer was one I would remember for a long time, "We love this place. Sometimes in life, you have to wear blinders."

I was relieved to hear that being gay was not why I was asked to leave. The irony in the situation was, as I later learned from one of my fellow interns, the whole operation was terminated soon after our period of instruction ended. The military decided that the area was no longer slated to be a replacement for Okinawa. Not needed anymore, even the old volunteers had to wind down their work. I had only missed out on a few weeks of this incredible, though disillusioning, adventure.

Foot & Mouth Disease & The Long-Haired Professor

On the way back home, I was flown to Honolulu where the government put me up in a hotel before shuttling me back to the mainland. I met a volunteer there who'd served on another island. Her name was Karina, about the same age as me. We went out together for a few meals in town on the Corps' modest per diem. Over a sashimi dinner, I asked her, "Where did you serve?"

She replied, "My assignment was on a tiny atoll in the corner of our district. It was so primitive, many of the women went around topless."

"Sounds like a Gauguin painting."

"It was as pretty as any he ever created, but the people were poor and malnourished. With my background in nursing, I was told to teach nutrition and hygiene. When I arrived, the life expectancy was low."

"That doesn't sound like where I was trained. The villagers had nice houses and ate well. I found their diet healthier than most Americans. They should come to our country and teach us a few things."

On the way back to our hotel, I asked, "How come you're going home by yourself? Aren't you part of a group?"

"Yes, but about a month ago, I came down with a strange disease."

I was curious. "What was it?"

"I don't want to talk about it. I had mouth sores and a facial rash."

"That sounds awful."

"It was embarrassing to be a health instructor and get sick. They say I'm over it, but I've been very weak. They're sending me home to rest."

"I hope you feel better soon."

"Thanks. After almost two years away, it'll sure be good to get back to the mainland again. My flight leaves tomorrow morning."

I did not share Karina's enthusiasm for returning home. After seeing her off at the airport, I explored Honolulu. I would have liked to stay there for a while and experience it fully. Suddenly, I had a splitting headache, so I went into a Safeway store to get some aspirin. I was struck by the contrast to where I'd been. After the tiny market in the small village, I was overwhelmed by rows of choices instead of one kind of soda, bread, or cheese that the little store carried. This huge supermarket was an embarrassment of riches, a virtual Disneyland of merchandise.

A couple of days later, I boarded a plane to take me to San Francisco and then back home to LAX. On this long flight, having been so far away from the influences of my family and society, I began imagining living an openly gay lifestyle. No more hiding and trying to live up to others' expectations. This desire was inspired after my meeting with the shaman. When the plane stopped over at the Bay Area, I considered moving there to begin a new life.

Not happy living back with my family, I made plans to move north. But I soon fell ill and had to postpone this. When I developed a facial rash and irritating mouth sores, this sent my mom into hysterics. Suspecting it might be something I'd picked up in the tropics, most likely from Karina, I wisely went to my college medical center instead of the family physician. I'd contracted a hand, foot, and mouth disease that a large university clinic had more experience in treating. Although easily cured, this condition was highly contagious. I was advised to quarantine myself for a couple of weeks.

I was confined to my bedroom in Chez Freberg. My dad was buried in his stereo business, my mom busy with volunteer work at Democratic Party meetings, and my sisters were out with their friends. So I lounged by myself, read a few books, and contemplated my future.

While I was coping with this illness, I got a phone call from the college where I'd studied before my Peace Corps stint. A guitar instructor there had left to go on tour and they were looking for a replacement. Because of my interest in folk music, my name had come up. Though my heart was set on a move to a freer life up north, there was the problem of making a living. I'd be starting over with private students, most likely having to scrounge up whatever odd jobs I could find in the interim. Here in LA was a position that could make use of my talents with some decent pay to boot.

One night, I had a high fever and dreamed that I'd bought a train ticket to San Francisco. When I arrived at the station, it wasn't in my wallet. As the train left the platform without me, I sat on a nearby bench and started sobbing. The weather was cold, dark, and menacing.

Suddenly, Mrs. B. sat down next to me and gave me a handkerchief to wipe my tears. "Honey, you weren't meant to travel north right now."

"What do you mean? This was my big chance. In the Bay Area, once I'm away from my folks I'll let my hair grow long, find happiness, and maybe even meet a boyfriend."

"Happiness is a state of mind. No place has a monopoly on it. You can find everything you want right here. You'll get to San Francisco at the right time. Meanwhile, you've just been given a great opportunity. Make the most of it."

She then disappeared as quickly as she came. The sun came out from behind the clouds. When I woke up, my fever had broken. I was greatly relieved.

It wasn't long before I became a college professor, one of the youngest on the campus. My lack of skill as a guitar player was compensated by an extensive knowledge of folk music. In the few weeks before class, I furiously brushed up on my technique.

The school had recently switched to the ten-week quarter system. After a couple of quarters had come and gone, I'd become a decent player. By this time, I'd let my hair grow long again, making me one of the very few hippie-looking professors on the campus. If I couldn't move to San Francisco, at least I could look like I lived there.

The music department not only tolerated me, they showed off my "Socratic approach" of breaking down my class into groups as a role model to visitors. When educators from other institutions came to observe our teaching methods, the administration officials used my example to demonstrate how "current" the department had become. I was one of the most sought after instructors in the school. I thought how my mom would be happy about this. I was finally popular.

CHAPTER 5
BROKEN HEARTED

Brian, Ram Dass, & Big Sur

Once I received a few paychecks, I resettled in Venice, moving into a modern apartment building on the boardwalk. With enough money to live on comfortably, thoughts of finishing my master's thesis disappeared in this laid-back environment. At the age of twenty-three, I resumed trolling for one-night stands, none of which went anywhere.

Then one day on the beach I ran into a tall, thin young man with long blond hair who was to make a few important changes in my life. Brian was a hippie with an ethereal build, a yoga practitioner and New Age follower who possessed an aura of mysticism. He attracted me with the line, "Our souls were destined to travel a spiritual path together."

I invited him over to my new apartment, lit some candles and incense, and put on some sitar music in the background. I really wanted to impress this new prospect. After a night of sensitive lovemaking, Brian headed for the door without a message of continuance. Before he could exit, I called out, "When can I see you again?"

"I live nearby, so I'm sure we'll run into each other on The Strand."

"Won't you give me your phone number?"

"I'm staying with people who wouldn't want to be disturbed."

"Well, let me give you mine."

"Just tell me. I've a good memory." Seeing my disappointment, Brian added, "Don't worry, we'll be together again soon."

It was strange to have my passions awakened, then followed by such uncertainty. I told myself not to be foolish like I was with Cherie. Despite efforts to get Brian out of my mind, I prowled the beach looking for him. Like a watched pot that never boils, this was unsuccessful. Just as I was about to give up the pursuit, I bumped into him at a local grocery. We went to my place and shared another mystical evening.

This time, he had a Baba Ram Dass book with him called *Be Here Now*, the hippie bible of its time. He left it for me to read. It was a guide to living in the present, not something I was good at. I ruminated about the past and worried about the future. Pop culture references to Buddhist philosophy had left me wondering. Brian motivated me to explore this path of consciousness. After a couple more unscripted meetings, he proposed hitchhiking to Big Sur together. I replied, "I'd love to, but I have to teach three days a week and can only take a long weekend."

"No problem," he reassured me, "so many people thumb up these highways, we'll be able to get there and back easily. Going on the road like this will teach you some lessons I feel you need to learn."

"OK, tell me what I need to bring."

Early one Friday morning, we stood on Highway 1 in Santa Monica, sleeping and duffle bags in hand with thumbs outstretched. It wasn't long before a ride was offered by a van full of hippies in tie-dyed garb. A young chick from the East Coast called out, "We can take you guys up to Oxnard. We're going to The Strawberry Festival there."

Once we climbed inside, a joint was passed around while everyone listened to Jefferson Airplane blaring on the stereo. I enjoyed getting high as I stared at the ocean and the local wildflowers. Declining an invitation to join them at the festival, we quickly found a ride up to San Luis Obispo with a car full of noisy college guys returning from a football game. Right after we were dropped off at the turnoff for Highway 1, another van stopped. A long-haired dude invited us the rest of the way, "We're going camping at Pfeiffer Beach. Come join us."

Young people from all parts of the U.S. were traveling on this route, brothers and sisters in a new Aquarian Age. Hearing "When the moon is in the seventh house and Jupiter aligns with Mars" on the radio, I was ready to become an official tribe member.

When we got to Big Sur, Brian had them drop us off at a spot north of town where a pine tree covered hill was bordered by a lush cattle pasture. Just as I finished setting up my tent, looking forward to a romantic evening, my companion said he was leaving. Suddenly, he was nowhere to be seen. I called repeatedly, but there was no answer. Darkness came quickly. I grabbed my provisions and went into the tent. Feeling abandoned, I crawled into my sleeping bag and fell into a desperate sleep.

Waking up in this idyllic location with the sounds of rushing water and mooing cows, what seemed frightening the night before was no longer upsetting. Making a meal out of trail mix, I walked to the village where many young people like me were congregating. I struck up conversations with fellow travelers and learned of a camping site nearby. Trading my store of raw nuts, fruit, bread, and cheese with others who'd set up camping gear there, I spent a delightful night with a gathering of friendly vagabonds.

The next day, concerned about having only two days to return to teach my classes, I got on the road early. Thumbing back to L.A. was as easy as traveling north. I arrived at Venice with a day to spare, emboldened by my adventure. Despite Brian's disappearance, I was thrilled to experience this new world and couldn't wait to do it again by myself.

Every evening, I searched in vain for him on the boardwalk. The longing in my heart was mitigated when I remembered the Ram Dass book. I poured through the text with its messages of freedom from attachment and living in the present. The words were easy to grasp on a superficial level. Truly letting go was more difficult.

The Draft, The Shrink, The Rabbi, & Dr. T.

A part-time professor and part-time hitchhiker along coastal California, I thumbed on some weekends and on others drove my van, picking up riders. Though I shared many encounters on hikes up sycamore-lined canyons and creeks, I had no sexual contact with anyone for a long time. I became a loner, a wistful refugee from civilization.

What kept me grounded was my teaching position. My classes were so popular the department doubled my class schedule. They continued showing me off to visitors. All seemed to be going well.

One day, I was shaken out of my routine by a letter from the U.S. Army. Since my stint in the Peace Corps I'd forgotten about them. I had to report for a physical to see if I was fit to serve. This sent me into a panic. Though given a fairly high lottery number, I didn't want to take any chance of getting drafted, which in those days meant going to Vietnam.

I confided this to one of my gay buddies, an older queen with his share of zingers. Matthew, or "Myrna," as we called him, told me that the only way "she" would serve "her" country would be down on "her" knees. "I've never been able to resist a man in uniform. You should have seen me with some of those horny midshipmen on leave in the San Diego harbor."

"What did you do, and how did you get them to do it with you?"

"A patriotic queen never reveals her secrets. I had a motel room nearby to invite them over for a free drink. You can imagine the rest."

My mind raced thinking about how much fun it could be to go to San Diego and do something similar with those military men. Not that it would ever amount to much more than "Wham, bam, thank you, sir."

Besides being a kneel-down version of a stand-up comic, Matthew had some practical advice. "Stay out of the army, even if this requires you to 'check the box.' That means putting an "x' in the military application form about being a homosexual."

I was skeptical. "Are you sure that will work?"

"Honey, it results in immediate disqualification. They don't want any queers like us in the military."

Afraid of revealing my sexual orientation to friends, students, or employers, I didn't want to let the government know. Checking the box was a last resort. One night, with anxiety mounting, I went out cruising and brought home a hippie who had some LSD with him. I hadn't ingested any drugs in a long time. That night became a significant exception. We swallowed our pills and had sex.

Soon after my companion departed, I began having hallucinations of young men marching off to war and being shot. This freaked me out so much I could hardly wait for the effects of the drug to wear off. The next morning, I realized that I needed to do whatever I could to get out of my military commitment. I made appointments with a social worker, a psychologist, a rabbi, and, at the suggestion of a friend, the orthodontist who'd put braces on my teeth when I was a teenager.

The social worker said that filing for conscientious objector status was futile without a long paper trail. The shrink counseled that even if manic-depression ran in my family, it wasn't enough to write a letter excusing me from service. The rabbi warned me not to check the box for being gay. In addition to being sent to Hell if I didn't change my ways, the legal ramifications would brand me for life.

The only alternative left was the orthodontist, an anti-war protestor. This man, Dr. T., put braces on my teeth and wrote a letter saying they'd fall out if the army removed them, forcing the military to pay for dental replacements for the rest of my life. He charged a big fee, but I felt better off free and poor than fighting in a war I didn't believe in.

At the physical, I nervously waited in line. When my name was called, I handed a clerk the letter and smiled, showing off my new dental hardware. The man barked, "Let me give this to the proper authorities. In the meantime, you need to fill out these forms."

When I saw that these were IQ tests, my anxiety increased. Skeptical about how they'd be used, I underperformed. These were followed by images of gears and mechanical parts. Truly inept at this, I didn't have to act dumb. Back in high school when given tests like these, I'd scored high on everything except mechanics, where I got a low score.

After these were completed, I was asked to fill out a questionnaire to measure if my personality would fit as a soldier. It contained questions like "Which would you rather do, smoke cigars and play pool with the guys or attend a ballet?" And "Who do you prefer to listen to, Elvis or Beethoven?" These were no-brainers. I wasn't military material. A question missing was would I rather date Marilyn Monroe or Sal Mineo. As "Myrna" would have said, "I'd rather be Ms. Monroe than date her."

I turned in my tests and waited. An hour later, a burly guy behind the desk said I was free to go. The army didn't want me. Dr. T's letter worked. Without checking any boxes I might regret later, I was dismissed.

Bruce, Pacific Heights, & The Christian Commune

With no more threat of military service, I tried to live in present tense. Treading water brought me neither great happiness nor undue sorrow. I'd often pass the beach where I met Brian, but no reunion took place.

Sometimes I noticed guys sneak under the local pier. In the dark crevasses where hardly any light made its way through the creosote-soaked rafters to the barnacle-encrusted pilings, gay men would grope each other's bodies in the caverns. This sometimes resulted in impersonal sex, occasionally with three or more guys at a time.

On a day I checked it out, the odor of amyl nitrate brought back the unpleasant West Hollywood party a few years back. I had little interest in this carnal amusement park. Though my hormones cried for release, feelings of loneliness were stronger than any horns pulling on my chain.

Just before sunset I sat on the outskirts of the pier cherishing a memory of Brian. Wrapped in reverie as the tide made its way up the shore, splashing onto my perch, I got lost in the last rays of sunlight streaking over the surf. I hardly noticed a stranger standing near me. Bruce, a handsome young man of medium stature, deep-set blue eyes, ruddy complexion, and brown curly hair, asked, "Mind if I sit next to you?"

Startled, yet pleased, I replied, "Why not?"

"The waves on the beach are so beautiful. Let's watch together."

"I'll take you up on that. I've been feeling a little lonely lately."

"Me too. I miss having someone to share something like this with."

We sat together and talked softly. As the conversation slowed, we held hands. With more gestures than words, I followed Bruce to his apartment a few blocks away. While sitting on the stylish sofa in his well-decorated living room, we awoke strong emotions in each other. What I'd long locked inside was released in a passionate night of lovemaking. We fell asleep in each other's embrace.

Waking the next morning, the chemistry ignited the night before was easily rekindled. Our steamy physicality was what I'd longed for ever since my encounter with Tim behind the bowling alley. Before he left, Bruce made a suggestion. "Next time we get together, let's share a joint first. I just scored some great stuff from Mendocino."

"If it's good enough for Ray Charles and Bob Dylan, it's OK with me."

Although Bruce was younger than me, being more sexually experienced, he introduced me to new foreplay techniques. He explained the WeHo handkerchief code. "One color is for active, another for passive, others for various fetishes. The meaning changes from time to time."

"So what's the point?"

"It's like being in a secret organization. Weeds out the riff-raff."

I didn't see any value in this code. We had no need for such signals.

Bruce worked in the financial district downtown as a stockbroker's assistant. On weekday mornings, he tied his curly locks into a ponytail trained to fall gracefully over the back of a crisp white dress shirt that was carefully tucked into pleated dress pants. A tasteful, colorful tie completed the outfit. I loved to feast my eyes on my chic partner, even though I had no desire to dress that way myself.

At my college job, I dressed informally, a tie never in my regimen. A fellow music instructor had warned me that the department could afford only one eccentric hippie on the staff. If another long-haired teacher came along, the faculty might become afraid and let both of us go.

Our bond grew as we spent almost every night together. One day, Bruce got a phone call from his mom who lived near Lake Tahoe, asking him to visit her. This was near the site of my first camping night under the stars. I wanted to show him Big Sur, so we incorporated both destinations. While driving in my van alongside Mt. Whitney, Bruce sat in the passenger seat sketching drawings of the mountains. We were in very high spirits.

Once in Tahoe, he introduced me to his mom, a reserved Midwestern woman. Though she knew of her son's sexual preference, she wasn't comfortable with it. But being a tolerant Christian, she felt it her duty to welcome me and put us up in a spare room in her modest apartment. Sensing that mother and son needed some time alone, I suggested, "Why don't you guys catch up while I go out and explore the lake?"

Bruce replied, "What a great idea. We could use time to ourselves."

As I exited, I overheard his mom comment on how thoughtful I was. I was pleased to have a relationship with the give-and-take this required. Considering other people's needs was not something I'd learned at home. It was an awareness I was picking up on my own.

We left for the Bay Area, staying in Pacific Heights with one of Bruce's friends, an artist who shared a three-story mansion with some students. This structure had amazing architectural details with hardly any furniture inside its huge rooms. That night with everyone out at an exhibition, Bruce took me to a sofa inside the living room. He had two sugar cubes laced with mescaline, a psychedelic he'd brought along. With no one else there but us, it was a perfect time and place to try the drug together.

I thought to myself, *a spoonful of sugar helps the medicine go down*. This turned out to be powerful medicine. An hour later, I became scared and shouted, "This drug is so strong, I shouldn't have taken it."

"Don't worry, just relax and enjoy where it's leading you."

"It makes me feel like that crazy acid trip I told you about."

"Yeah, and didn't it ultimately lead you to a good place?"

"Yes. But I hate losing control. How much longer will this last?"

Bruce hugged me, and in a soothing voice advised, "Guy, this may be a long ride. Relax, I'll put some Hendrix on the hi-fi."

When I stopped resisting the drug, I was filled with vivid imagery as I changed into animal forms, plants, and seaweeds. I became a lotus blossom unfolding in the sun. In a trance, we shared some ecstatic sex.

We awoke in a private room Bruce had led me to that night. When he wanted us to try more mescaline I declined, saying it was so intense I needed time to assimilate it. He reluctantly abstained. We slept off the drug's effects and toured the city's many sights the next day.

The following morning, we drove down the coast to Big Sur. Once there, we slept in my van. Bruce acted strangely detached, not matching my enthusiasm. Even the sex we shared that night seemed forced. By the time we returned to L.A., the bloom was off the rose. Bruce said he needed time by himself. Miffed, I concentrated on updating my lesson plans while he returned to the structure of his brokerage job.

One morning, sleeping by myself, I awoke to a jolt that threw me out of my bed onto the floor. I saw some bright lights flash. Sensing a disaster, I prayed it wasn't atomic. The tremor was followed by a rolling sensation. *An earthquake*, I thought. The power went off. On a transistor radio, I heard that one indeed had occurred.

Outside of a few cracks in my apartment, I didn't suffer any damage. This couldn't have been said of Bruce. Not that his dwelling had any injury. But the day before, a group of Evangelical Christian activists had protested on the street in front of his brokerage house. Their signs had dire warnings that the world was coming to an end with proclamations that homosexuality was a sin and gay people were going to Hell. This really upset him. The earthquake reinforced his fear.

The day after the quake, he phoned me. "Meet me at our bench on the boardwalk. I need to discuss something." Once we were seated, he related, "Remember those people downtown I told you about?"

Sensing trouble, I answered warily, "What about them?"

"I was so disturbed by their signs, I couldn't sleep all night."

"So?"

"I haven't shared much with you about my Christian background."

"You're Christian, and I'm Jewish. So what?"

"Seeing my mom started me thinking how I'm going down the wrong path." He took my hand and squeezed it, adding, "I need some time to think things over. I'll call you when I've sorted it out." He kissed me on the cheek and walked away without looking back.

For several days I didn't hear from him. Every time I called, there was no answer. When we finally spoke, the news was not good. He said, "I'm quitting my job and moving to Northern California to a Christian commune. Those activists awoke a calling I need to answer. Being gay is a weakness I have to change or I'm going straight to Hell."

"Those people are wrong. Don't let them tell you that being gay is evil. God made us this way. Jesus never put us down - his followers did."

"What we are doing is immoral."

"According to whom, a misguided prophet? You're not only punishing me, you're hurting yourself. I pleaded, "You'll be sorry. You can't run away from yourself. Don't leave me. I love you."

He sobbed, "I love you too, Sam, but my mind is made up. I'm leaving this weekend. I'll write you once I get there. I promise."

I never heard from Bruce again. This abrupt breakup turned my world upside down. When Brian had disappeared, I was disappointed. This time, I was totally broken-hearted. With emotions ripped apart from me so suddenly, love was not just a glance away. It was hundreds of miles more distant. I would not be the same for a long time.

CHAPTER 6
ARRESTED DEVELOPMENT

Vernon, Paul, & Lucas

In the early '70s, I had a winter of discontent. It was an El Nino year with double the average rainfall, and the hostile weather matched my downcast attitude. Carole King's hit recording "I Feel The Earth Move" only brought tears. She had no idea how an earthquake helped to end my relationship with Bruce. I was left for Jesus. Ms. King's songs being too warm and fuzzy, I listened instead to sad recordings by James Taylor and Jackson Browne, and identified with Joni Mitchell losing yet another lover.

My interest in teaching waned. Even my hitchhiking fell by the wayside. Rather than escape to the fog banks of Big Sur, I frequented the back alleys of WeHo and the notorious Selma Avenue in Hollywood. On cold damp nights, I'd cruise the streets half hidden in a pea coat and scarf, darting my eyes towards and away from strange men with hardly any communication. The few times I managed to connect with someone, it was a "hit and run" event at best.

At the Santa Monica Boulevard bars, I had no better luck. I wound up like many other sad souls sitting on our barstool thrones, playing a game of "I'll reject you before you can reject me." Often, I finished the evening taking out my frustrations at a greasy hamburger stand before going home alone. The body that once was my temple accumulated infusions of late night cholesterol without religious services. If there were any rites, it was the worshipping of false gods.

Near Decorator Row, I drove around in my van picking up strangers for quick sex in the back of the curtained vehicle. I'd park on a dark corner of a deserted street in a futile attempt for a connection. I spent my nights alone in a crowd of loners, chasing what fleeting pleasure I could get, far from my heart's desires. This was the tawdry homosexual lifestyle described in books and movies, a far cry from the joyful experiences I'd shared not long before. I related to the words in a song very popular then, "Nobody Brings Me Flowers Anymore." In those days, nobody brought me anything but rejection and abandonment.

One night after the bars had closed, I saw a stocky guy with long red hair hanging in dreadlocks lean against a lamppost in front of a hustler hangout. I parked around the corner to entice him to come over, and the ploy worked. Not looking to purchase company; paying for sex was not in my vocabulary. I wasn't even feeling sexual, just lonely. After gestures and window rolling down, the stranger entered on the passenger side. Neither of us had any expectations.

"Your place or mine?"

"Mine, I live just a few blocks away."

The guy directed me to an old brick building in a dark pocket of what was sometimes referred to as Hollywood's rock-n-roll ghetto. On the way up the dingy urine-stenched stairway to this fellow's dimly lit apartment, I learned that my "date's" name was Vernon. If this was "Hotel California," it was not one with a "Tequila Sunrise."

Instead of an erotic connection, we took a different course. From New Orleans, Vernon was a rock musician, a bass player. Since moving to L.A. to pursue a career, he wrote a song that had made its way onto the charts. Impressed to meet someone with success in the field, I asked its name. Finding out, I shouted, "I heard it on the radio. You must be getting lots of money. Soon you'll be moving into fancier digs."

He replied, "Not so. I've got nothing to show for it."

I was astonished. "How can that be?"

"I signed it over to a crooked publisher. That motherfucker stole the rights to the song, even put his name on it as co-writer. I probably won't see a cent. Looks like I'll be staying in this fleabag for a while."

"That's terrible, man. Didn't you go over it with an attorney?"

"I couldn't afford a lawyer. That dick hyped me so much about my song being a hit, I let him pressure me into signing a bad contract."

"What a bummer."

"There's lot of thieves in this town. I've got more songs I want to sell. Next time, I'll be more careful."

I looked at my watch. "Hey, I've got a class to teach in a few hours. Here's my phone number. Call me. Maybe we can get together soon."

"Sure, I'm not busy. I've got nothing but time."

"Good. I'll bring over my keyboard and we can jam."

This began a successful friendship. We'd each taken some lumps and needed to vent our frustrations. Vernon told me about his problematic past. In Louisiana, he'd gotten into a fight, was thrown in jail, and had more scuffles in prison. I was fascinated with his jailhouse stories. On the weekends, we hung out at his apartment and jammed together.

One night, he invited a guitarist to join us. Paul, a tall lanky dude in his 20s, had long dark hair hanging down to his slim hips. A World War II pilot's jacket, pipe, and Fender Stratocaster in its case complemented his striking appearance. He was an amazing guitarist with a distinctive tone and melodic expressiveness that I admired. He also had an uncanny ability to improvise.

Vernon needed to return to New Orleans to take care of some legal business, so Paul and I started playing on our own. I drove to Hollywood to bring him to the beach. The apartment next to mine was empty. We played to our heart's content as long as it didn't go late, trading riffs, changing keys and tempos in a symphonic manner. This was as intimate as good sex, and we got together often.

Sometimes Paul brought his girlfriend Arlene along. She was a sweet hippie chick devoted to him. She'd bring some groceries and whip up a veggie stir-fry in my kitchen for us to share after a jam. We'd smoke a joint and listen to rock albums like Pink Floyd and Led Zeppelin.

One day, I got a call from her. "Have you seen Paul?"

"Can't say that I have. It's been a few weeks since we've played."

Her voice was troubled. "I haven't seen him either. He's been staying at a hippie commune out near Malibu where they're into heavy drugs and communal sex. He's lost all interest in me."

"I wonder what turned his head around. You guys had such a good thing going. Frankly, I've been envious."

"He's fallen under the spell of the group's leader. I met the guy and can tell he's bad news. Paul doesn't see that. He idolizes him."

"Sorry to hear this. Is there anything I can to do to help?"

"Maybe you could visit there and talk some sense into him."

"Why don't we go together?"

"I've tried several times without success. Please, I'm desperate."

"OK. Tell me where he is. I'll give it a try."

Speaking to Paul over the phone, I could tell that he'd changed. I drove to the commune where a ditsy teenaged girl said he was busy and couldn't see me. The next visit, when told the same thing, I said I'd wait. While sitting on cushions in the front room, I picked up an acoustic guitar and strummed a few jazz chords. When the curtains opened, instead of Paul it was Lucas, the head honcho of the commune. This gnarly guy was drawn by my playing and reached for another guitar. He fingered some bossa nova licks and began singing the words to a jazz standard.

From the minute we met, I did not like him. He had a scraggly beard and a manner that rubbed me the wrong way. It was odd jamming with someone who gave me the creeps. When Paul entered with two teenaged chicks, one on each arm, Lucas, realizing his music was passé to these girls, switched gears and started playing a faux raga style to support his guru image. There was something sinister about him that I could not put my finger on. Paul led the girls into an adjoining room without saying a word. Left alone with Lucas, I excused myself and drove home. Arlene and I agreed that Paul was a lost cause for both of us. Wisely, we stopped all contact with him.

A few months later, a newspaper headline reported that a crazed cult was creating mayhem and murder in the Hollywood Hills. Paul's photo was at the bottom of the page. I put the paper down immediately, not wanting to know any more. I remembered what the Peace Corps couple had once told me, "Sometimes in life you have to wear blinders." I needed to shield my vision from an age growing murkier and murkier with each passing year.

Griffith Park, The Vice Squad & The Public Defender

I descended even further, replacing my former dreams with a "screw everyone before they screw you" attitude. I was not out of step with my times. After the Kennedy and Martin Luther King assassinations, the wind was driven out of the sails of the flower child movement. A bitter cynicism filled the '70s as expressed in the lyrics "Desperado, you ain't gettin' no younger. Your prison is walking through this world all alone."

The only thing helping me through this period was my teaching position. My downcast attitude was reflected in lectures about long-suffering blues musicians, plaintive Negro spirituals, and sorrow-filled ballads from the British Isles rather than more uplifting folk songs.

In the beach community, people told stories of gay guys getting beaten up by homophobes. The police rarely sided with the victims, letting the perpetrators off easy. The L.A.P.D. had a long history of anti-gay bias. When a new chief had recently taken over the reins, arrests for public pursuit of sex partners increased.

One afternoon, after finishing teaching my last class of the semester, I stopped at the hills above Griffith Park on the way home. Though I'd read about the cops harassing gays cruising there, I forgot this. Far from where most people visited, I parked where men my age were milling around. I got out of my van and leaned against it, striking a seductive pose. A muscular guy wearing a T-shirt and levis walked by. He motioned for me to follow him to some bushes away from the road. Once behind them, the man undid his zipper, pulled out his member and started masturbating. I asked if we could go to his place and get it on.

As soon as I spoke, another man knocked me to the ground. Suddenly, handcuffs were slipped on my wrists and I was asked to get on my feet. I was so stunned I couldn't stand up. The man who'd been playing with himself put his schlong back in his pants, pulled up his zipper, and the two cops started beating me into a pulp, calling me a faggot and a pervert. They led me into an unmarked car and said that I was under arrest.

I cried in disbelief, "For what?"

"For propositioning a police officer and resisting arrest," was the reply.

At the police station, I was processed. Having no prior experience with law enforcement, I had no clue how the legal system operated. When questioned about my employment, I mentioned my instructor position, hoping this would lead them to treat me with more respect. Instead, thrown into a holding tank and given the opportunity to make just one phone call, I didn't know whom to ask for help. Not my parents or employer. Having little connection to the gay community, and not "out" to most of my friends, I didn't call anyone.

I spent the night in a room full of loud noises and only a cement bench to sit on or lay down upon for the night. A homeless vagrant with the stench of alcohol and strong body odor was also admitted that night. All I could think about was how I could get out. The next day a public defender arrived. Since I hadn't called a lawyer, the court provided one who advised, "Because this is your first offense, if you plead guilty I can get the charge reduced to trespassing. It's a misdemeanor and you won't be labeled a sexual offender."

"Offender?" I protested, "All I did was ask another adult man if he wanted to go to his residence and have sex. We didn't do anything. It was the officer who exposed himself, not me."

"That's not what's on the police report. It says that you were masturbating wildly in front of him like an out of control pervert."

"It's a lie."

Trying to help, the lawyer asked, "Were there any other witnesses?"

"Only the other policeman."

"Then it's your word against theirs. You'd better plead guilty."

"But I'm innocent. If I plead guilty, will I lose my teaching job?"

"Once I get the charge down, you'll be all right. There'll be only a fine and some probation. Just don't get arrested for this again."

I pled guilty to trespassing at the arraignment and was soon free to leave on my own recognizance after agreeing to return for sentencing in a month. I took a bus to Griffith Park, walked a few miles to where my car was parked, and drove home in a mixture of shock and relief.

That night I dreamed I was still in the holding tank, a dark, depressing room without any windows. Suddenly, a bright light filled the room and Mrs. B. appeared. I shouted, "I would've called you, but I didn't have your number on me."

She replied, "No need. I knew where you were."

"This place is miserable. Can you get me out of here?"

"Sorry, escapes are not in my job description. But I can offer you this." She reached into her purse and pulled out a large gold key.

"What's that for? Will it unlock my cell?"

"Not really. It's a key to understanding. You can't see it now, but you've been given a gift." I was too flabbergasted to speak, so she continued. "The last time we met, we talked about happiness. Incarceration is also a state of mind. You've already been in prison for a long time. Deep inside you is a place that knows the truth. Believe in what it reveals, not in any judgment brought against you."

"How do I accomplish this?"

"That's for you to find out."

She handed me the key and soon was gone. I woke up in my bed with more questions than answers.

After turning in the final grades for my class, I was glad it was semester break and I had some time to mull things over. Then I got a call from the department chairman to come over for a meeting. I tried to convince myself it was about adding another class. This was correct, but not for the reason I'd hoped.

Well before my court date, the police had contacted the school about the arrest. The chairman's emotions were mixed; I was well liked by the staff. However, Governor Reagan and his cronies in Sacramento were committed to weeding out gay teachers in the schools. At this stage in California's politics, any gay activity, guilty or innocent, could cost an instructor without tenure his or her position. The best the chairman could offer me was an additional class to help defray my legal costs. After that, the department couldn't renew my contract.

I'd been lied to by the public defender. My day in court hadn't even come up and the department was already letting me go. I reached out to a gay center for legal advice, but before I could meet with someone, the court sentence was a *fait accompli*. The counselor said I had been the victim of entrapment, a common practice at the time to which the courts were unsympathetic. There was nothing anyone could do. My new mantra was "Help, I need somebody, Help, not just anybody, Help!"

Back on campus, word got around. A faculty member came to my aid. I'd suspected that this married, tenured professor was a closet gay. The man asked, "Why didn't you recruit partners here at school?"

"I've always thought it improper to combine work and play."

He responded, "That never stopped me from trying."

Another instructor, an activist who liked stirring things up politically, suggested that I confide this entrapment to my students and have them march in protest. He guaranteed this would make the local, if not national news. I hadn't yet told my parents about the arrest and didn't want to cause any uproar. All I could think of was digging a hole and climbing in. I put on a brave face for the rest of the semester and retreated to my beach community a broken man.

I Feel The Pain & I See The Light

My extra course earnings went into court costs. The fees plus extra "police protection funds" were steep. But this was chump change in comparison to what it cost in self-esteem. Once my job was terminated, I rarely left home except to teach private students. Meanwhile, in Washington D.C., Nixon was nabbed for covering up surveillance at the Watergate

Building and run out of office. Gerald Ford replaced him. The post-Watergate era was not a proud period. Neither was my life during this time.

Faced with an empty nest, my folks sold their home and moved into a swanky apartment in the nicer part of the Valley. A few months before the arrest, I'd inadvertently come out to them. One night when I was visiting, my mom did her usual nagging. "When are you going to get a girlfriend and settle down? Your father and I are no spring chickens. At our age we should be having grandkids to spoil rotten."

"Ma, don't hold your breath."

"I'm not holding anything. Honestly, Sammy, is this because you don't like children or you don't like girls?"

My eyes started tearing. "I really like kids. It's just that…."

"Oh my God in heaven, Irv is right. You are a *faigele*."

"I'm not a fag, Mom. I'm gay."

She screamed hysterically, "Irving, come in here right away!"

"This better be important. I'm listening to a Brahms symphony."

"Brahms can wait. You bet this is important."

When he entered, she said, "Tell your father what you said to me."

I swallowed hard. "Mom asked why I haven't brought any girls over for a long while. It's because I'm not into women. I'm gay."

"I knew it, I knew it," he raged as she sobbed hysterically. "I told you he would bring us *tsuris*. It's all your fault for being so soft."

"The way you treated him, I knew he'd strike back. It's your fault."

"You had his eyebrows plucked, tried to turn him into a pretty boy."

"You're to blame, stripping away any manhood he might have had."

I protested, "It isn't anyone's fault. This is just how I'm wired."

"Don't give me any crap about you being born this way. You purposely chose this lifestyle to punish us."

They continued arguing, ignoring my pleas for understanding. I knew that to live under false pretenses would only bring harm to whomever I was involved with. Mrs. B's voice came to mind. "Leave others to their own opinions. What they think of you is none of your business." I slinked away, leaving them to rage on.

Later, when I finally told my mom and dad about the arrest, they fell into another blame game. She yelled at him, "If you had a heart, maybe he wouldn't have become such a criminal.

"I tell you he's a radical like my father."

"He's a rotten beast like you. I'm not giving you any for the rest of the week. For the rest of the month, even!"

They hadn't listened to a word I said. Again, I exited unnoticed and unheard. My sisters also weren't sympathetic. Desperate to find some support, I remembered Uncle Ernie and called back East. Crying on his shoulder, I explained my situation. He replied, "We knew you were gay, but no one wanted to talk about it."

"You mean I was hiding all this time for no reason?"

"It's terrible how our society treats homosexuals. I have a gay cousin who was an outcast his whole life. He and his partner had to lie about themselves, pretending they were roommates for thirty years."

"That's terrible. Will this ever change?"

"Maybe, but slowly. With so many churches preaching hatred and condemning you guys as sinners, how do you expect people to act?"

"You're telling me? I belonged to a college Jewish group where I had to keep quiet. You'd think with them I could be myself."

"Our religion can be just as bad as the rest. There are a few reform rabbis trying to change this. Thank God, some of your brothers and sisters are fighting back. Sam, did you ever hear about Stonewall?"

"No. Tell me."

"Stonewall is a gay bar in Manhattan where the customers, many who were drag queens, were harassed by the police and arrested just for hanging out there. A few years ago, these brave souls had enough of this discrimination and organized a protest that made newspaper headlines around the globe. A new social movement grew out of it. I fully support this. Your father and I have had many arguments over gay liberation."

"I'm not surprised. Dad doesn't like anything progressive like civil rights, women's lib, or gays. Why is he so damned homophobic?"

"Don't ever discuss this with him. Zelda told me he was molested by a group of young men when he was growing up in Brooklyn. He's never come to terms with it. If he acts crazy, try to give him some slack."

"Are you kidding me? That explains a lot. I'll keep it secret."

Uncle Ernie's revelation made sense. Though this brought me some solace, it didn't take away the rejection. Unlike my father, I'd never lashed out at anyone. I didn't deserve to be treated so harshly.

I abandoned my dreams and plans, living a day at a time. One afternoon, I remembered unfolding like a lotus in Bruce's arms in San Francisco. I decided to study yoga to retrieve some of the peace I'd glimpsed so briefly. Maybe this could help relight my inner fire.

Yoga, The Swami, & The Weekend Retreat

In the 70s, the Venice area was filled with yoga classes. Though fairly agile, I found many positions challenging to get into. A helpful instructor taught me that yoga is done at one's own pace, an evolution of self-improvement, not a competition or a Western race to the top. This philosophy and these practices helped me to laugh at the foibles in the world around me. This laughter was good medicine as I began dissolving much of my gloom.

At one class, I heard about a retreat in Northern California, four days of postures and meditation instruction. The cost was reasonable and I signed up right away. A week before the retreat, I had a weird dream in which the event was led by a recovering Jew named Swami Nachesnanda. This long-nosed mystic had written a bestselling book called *Turning Your Oys Into Joys*. He merged yoga and Hebraic traditions and taught his adherents Sephardic chants to help them achieve better lives and pray for the opportunity to drive nicer cars.

After starting his career by publishing the bumper sticker "Keep the 'C' in Chanukah," Nachesnanda turned his profits into prophecy. While on a trip to India, he met the renowned Sri Schlepabanda, proprietor of The New Delhi Deli. These "Two Gurus from Brooklyn" created a vegetarian pastrami that attracted palates from all over the world. This invention lined his pockets with even more funds. As he continued his studies, Nachesnanda felt there was too much guilt to be expiated in just one Day of Atonement at Yom Kippur. So he formulated a course of study to expand this into a full week of intense self-sacrifice and immolation.

This enterprising Swami opened up an ashram in Manhattan's Upper West Side, attracting Jews and Gentiles alike. He then went around the country giving retreats for devotees on a budget. When he saw me enter one of his workshops, he used this as a teaching moment. "Are you a good Jew?" I was speechless. "When is the last time you ate bacon?" I remained silent. "And I've been told that you don't like cheesecake? What self-respecting Hebrew could refuse such a thing?" I shrugged my shoulders as the Swami chanted "*Feh! Feh! Feh!*" Soon, the room of yoga practitioners joined him in a chorus of *"Fehs,"* peppered with an occasional *"Oy Vey Iz Mir."* I awoke from this spiritual nightmare drenched in sweat.

I didn't let this bad dream dampen my enthusiasm. Packing my van, I drove to the retreat. I parked in a lot replete with other hippie vehicles plastered with counter-culture bumper stickers like "Peace. Love & Freedom," "Make Love, Not War," and "Meat Shall Never Touch My Lips, But You Can If You Want To."

Walking inside, I was given a schedule of activities. No talking was allowed during the weekend, except in Q&A sessions after each class. Anyone who uttered a word was asked to leave with no refunds given. I remained silent the whole time. I didn't even ask questions for fear of saying the wrong thing. Not talking built up an amazing amount of energy. The weekend culminated with a vegetarian feast where the participants were allowed to speak freely, but few words were spoken.

By the time the event was over, I was ready to burst. On my drive home, beaming with radiant energy and awareness, I stopped in San Francisco and wound up by accident in the Tenderloin district with its homeless people living on cardboard pallets out on the street. I was filled with pain and compassion for these hopeless drifters. By the time I returned to my home by the beach I was grateful for all I had in my life, not sorry for what was missing.

Cedric & The Free Theater

Continuing with yoga classes back home, I experienced fleeting moments of serenity even if I didn't achieve any lasting peace. Aligning my mind, body, and soul helped me open up new directions in my life. Having written songs in high school, it wasn't much of a stretch to go from creating lyrics to poems. Stringing together a few rhymed verses, I attended some open mikes in the area.

At one of these readings I met Cedric, a tall bohemian guy with long jet-black hair, the regular emcee who introduced each poet. After an inspiring session, we had an intense discussion about creativity and where it comes from. Ten years my senior and an unorthodox Christian, Cedric tried to convince me that my poems came from a divine source, not products of my mind alone. I intuitively sensed this. Sometimes when improvising I seemed to be channeling what was being sent through me. But the mention of

Christ turned me off. Being an aware person, he dropped the Christian references and used higher power terms I could better relate to.

He became a father figure. I invited him to my place to share some poetry aloud. Impressed when I sat down at the piano, he remarked, "I had an idea you had talent. Now I see just how special you are."

"That's very flattering coming from someone I admire."

He sat closer to me and confessed, "I was attracted to you at the readings, but was hesitant to tell you this because I already have a boyfriend. You met him. Shelby is the guy with the blond ponytail who helps me set up at the coffee house."

"Lucky you. He's a hunk. I've always had a thing for blonds."

Cedric gently grasped my hand. "Shelby and I have been living together for several years, but for the past two we've only been roommates. I miss having someone to share being physical with. I'm certainly not blond, but I was wondering if…" Without warning, he reached over and kissed me on the lips.

A new romance was born, spiritual on one hand and carnal on another. Cedric was a wet sloppy kisser, slower and more deliberate than any partner I'd ever been with. There was a solid quality to his touch. He provided a sanctuary that I really needed at the time.

Among his many interests was acting. He led a local theater troupe and invited me to come to a rehearsal of one of their upcoming productions. With not much on my plate, having the time and interest, I readily agreed. He'd assembled quite a collage of creations from the troupe members. Joining the production, I contributed some original material. We rehearsed for weeks. The project blossomed into a festive celebration of music, poetry, and choreography. Many of the performers sang songs I'd written.

In a few months, we performed this work at a beach amphitheater. Aimed at the neighborhood crowd, it was offered for free with suggested donations. Many of the locals volunteered time, apparel, and sound equipment. A few musicians formed an ensemble to play behind the production. It was a spectacle. Imagine *Hair* meeting *The Rocky Horror Picture Show* and add some dancing, spinning hippies.

After each performance there was a dance party onstage afterwards. It ran for several weeks, playing to full houses. Receiving good local reviews, we became the darling of the Venice locals. Exhausted from all the commotion, all I desired was to drive up to Big Sur with Cedric and wind down. He also wanted time off, but to my dismay, not with me. Not long after everyone recovered from the hoopla, he gathered the cast together and to say he was leaving the troupe. Later, he told me he was moving to Seattle with Shelby where they were looking for a place to live together.

Like before, when I least expected it, I had a carpet pulled out from under me. Nothing in my life seemed meant to last. Jobs, apartments, friends, and lovers all fell by the wayside. Gracie had her chocolate greasy baby, Cherie went back to her ex, Brian disappeared into the cosmos, and Bruce fled to his Christian commune. At least this time, I wasn't so enthralled by Cedric that I was devastated. Yet all this abandonment weighed heavily on my mind. Something was wrong with me, and I needed to figure it out.

CHAPTER 7
PHOENIX RISING

AAA Interruption

Once again, this journey through my past was interrupted by a phone call. "Mr. Freberg, this is your driver from Triple A."

Startled, I muttered, "Give me a minute. What did you say?"

"This is your Triple A guy. I was only 10 minutes away from you when my tow truck was sideswiped by a passing car."

"Oh my God, are you all right?"

"I'm OK. Thanks for asking. But I can't help you today. I have my own mess to take care of."

"But how can I…when will…"

"I've sent for another driver to help you. He should be there soon."

"I won't hold my breath."

Exasperated, the guy hung up after saying a perfunctory "Sorry."

I called Darryl and complained. "Fate is against me. My driver had an accident and had to send for a sub. It'll be at least another half hour before I can get going."

"I'll tell everyone. It's an extended meeting, so we still have plenty of time for your presentation. You're not even scheduled to speak until the second half."

"Yeah, if I do make it, I'll be in great shape for a speech."

"Keep cool, dude. Higher Power works in mysterious ways."

"I'll try."

After hanging up, I went back to revisiting my life. This time, the downward paths I'd fallen into were starting to change course.

Therapy & Self-Discovery

After so many losses, I was filled with self-doubt. Yoga and meditation were not enough. Like Sisyphus, no matter how many times I rolled my boulders up any hill, they dragged me down again. An old college friend saw my sad state. Currently going through therapy, she recommended Annette, the woman she was seeing. While this shrink was expensive, living near Beverly Hills, she worked on a sliding scale that fortunately slid down to my level. I decided to give her a try.

From our first session, we clicked. Annette saw how my creativity was blocked by low self-esteem and a pattern of mood swings. I saw in her the stable, supportive mother figure my mom never was. She probed me in a soothing manner. "The way you describe your relationships is that you seem to rush into them without getting to know your potential partner first. Why do you think this happens?"

I confided, "Once we have sex together, I seem to lose control over my emotions. I try not to fall in love, but I can't stop myself."

"And how soon do you have sex with them?"

"Usually on the first date. If not, I wouldn't have seen them again."

"What would you have lost out on if you had waited?" I was silent. She added, "Was it worth all this disappointment?"

I broke out in tears and admitted, "I don't know. Maybe not."

She went on. "Before our next meeting I'd like you to think about why you cruise for sexual encounters. You might ask yourself if you're trying to get all the good stuff right away without working for it."

"Do you mean like having dessert before the meal? Are you saying I have too much of a sweet tooth?"

"You're a bright young man, Sam. I think you can answer this question yourself. Mull it over."

At our next session, I confessed that my cruising habit probably led me into these failed relationships. "Hoping against hope that love happens overnight certainly hasn't worked out for me."

Another sore point was how I related to authority figures, putting too much trust in people who didn't deserve it. She advised, "You can meet people half way, but if they want you to cross a bridge by yourself to be with them, you ought to think twice. Ever wonder why you get let down so often? Maybe you set yourself up for it."

I'd trusted my parents, Cherie, Brian, Bruce, the public defender, the shrink, the rabbi, and the Peace Corps people. The only one who came through was my orthodontist. And oh yes, Uncle Ernie.

In the next few months, Annette opened my eyes to how my inner tree had been bent to the sagging point. She gave me some trellises to help train my trunk in a taller, prouder direction. My new favorite song lyric was "Doctor, my eyes have seen the years and the slow parade of tears without crying. Now I want to understand."

During one of our more intense sessions she asked, "What do you do when you get let down by someone or something?"

"I try not to dwell on it."

"Maybe you need to feel your feelings instead of stuffing them. Your emotion seems to come out sideways, not directly to the source of your irritation."

"My parents yelled at me so much, I try not to do the same thing."

"You might learn to express your grievances before you explode with rage like they did or go out and do something self-destructive."

Annette was trained in Jungian psychology with its emphasis on folk archetypes and the collective unconscious. She worked with a professional astrologer and had my horoscope done. This revealed clues to some of my problems and how to rise above them.

This report described an adventurous free spirit. I had several planets in Scorpio, a sign many people think of as deviant. Its other side is the phoenix, an eagle with a spiritual energy of rebirth. "Sam, you have it in you to rise above the ashes and transform your life into a shining example for others."

Not sure if my life was predestined by planetary placements, I tried my best to learn from these tendencies. This therapy took work, time, and money, even at Annette's reduced rate. After a while I could barely afford to see her and reduced my sessions to once a month. Finally, I had to quit entirely. Though a diamond in the rough, I began to see the path ahead of me and resolved to continue this journey through any bumps in the road. Many challenges were waiting ahead, but there were also some bright spots.

Leo & The Silverlake House

Not long after my last session with Annette, I stopped by the university where I'd gotten my degree. Feeling shaky after unwrapping yet another layer of camouflage around my vulnerable soul, I sought refuge at the sculpture garden near the art department. As I sat between a colorful Alexander Calder mobile and an organic Henry Moore statue, I noticed a gangly, dark-haired young man with horn-rimmed glasses gazing in my direction. This fellow seemed to need to give someone attention as much as I needed to receive it.

When our eyes met, it was more than casual curiosity. Our radar, or "gaydar" as it is sometimes called, made it obvious that we were brethren. The young man sat down next to me. "Hi, my name's Leo. Isn't the artwork here fabulous? I'm a real fan of Calder."

I responded, "Me too. Sometimes I come here to seek consolation. Sitting next to these works of art, I don't feel so alone."

"I know what you mean. Artists put so much of themselves in their work, coming here is like being with them. Say, why don't you join me for some espresso at the student union? It's a great place to hang out."

"Why not? You said your name was Leo, right?"

"Leo Bonelli. I come from three generations of Sicilians."

I shook his hand. "Sam Freberg, great to meet you. I'm also third generation. I'm descended from Polish and Austrian Jews."

"Italians and Jews have a lot in common. We appreciate the arts, talk with our hands, and really enjoy food."

"You got that right. My mother follows guests around with a bowl of fruit that never ends. She always says to eat a little something."

"Sounds like my nana. She gets insulted if you don't finish what's on your plate. My grandma is the world's best cook. There's nothing like her Italian pastry. You should try some."

"I never turn away a good dessert. A sweet tooth seems to run in my family." As we made our way across campus I asked, "What brings you here? Are you a student?"

"I was, but had to drop out to make a living. I'm a painter when I have time. Since I left school, I can't follow my passion as I'd like. Doing displays for a discount store is not my idea of creative expression."

"I can relate. I'm a pianist. I'm lucky that my work as a music teacher uses my creativity."

He purred, "Seems like we could get along, you and I."

Feeling similarly, I chimed, "Sure looks like it."

By the time we reached the coffee place, we had much to share. The loneliness we'd felt a short time before quickly disappeared.

Although coming from a devout Catholic family, Leo was as devilish as his religious parents and grandparents had hoped he would become angelic. Raised to become a priest, he'd rebelled against his upbringing by acting like an outrageous in-your-face queen half the time and a people-pleaser trying to atone for his bad-boy behavior the other half. Leo was a classic Gemini with one twin responding to a situation one way and the other soon acting out its polar opposite. He'd infuriate people by agreeing enthusiastically with them and then stubbornly argue the other side of the coin afterwards.

I was attracted to this complex person (and soon-to-be lover), even though he was far from the kind of swarthy, athletic guy I usually liked. But he was very entertaining, crooning a romantic Frank Sinatra ballad one minute and a raspy AC/DC rock vocal the next. With him, if you didn't like the person you were hanging out with, just wait a half-hour and an entirely different human being would be your new companion. In his presence there never was a dull moment.

After two cups of java each, we both were wired. He invited me over to the place he shared in West Hollywood with two roommates. I had to work the next day and took a rain check. As I drove home to the beach, little did I know how much my life was about to change.

The next weekend, we went out for dinner and a movie. After the film, we arrived at his place where a wild party was in progress. We had to fight our way past a crowd of gay men gyrating to disco Donna Summer music in a strobe-lighted living room under a rotating glass mirror ball. Drugs were passed around. The odor of amyl nitrate leaked from a den that was set up as an orgy room. I was put off by this activity. Noticing my discomfort, he whisked me immediately past the throng of revelers through the back door and over to the private guesthouse where he lived by himself.

Once safely inside his immaculately clean, color-coordinated living quarters, he poured us each a drink. We stared at each other's eyes and kissed briefly. Then he motioned to the bedroom. "Before we go inside and get comfortable, would you like a hit of poppers?

I replied, "No way! I'm allergic to amyl. It makes me sick."

"Sorry, it's protocol here. Everyone takes poppers before sex."

"I don't."

Leo realized that if he wanted to keep me in his life, he'd have to tone down his lifestyle. He played a softer side of Donna Summer on his stereo, "Love To Love You Baby." I was wary, especially after what I'd learned from my sessions with Annette, "I'd enjoy having sex with you, but let's talk more first. OK?"

Leo teased, "I can wait." Then he added, "At least a few minutes."

After we both laughed, Leo showed me his paintings. Using the tiny residence as a studio to display his artwork, his amazing creations were as varied as his fractured personality. Realistic, surrealistic, and abstract canvases hung on the walls. I liked some paintings more than others. Though impressed with what I saw, I managed to put off our initial sexual encounter until our next date.

As much as we enjoyed each other's company, the sex we shared lacked some of the carnal intensity I'd experienced with prior lovers. Intensely drawn to each other, we often needed time away, commuting regularly from bliss to overload.

The following weekend, he visited my beach pad.   Smitten with limerence, he liked my bright-colored apartment even if he had to overlook the fact that it was messy. When I sat down at the keyboard and played, he realized he was in the presence of someone with talent to match his own. He gushed compliments in his customary fashion, "You're so creative. I adore these colors. That photo of the guy with his hair down to his waist playing in a rock band, is that you?"

I answered, "Yes."

"You were a real hippie, weren't you?

"Yes. In some ways I still am."

"I'm a *boho*, one foot in the art world, the other in the avant garde. "

As we continued dating, he suggested that we find a place to live together. Neither of our current homes was suitable. Besides the limited room of his guesthouse, Leo was tired of the party environment there. He longed for a domestic situation with a home to decorate and a large flower garden like the one his grandparents had out in the suburbs. I was tired of Venice, having lived there for over a decade. Searching for a place became a fun thing to share like many same-sex couples were doing at the time. Gay parlance often described this as "hanging up curtains with a hard-on."

It took several months of house hunting to find one in a neighborhood that appealed to both of us. The beach was too distant from Leo's work, West L.A. was too expensive, and I would not hear of locating anywhere near WeHo. The Hollywood area was too grungy, so we looked farther east and discovered Silverlake. Its palm tree lined streets were close to downtown L.A., yet convenient to the Westside.

Though not as gay a neighborhood as Decorator Row, it was trending that way. Silverlake's vibe was more butch than femme, which pleased us both. Here we found a Spanish style, tile-roofed house with large rooms, arched entryways, craftsman windows, and a nice fireplace. The rent was reasonable. We settled happily in our very own nest.

From the moment we moved in, we were like Neil Simon's "The Odd Couple," he a compulsive clean freak, and me picking up after myself when and if I felt like it. It was not uncommon for him to complain, "I get so tired of your 'whatever, however' attitude. The way you scatter things around makes this place look like a pigsty."

I also voiced my concerns. "I'm trying to be neater. The way you have to keep things so spotless, I feel like I'm living in a store window display. This is my home too, you know."

Another thing causing friction between us was his need to plan everything we did in detail, leaving little to chance. Our trips, even to the supermarket, were scheduled to the minute. My ad hoc approach led to frequent clashes. A saving grace in these conflicts was that we knew we were both extreme in our habits and had much to learn from the other. Over time, he loosened up and I became more organized. Our relationship was a case of opposites attracting. These differences kept us fascinated with each other.

For the first time in my life, I had a real partner, even if sometimes we fought and bickered like my parents. We may not have had a formal ceremony or civil license and wore no rings, but in many ways we were much like a married couple. Now I finally had someone to bring me flowers and sing me love songs.

Two Sets Of In-Laws

One thing Leo contributed to our domesticity was involvement with his family. An unintended surprise for me was a reintegration with my own brood. We soon became part of each other's households.

I was introduced to Leo's clan in an unexpected way. One day after we moved into our house, while most of our belongings were still in cartons, we fell asleep late one night in our new bedroom. As the sun's first rays shone through the sheet-covered window, we awoke to loud knocking on the front door. He forgot that his grandparents who lived in the hills above La Habra in Orange County and rose with roosters crowing were coming over. "Get dressed!" he cried. "Pablo and Nina are here. They can't see us like this."

As we hastily threw on some clothes, their knocking continued. We could hear Nina's voice shouting, "Rise and shine, boys, rise and shine!" He went to greet them while I moved boxes and hastily put out some chairs on which we all could sit. After being let in, the two grandparents were all smiles as they boisterously celebrated our new residence. Though put out for being awakened so early, I immediately liked their joie de vivre.

After Leo made introductions, Nina shouted, "Clear more space in the living room. We've something special to bring you guys." The septuagenarians excused themselves as they returned to their RV parked in front of the house.

I was clueless, but Leo knew what was up. Pablo carried in a large folding table that he quickly propped up. Nina brought in a few shopping bags filled with provisions, putting them down on the table. A second trip produced plates, glasses, silverware, and a large bottle of pink chablis. Pablo grinned wildly and Nina hummed Italian tunes while they quickly spread out a tablecloth and place settings for a meal. Before long, a pasta dinner complete with Nina's homemade sauce was laid out. Wineglasses were set out and filled.

Nina cried, "*Mangia, mangia*, it's time to eat."

Pablo added, "She prepared her homemade ravioli for you guys."

I was touched. "For us? You didn't have to. I love ravioli."

With his typical gusto, Leo bragged, "Nobody cooks like Nina."

I couldn't believe my eyes. An Italian dinner was served in our honor at eight in the morning. This was like my rambunctious welcome to the islands in the Peace Corps after a similar sleep-deprived night. Needless to say, the meal was wonderful. With Jews and Italians, holidays and occasions revolve around food. I was gratified to be treated as part of a family, a feeling I hadn't experienced in quite a while.

On our first visit to Leo's parents in the Chino Hills area forty miles away, I was welcomed with open arms. They knew he was gay. Unlike my folks, despite their misgivings, they were concerned for their son's happiness and glad to see him with a stable partner. Mrs. Bonelli said cordially, "Sam, would you like to join us for Christmas?"

I responded enthusiastically, "I'd love to."

In college, I'd been to some Christmas parties, but it was not the same as a traditional holiday with its feeling of togetherness. Although we Frebergs were Jewish, my mom taught us to believe in Santa Claus when I was young In addition to lighting menorah candles on Chanukah, we observed Christmas with modest presents. In contrast, the Bonellis went overboard buying expensive gifts. They even gave me a tie, a wallet, and some handkerchiefs. For once, I enjoyed rather than cringed when I heard "Chestnuts roasting on an open fire."

By the end of the year, our house was set up, and, thanks to Leo, the front rooms were impeccably decorated. Redoing the dining room was next on the agenda. Although he behaved like a queen on occasion, he had a macho side, a master craftsman with a complete set of tools. He wielded a hammer and saw, creating accessories for the house and talking me into helping with the construction. For someone who was all thumbs, I was glad to pick up some practical skills.

Seeing how successfully his family had accepted me, I wondered about my own. I invited my mom to see our new residence, but wasn't ready to subject us to my dad's likely disapproval. My mother was so impressed with the cleanliness and decor, she told my father what a fine home we had and what a good influence Leo was for me.

On her next visit, she brought my dad along. He also was impressed with Leo's charm and delighted to discover his construction abilities. Leo had a talent for relating to the older generation in a way I'd not mastered. He subtly referred to us as roommates, playing down our lover relationship. In addition, he programmed background music like cuts by Barbra Streisand. A hot dance record by Lady Marmalade had to wait for another time.

The next holiday season, we spent time with each family in split shifts, celebrating both Christmas and Chanukah. Appropriate gifts were given and received. Leo's repartee was well liked by the Frebergs, especially my sisters. I got along with Leo's sisters as well. It was great having two families and two sets of in-laws.

Beverly Boulevard & The Street People

Leo painstakingly redecorated every room in the house, not stopping until he was done three years later. When it was time to take a breather, he found it difficult to relax. I suggested that we take a trip together. After my sad experience with Bruce at Big Sur, I had no desire to go up the coast, so I proposed that we travel to Yosemite National Park instead. A compromise was worked out, spending half our time in a nice hotel, and half in the kind of campground Leo found comfortable, a site with amenities like flush toilets and hot showers.

As much as we squabbled at home, we set up camp, cooked on a propane stove, and organized our travel with few disagreements. Staying at an old inn, we shared a few romantic meals. On the way back, a memorable feast at a Basque restaurant in Bakersfield capped our trip. It was a shame my family hadn't patronized one of these eateries instead of the many coffee shops on our excursions there.

While we were away, Leo realized how unhappy he was with his job at the discount store. With his parents encouraging him to go into business, he decided to open up an art supply shop. Nearby Echo Park had a growing community of artists, and low-rent storefronts were plentiful. Leo soon found a suitable space. With his merchandising experience and outgoing personality, he established a successful enterprise. It wasn't long before he needed help with this growing establishment.

Since I was busy teaching piano and didn't have time to assist him, Leo put an ad in an underground weekly for an assistant. He filled me in on the applications received, especially one from a lively young woman named Beverly, who had an offbeat sense of humor. When he noticed on her form that she'd written down Boulevard as her last name, he asked if this was a put on. She told him it was her legal moniker, changed from the original one given to her as a child. He wanted to know why. In a thick southern drawl, a remnant of her Georgia heritage, this is the story she related.

"I was born in an old three-story Victorian house not far from here in a once fashionable neighborhood called Angelino Heights. I'm the third child of Thomas and Meryl Street, hard-working descendents from an old Southern family that had once lived in what remained of an antebellum cotton plantation outside of Valdosta."

Impressed, he responded, "That sounds like Tara, Scarlet O'Hara's plantation in *Gone With The Wind*, my favorite movie."

"Oh my, it was very much like Tara. The house had real Southern charm, three stories high with tall white columns, a gable roof, and a large front porch where the family sipped mint juleps in the summer."

"Sounds simply devine," he interjected.

"Grandpa Chester Street sold the estate for a goodly sum and moved with his wife Bertie to Los Angeles in the 1920s when Angelino Heights was in its prime. They had their pick of the Queen Anne and Victorian mansions on the market. Although the Depression era wiped out the family assets, we held onto our home."

"That's good."

"They had three children, the oldest was my daddy Thomas. When he was in his teens he fell in love with Meryl, who lived a few blocks away. They became high school sweethearts, attended the same college, and earned degrees in urban planning. After school, they went into business together doing community reconstruction projects. My older brother, sister, and I were born in the 1950s. Thomas, being a practical joker, named us kids First, Second, and Third. At home, this was no problem, but at school we were always teased about it. Being the youngest, I had the godawful name of Third Street. I hated it."

"I can only imagine."

"My brother First was an enterprising fellow. He found an attorney to officially change our names. Like Daddy, First had a wicked sense of humor. Inspired by L.A.'s Thomas Street Guide, he reinvented us as Wilton Place, Melrose Avenue, and me, Beverly Boulevard."

"Really? I'm beginning to understand."

"I was thrilled to say farewell to my former name and proudly flaunted the new one. Beverly is so much more feminine than Third, ain't it? After graduating high school, I attended a local college and got a BA in home economics. I also took art classes and learned graphic techniques to help me design and print street scenes."

"That only seems natural, coming from a family of Streets."

"I signed them at the bottom followed by an issuing number such as 33/200. I was able to sell some of these to local real estate agents and banks that hung them up on their office walls. To my regret, not one was ever bought by a business owner whose establishment was located on the street that shares my name."

"What a pity."

"When I left the comforts of Angelino Heights, I wasn't able to make a full-time wage as an artist. Having difficulty finding an instructor position, I taught classes at a learning access facility. These courses attracted rich people from the west side of town, disaffected children of the upper class like I'd been, curious to see what lay on the other side of the tracks. My course was called Slumming 101, and it was very popular. As my reputation spread, I became a guest on local radio and TV shows. I gave advice on where to find thrift stores, cheap eats, breadlines, and soup kitchens for privileged and underprivileged alike."

Leo was taken with her story. "That's amazing. But with all this success, why are you applying to work for me?"

"I'm getting to that. The proprietor of the outfit that set up my classes was busted for lining his pockets while getting grants from the federal government. We instructors were dreadfully underpaid. The F.B.I. investigated, there was a scandal, and he was put out of business. My reputation was ruined, and I had to move back in with my folks. Mr. Bonelli, I really need this job."

"I could use someone on the ball like you here. You're hired."

Beverly's outgoing personality helped expand Leo's customer base with her ability to relate to artists from all walks of life. When I visited the shop to pick up things for him, I'd often run into her. She always had a wisecrack waiting. I'd respond with something equally off the wall. We were cut from the same cloth. One day when I entered, she said, "Look who just walked in. It's the other half."

"The other half of what?"

"I'm not telling. Here's a clue. Half of none is better than what?"

"That sounds like a Zen koan. Should I respond half-heartedly?"

"That's determined by which half you're talking about."

"The better half."

"Better than what?"

"Better than the other half."

"But I thought you said I was the other half."

"Yeah, but I only half meant it."

"I think we better start over."

We enjoyed building on each other's silliness, running a good thing into the ground, much to some people's amusement and many others' dismay. One day when we were cracking jokes, she invited me to go to one of her cheap eateries and share some lunch. Over Thai noodles, we decided to research the bottom rung of L.A.'s inexpensive street businesses. Soon afterward, we wrote a small tome for rich folks who wanted to roll up their silk sleeves and get their two-hundred-dollar shoes dirty. We self-published the book and had a following of street devotees.

Leo did not share these humble desires, wishing he could move his art store to West Hollywood and be a big shot supplying trendy interior decorators. Over time, there was a growing distance between us - he, an ambitious social climber, and I, an easy-going proletarian. This disparity slowly ate away at our domestic bliss.

Good Times, Inflation, & Selma Swenson

My music teaching flourished during this period. President Carter replaced Gerald Ford in the White House, and the country's finances recovered from the sinkhole of the first part of the decade. After surviving the 1974 Oil Embargo, people started spending and partying like there was no tomorrow. It was the age of *Saturday Night Fever* and couple-swapping films like *Bob & Carol & Ted & Alice.* The sexual revolution and other social movements were in full swing. Like the civil rights marches in the '60s, women protested to achieve equality with men in the '70s. Helen Reddy released her single "I Am Woman."

Leo and I did well enough to continue dining out at trendy restaurants and see first-run movies on a regular basis. If we'd known the speed bump the economy would soon take, we'd have squirreled away some money to save for a down payment on a home. However, life was good. We spent every penny we made, often taking Beverly along, as well as a friend of hers named Selma.

This new addition, whose last name was Swenson, became Beverly's pal when the two women took a cooking class together at an adult high school extension. They bonded, discussing nutrition and saving money at ethnic markets, two of their favorite subjects besides "men," a topic they could discuss endlessly. One day when they were shopping at Von's, Selma started a little gossip. "Guess who I saw squeezing the tomatoes and sniffing the cantaloupes the other day?'

Beverly was intrigued, "I have no idea. Spill."

Selma responded playfully, "Remember that hunky guy in the dark blue shirt with those bulging muscles we ran into last week."

"Drool city. Didn't you say you thought he was a fireman?"

Selma spoke softly as she subtly pointed in the guy's direction, "That's him. I found out from my neighbor that he is L.A.F.D."

"I'd like to see him in his working clothes. I love a man in uniform."

Selma waited until he disappeared from view and whispered, "I'd rather see him take his uniform off."

"Figures, you slut."

"Look who's talking. You were ready to ask one of the boxboys over to your place on his break."

"They don't call me a wannabe supermarket checker for nothing."

"Men, you can't live with 'em, and you can't live without 'em."

"I'll second that emotion."

The two women were tickled when they realized they each had names that coincided with local streets. However, Selma's last name wasn't Avenue, but instead typically Swedish. Beverly suggested that she change her name to Circle or Court or Drive. Thinking of putting out a personal ad looking for a male partner with such a surname, the two got out the white pages to see if there were any listed. Beverly wanted to be a bridesmaid at her "street" wedding.

These good friends often tagged along with us. When our foursome ate in local cafes, many thought we were two married couples. What people didn't know certainly didn't hurt anyone.

Gay Lib, Divine Miss M, & The Advocate Experience

As my music students increased, I began teaching workshops in our living room. After a while, the commotion got on Leo's nerves. He encouraged me to do what he did, find a little commercial space to accommodate my business. As much as I understood his concern, I was skeptical about this suggestion.

During the Carter years, the economy ran into hyperinflation. Prices went through the roof. Leo's store had its rent raised twice. When I went out looking for a place, what once seemed reasonable was priced out of my reach. Concerns of "location, location" were replaced by "overhead, overhead." Meanwhile, our relationship began unraveling.

It was still early in the Gay Liberation movement and the party environment in the gay scene reigned supreme. Same-sex couples staying true to each other were considered to be squares. Everyone seemed to be on the prowl for new partners, many even patronizing the popular sleazy bathhouses. At first, we were monogamous, but we eventually fell prey to the many temptations surrounding us.

This started with an occasional *ménage a trois* when one of us brought another man home, often a former trick. Leo had a stable of men when he lived in WeHo. My previous encounters were less personal, but I knew where the action was. At first, we entertained these sexual partners as a shared experience. But this didn't last. Our spare room housed covert trysts when he was at work or I was away teaching. It wasn't long before we officially opened the relationship to extracurricular activity.

One evening, I griped, "Where in the hell are you going?"

"Out."

"But I thought we were watching *The Naked City* together?"

"I'm going to the city to find someone to get naked with."

"Maybe I should get a dog. At least I'd have companionship."

"Find yourself a playmate. There's a lot of dogs out on the street."

Along with the return of our cruising habits came his re-involvement in drugs. In addition to pot, he began indulging in heavier stuff. I tolerated this destructive behavior against my better judgment. That summer he bought three tickets to a gay lib fundraiser at the Hollywood Bowl featuring one of our favorite performers, Bette Midler, with Richard Pryor as her opening act. In full rebel mode, Leo brought along one of his tricks with the third ticket and some cocaine to enhance the event.

"Here, Sam, have a hit."

"No, you guys go ahead. I don't want any."

"Don't be a party pooper. You'll enjoy tonight better with this."

After he and his buddy snorted a line, I gave in and followed suit. Soon, I was high as a kite.

"I can't believe it. This is great. I can't wait for Richard Pryor to begin."

We laughed hysterically through Pryor's drug-laced routine. Everything was perfect until the comedian suddenly changed course and launched into a diatribe against gays. He complained that we didn't march in the civil rights movement, so why should he support our cause now. Then he turned his back to the audience, dropped his pants, and mooned the crowd, saying, "You can kiss my fat black ass," and stormed off.

The audience was outraged. What had been an intense high became an extreme low. The only thing that saved the night was when the Divine Miss M came onstage and mimicked Pryor by pretending to moon the audience. She sassed back, "Mr. Pryor can kiss my big fat white ass." The resulting laughter was welcome, but the damage to the event had already been done. Such were the early days of gay liberation.

I swore never to do coke again. I also resolved not to put up with my partner's bad habits much longer. They continued, leaving me to pray that, unlike my abusive father, Leo would outgrow this phase. Not ready for a total break from the relationship, I became anxious to move my business out of our residence.

During this time, transformational weekends such as EST and the like were the rage. The gay community had a spin-off called The Advocate Experience. Knowing that I needed new input, I enrolled. Two days of workshops promoting gay pride and following one's dreams ensued.

This well-attended event was held in a large corporate banquet room near downtown L.A. The facilitator suggested, "Close your eyes and envision something you want in your life. You are a confident, powerful person. The world will respond to what you ask for and give it to you. Imagine there's nothing blocking you from your desires."

I shot up my hand and commented, "Whenever I reach for the stars, I only fall back to earth, wounded and disappointed."

The leader advised, "Keep trying. Don't hold onto your wounds. They only block your potential."

"But as a homosexual, I've been harassed, ridiculed, and arrested."

The man up front had heard this many times before and had a ready answer. "We gay people have been told we can't have what we want, what most straight people take for granted. We all deserve to be fulfilled. The biggest obstacle to realizing your dreams is you."

After this motivational weekend, the world was my oyster. There was nothing I couldn't conquer. Not letting Leo get in my way anymore, I pounded the pavement searching for a space to teach music. I enlisted the help of Beverly, whose knowledge of L.A.'s streets was unquestioned. She suggested that I check the mid-town area on Wilshire Boulevard (no relation). It had fallen out of favor to the Westside. The occupancy rate was low and rents were reasonable.

The instincts of this maven of the street scene were right on. In an old deco-style building with a rickety elevator, I found an office located over a storage room where nobody would be disturbed by music. It even had its own tiny bathroom, a functional port in a storm.

While weighing whether or not to rent this space, I had a nightmare. I was sitting in the audience for the Phil Donahue TV Show. Suddenly, my name was called and I was asked to come on stage. The studio audience chanted "Sam! Sam! Sam!"

My old blues band by the beach played Lou Reed's "Walk On The Wild Side" and I was asked to lip sync the lyrics. Then Vernon and Paul joined the group as we all segued into "Born Under A Bad Sign." Next, the studio crew rolled out an upright keyboard for me to play. As soon as I joined in, a posse of vice squad members arrived with guns drawn. I cried out "Don't Shoot The Piano Player." Leo arrived with one of his tricks and both of them tried to get me to ingest some cocaine. When I refused, they tackled me and tried to force the drug up my nose. Pandemonium broke out.

Phil attempted to restore order, apologizing to the crowd for his show getting out of control. The station cut away for a commercial break. As the cameras faded, I awoke in a deep fright, still hearing the chants of "Sam! Sam! Sam!" ringing in my ears.

The next day, I realized I needed to take a course of action right away. I went to the rental agent and put money down on the new studio. A transition to a new chapter in my life had begun.

Personal Ads & Impersonal Rejection

Not long after I got my new space, Leo came over to help me decorate it. One of the motivations in moving my workplace was to detach from him. He'd been so controlling, my creativity was squelched for many years. It was time to make my own choices and find my own style. Several times I had to escort him out the door. Much to my surprise, I prevailed and successfully completed the work myself.

By then, President Carter had run into a frustrating confrontation with Iran's revolutionary government. A group of Americans were held hostage in Teheran for 444 days. This would eventually bring about his downfall and launch the Reagan administration.

As tension mounted in the geopolitical theater, the vibes grew ever darker in our Silverlake house. Leo resented being shut out of my life. The few times we still dined together, our conversations became ugly. One night, he was so angered by something I said that he picked up a kitchen knife and lunged forward.

"Take that, you ingrate. After all I did for you, you're treating me like a piece of shit."

"You don't own me. I'm a free man. I don't owe you a thing."

After a second lunge, in self-defense I threw a plate of spaghetti at him that missed and hit the wall, breaking into pieces. It filled the room with red greasy sauce, which sent him into tears. "You've ruined the dining area. The walls are a mess, and so are the curtains. I'll have to decorate the whole room over again."

"The way you came at me, I had no choice. I'm sorry."

He put down the knife. We hugged each other as he continued sobbing, "I don't know what got into me. I'm sorry, too."

I asked plaintively, "What in the hell has happened to us?"

He whimpered like a child, "I hate it when we fight like this."

"I do, too."

Nine years previously, Pablo and Nina brought over a similar sauce in such good spirits. Now it was staining our dining room as well as our life together. A life once full of flowers and love songs became a pile of dirty sheets and drug paraphernalia. Our relationship deteriorating, I bought a futon and started sleeping in my studio. I knew how to get by on very little and began adjusting to a bachelor's existence once again.

Tired of paying rent for half a house I barely used, I found a small flat in an old building near my studio. It was cheap and convenient. I moved in the rest of my stuff.

This was a bad time for a new business. During the early Reagan years, a deep recession put a damper on the economy. People tightened their purse strings. When many of my students dropped their music lessons, I could barely make my overhead. Not having much left after paying two rents, I had to get outside work to afford my studio. It was a good thing I had the skills to find a few temp jobs as needed.

The Mid-Wilshire area was not close to the action of the gay community. Most of the WeHo crowd I'd run into there would not leave the area unless someone was hung like a horse or had a large bankroll. I had neither to offer. Feeling a need for some male companionship, I put a personal ad in a gay newspaper.

This began a parade of correspondence and blind dates. Most gay men were into fantasy like I'd been, and they misrepresented themselves in their ads. Their expectations were either too high or too low. Someone looking for a lover would turn out to be a frog wanting to be kissed by a prince and become royalty overnight. Other ads were more appropriate for the movie *Looking For Mr. Goodbar*, seeking a midnight snack, not interested in a "long-term relationship." Even when the words were aimed in the right direction, they seemed to be plagiarized.

I'd already been around the block in an "ltr," as this was abbreviated. Other abbreviations such as w/m, gp/fp, s&m, and no p&p littered the ad space. One needed a glossary to understand what they all meant. Having been in this rodeo before, I just wanted to meet a decent guy to spend quality time with. It was no easy task.

I wrote countless letters, answered many phone calls, and knocked on quite a few doors. Most of these guys were off the mark with descriptions that deducted 10 or more years from their age and 20 pounds off their weight. They added a few inches to their height and padded a couple inches to their private parts, if things ever were to go that far. Some greeted me in chic outfits, muscle T-shirts, 501s, and a few in a speedo or g-string.

Once, a guy came to the door in the buff. If he had something to flaunt, it might have been worth the visit, but this queen substituted lack of attributes with bald outrage. Then there were the door slammers, like the barstool crowd that rejected you before you could reject them, a tactic used by people who needed approval the most. Disheartened, I was tempted to give up the quest.

One night, after yet another disappointing encounter, I dreamed I was in a gay bar after closing time, sitting on a stool in a back corner of the room. I was so absorbed in self-pity I didn't notice that even the employees had left. The place smelled like stale beer and amyl nitrate. I was alone and miserable. Suddenly, Mrs. B. appeared and tapped on my shoulder. "Sam, don't give up. You've been looking for love in the wrong places. Search instead for someone with better credentials than a barfly or an alley cat. You deserve a handsome loving partner."

Then she disappeared as quickly as she'd arrived. Though loneliness kept haunting me, like the little engine that could, I kept trying.

The Passing Of Sheila

A few months after my breakup with Leo, I heard that my mother was seriously ill with cancer. It had spread to her liver and was terminal. She had a previous bout, but it was caught early and she recovered. Back then, detached from her and very self-involved, I didn't allow myself to be affected by the news. This time, upset to hear how serious her current condition was, I responded with much more concern.

On one visit I asked, "Mom, how are you feeling today?"

In a pained voice she answered, "I have my better days and my not so good ones. This one is not so good. What did I do to deserve this?"

"You didn't do anything. It's part of life."

"Easy for you to say."

Instead of my usual comeback quip, I was silent and just smiled. Appreciating my support, she softened, "You're so nice to visit me. When Judy comes over, she gets nasty. I can't figure out what she wants, she carries so many grudges."

"She's got a lot of stuff against me and against Leslie, too."

My mom declared angrily, "When it comes to Judy and your father, it's a different story."

"The two of them act so much alike, you'd think they had a conspiracy."

She motioned for me to come closer. "Sammy, to be honest, I never loved her the way I love you."

I tried to refute this. "I know you care for her, maybe in a different way, but you do." Tears welled in my eyes as I reacted, "You never told me to my face that you loved me before."

"I always thought of love as weakness. I always had to be strong, especially around my father. Not to mention Irv."

"But love is the real strength. It conquers all."

"You're just saying that because you read it in a book somewhere."

"I'm just beginning to understand some of what I've read."

Changing the subject, she uttered, "I'm sorry you broke up with Leo. I always liked him. He was so good for you. Even Irving liked him."

Amazed, I asked, "Really?"

"There's a lot your father has never told you."

Suddenly, she grimaced in pain and turned to me as she moaned, "I'm very tired. I need to rest."

Gently, I spoke, "I love you, Mom."

In a fading voice, she acknowledged, "I know. You're such a good boy. You always were. Oh, here he comes now. You have to leave."

In a few weeks, my mom's cancer ran its course. Leo came to the funeral ceremony to pay his respects. Though we were estranged, our family bond was still strong. My dad was his usual stoic self. My sisters were in tears as I gave a eulogy.

"Sheila Freberg was a strong woman who ran a tight ship. She pursued her goals with determination and had our interests at heart. Sometimes she made us do things we weren't sure we wanted, but with her support, we were able to accomplish more because of her efforts. As she got older, she softened her emotions and opened her heart. Now that she has made her transition, we all wish her well. May she finally rest in peace."

Little did I know that memorial speeches like this were going to be a familiar activity, eulogizing departed loved ones on a regular basis.

Jim, Ostracism, & the Court Battle

While I was grieving my mother's departure, I was too busy to look for another partner. I wasn't sure I wanted one. Occasionally, I'd open up a gay rag and browse through the classifieds skipping past the "hot stud seeks the same" listings.

Then an ad caught my eye. A young chiropractic student w/m in his 30s living near Malibu was into natural foods, yoga, and meditation and seeking a relationship with the same. I thought *Now only if this guy is tall, dark, and handsome, it might work out.* I was through with blonds by that time, especially the bottled WeHo types.

Jim turned out to be tall, dark, and handsome. Not very athletic, but you couldn't have it all. Recently divorced with shared custody of a young boy, he was looking for a partner to spend time with and help him raise his child. Being a step-dad never occurred to me, but ever since Gracie and her baby, I was intrigued by the idea of parenthood.

Our first date was at a coffee shop on the Westside, followed by a walk on a nearby beach. It had been a while since I'd smelled the salt air and felt the sea breeze on my face. The return to this environment plus my attraction to Jim gave the night a wonderful feel. I expressed, "You're so lucky to live near the ocean. I miss it so much. How far up the coast is your place?"

"It's a few miles north of here. I'm not really that close to the water, but up in the hills above it."

"I used to live right on the beach. How I miss the openness and those beautiful sunsets. I loved falling asleep to the sounds of the waves crashing. It seems so long ago."

We walked quietly along the seashore until he broke the silence, "I don't hear the waves, but I drive past them all the time when I pick up my son Jonathan who lives with my ex-wife in the Valley."

"How old is he?"

"Six."

"I'd like to meet him. I really enjoy children."

"You do? Most of the guys I've met can't stand kids."

"Not me, I'm still one myself. Now tell me more about your weaving. It sounds so fascinating."

Our conversation continued in this respectful manner. We made plans for a second date, which led to a third and a fourth. Neither of us was eager to jump into a relationship. Jim's ex bitterly left him for another man after she found out that he was gay. I was smarting from my breakup with Leo. So we approached each other gingerly.

Jim was a fascinating person involved in the arts, New Age healing, and self-realization. We had common interests in shamans and Native Americans. Laid back and quiet to a fault, he was a real contrast to Leo's overbearing intensity. Being with Jim helped me mellow out.

I drove out to the hilly area where he lived in a converted flatbed truck that he'd fashioned into a home. This hippie-like structure appealed to me, a welcome departure from my recent urban environment. He enjoyed the old deco architecture of my flat and my office with its antique elevator. After a period of courtship, we started sleeping together. Like it had been with Cedric, warm, not hot, was the word. Warm was good enough for both of us at the time.

On a visit to Malibu, I met Jonathan. This rambunctious kid was as full of spirit as his dad was restrained. We liked each other immediately and developed a strong bond.

Jim and I soon grew tired of our cramped living spaces and decided to share a place. We found an inexpensive rental in the West Adams district of old duplexes near an African-American neighborhood. When we moved in, the Carpenters' song "We've Only Just Begun" played in my mind. I'd never used the term soulmate, but I was beginning to think that he might be the one.

When Jonathan stayed at our house, I cared for him while Jim was busy with work. I took him on outings to the observatory for planetary shows and to a bowling alley where I taught him how to aim the ball properly toward the pins. He even got a few spares and strikes, much to our delight.

One weekend when Jonathan was over, the three of us went to visit my dad. I hoped my father would like my new family, thinking he might be proud to see I was helping to raise a little boy. He didn't say anything right away, not until a short time later when my sisters returned home for semester break and the Freberg clan was planning a dinner. After hearing abut this, I called my dad to ask if I could bring Jim over. My new boyfriend was certainly as interesting a man as Leo.

He responded harshly, "Jim is not invited."

Shocked, I asked, "Why not?"

"I hate queers. I only accepted Leo because of your mother. Now that she's gone, I'm not going to tolerate your lifestyle anymore. From now on, homosexuals will not be allowed in my home."

"Wait a minute. Does that include me? I'm your son."

"You I'll deal with, but don't ever bring any of your kind with you."

"I refuse to be treated like a second-class citizen, especially in my own family. Until you change your mind, I'll have nothing to do with you."

I slammed down the phone. I was so shaken I could barely sleep that night. I left Jim alone in our bed and sought refuge on the living room sofa. When I called out in desperation for Mrs. B., she appeared dressed not in her usual chic clothes, but in rags.

Shocked, I quizzed, "What in the hell happened to you?"

She responded, "Honey, I also was an outcast in my family. I'd married a handsome well-established man that my parents were very fond of. We got along fine at the start, but when I wanted to finish college and get my degree, he demanded that we raise a family first. My folks put a lot of pressure on me to comply. Women in those days were supposed me to be subservient. When I insisted on staying in school, he filed for divorce. Afterwards, my folks wouldn't talk to me. All they wanted was grandkids. Didn't care a whit about *my* happiness."

"I'm sorry you had to go through this too. It's so painful to be cast out."

"Yeah, ain't it a bitch?" We both shared a laugh. "Don't worry, 'hon. It won't be long until gays will be given more rights and shown more respect. Stay strong. You'll see."

For the next few years, though I lived only a half hour away from my father, we didn't see or speak to each other. Family birthdays and holidays were celebrated without me. I was furious that my sisters supported him over me and I had little communication with them either. I doubted that they felt the same way as my dad. Yet, afraid to challenge him, they obeyed. I became a pariah at home.

Meanwhile, I helped Jim look after Jonathan as I tried to bury the rejection of my blood relations and invest in this family unit. We dug out a plot in front of our duplex and planted some organic vegetables. We took turns cooking soups and stews, mostly vegetarian, and baked hearty homemade breads, another interest we had in common.

However, our domestic situation ran into its own snags. In the divorce settlement Jim had negotiated with his ex there was an informal sharing of custody over Jonathan in return for him sending her some financial child support. When she remarried, her new husband was a homophobe who hated Jim and wanted to halt all contact between father and son. When Jim fell behind on payments, he took advantage of this to deny him access to the boy. Jim had to hire an attorney to contest this.

When the matter came to court, I volunteered to be a character witness. The official presiding over the case invited all four "parents" to a mediation appointment. She asked each of us what we wanted for the child. His mother didn't say much. The supportive language from Jim and me contrasted greatly with the stepfather's angry words.

Jim began, "I know how much my son enjoys attending the symphony, seeing art galleries, and exploring the architecture downtown."

I continued, "We take him to the beach, go rock climbing, and visit gardens like the one at the Huntington Library."

The stepfather protested, "I want to keep him away from these two men. They're a bad influence."

In the Midwest or South, we wouldn't have stood a chance, but in L.A. it was different. The mediator confronted the man, asking him the real reason he wanted to deny Jim contact with his son. "Because they're a couple of faggots. I don't want a kid of mine to be near these perverts."

We had to restrain ourselves from yelling at this bigot. Our cool heads prevailed. The mediator said she'd heard enough and asked us all to wait in the hall while she wrote down her decision. A half-hour later she returned and gave Jim standard custody rights, including weekends, every other holiday, and two full weeks vacation a year. This was more time than what had been worked out in the original divorce agreement. We left the court overjoyed. A decade before, I felt like I was treated like chopped liver in the legal system. Now I was valued like an entrée.

Open Relationship, Advocacy, & Parades

I continued helping Jim, supervising his son when needed. Life was simple with plenty of time to smell the roses. A typical afternoon would see Jim calling to me, "Can you pick some arugula from the garden? I want to make a green salad to go with our stir fry."

"Sure. Do we have any of that multi-grain bread I baked left?"

"Half a loaf."

"Yum! And how about the goat cheese?"

"It's all gone, but I bought us some Emmentaler."

"I can't wait to eat. Should I ask Jonathan to come inside and join us?"

"Sure. And snip a few rosebuds for the table, will you?"

About the only fly in the ointment of our life style was that Jim was not experienced in gay sex and had been with few partners. I was content seeing only him. When Jim stated a desire to go outside the relationship, there wasn't much for me to do but let him. It was a party out there. Sexual liaisons were as easy as picking fruit off a tree.

What was good enough for the goose was good enough for the gander. This was not my first choice, but I also treated myself to an occasional fling. We agreed not to bring anyone home. What we did on the outside was fine, just as long as the activity didn't get out of hand. Nothing was ever done whenever Jonathan was around. I ditched my soulmate fantasy about Jim. I prayed our relationship wouldn't become a roommate situation like it was with Leo.

I heard about a Gay Pride Celebration with its colorful parade and festive fair afterwards and dragged Jim along to see it. Besides the display of drag queens, leather dudes, and dykes on bikes, members of various social organizations in the community marched as well. Included were church and civic groups, business associations, a Great Outdoors chapter, and a local track club.

We had a great time. The parade started at one end of WeHo, wove its way down Santa Monica Boulevard (no relation to Beverly), and finished on the other side at the entrance to the fair. Among the many booths was one for the running club. I had always enjoyed jogging, and though I was now hitched, the thought of hanging out with gay athletes appealed to me. I joined the club soon afterwards. This became a regular activity and welcome social outlet.

A year later, I marched with the group in the next parade. Despite the fact that my disapproving family hadn't changed their mind about my ostracized state, I was proud to be an openly gay man. If my face was captured on the television cameras, so be it. I shouted with pride, "Uncle Ernie, this smile is for you. Hey mom, if you can see me from wherever you are, look, no hands!"

PART 3
CLIMBING OUT OF SHADOWS

Chapter 8
HIV

From WeHo To The Navajo

One night that summer I had another strange dream. I was back on TV. This time, the program was narrated by Jack Bailey, the famous emcee of the vintage television show *Queen For A Day*. Jack had been watching the Gay Pride Parade looking for a contestant to feature on an upcoming telecast. He'd been in the judge's booth when my track club passed by. At the moment he mentioned to an associate that they needed a damsel in distress to rescue from her plight, I tripped while waving to the judges and twisted my ankle.

Jack exclaimed, "There's a poor queen who needs our help. Not only does she have a limp wrist, she's limping all over."

His assistant replied, "I'd say she's a real basket case."

By the time the two men approached me, I was in such pain, I fell down on the asphalt and tore my tank top, exposing a nipple. "Perfect!" cried Jack. "Grab her."

The next thing I knew, I was sitting in a wheelchair being led onstage at the television studio while "Pomp and Circumstance" was being played in the background. The audience was crying "Sam, Sam, Sam" while Mr. Bailey tried to support me by saying, "It doesn't hurt that bad, does it? Is your other foot is okay?"

I responded, "It only hurts when I carry my purse."

This caused the studio audience to break into spontaneous applause with many reaching for the free box of Kleenex placed next to every seat. Over much sobbing, Jack begged theatrically, "We must get this poor queen back onto her feet. Is there a healer in the house?"

Just then, the shaman from my Peace Corps days appeared, wearing a gaudy muumuu, a lavender lei, a beehive wig, lipstick, and costume jewelry. He placed his hands on my shoulders and told me to stand up. I rose onto my feet successfully while the studio assistants took my wheelchair away. Jack then announced that a miracle had taken place. He put a tiara on my head and crowned me Queen For A Day. The audience gave this a standing ovation.

Immediately, two drag queens from the parade came onstage and tried to grab the tiara away, claiming that they were queens for the day - not me. Panic and pandemonium rang out as they chased me around the stage as the crowd kept yelling "Sam, Sam, Sam!"

I woke up screaming, "I'm the queen! Leave my tiara alone."

Surprised to hear me begging to be a queen, Jim said nothing. He had a week off from chiropractic school. During this break, he'd planned a trip to the Navajo reservation to buy wool for spinning and meet with a few tribe members to discuss weaving techniques. He invited me along.

There were news reports that week about a few gay men on the East Coast who'd come down with a medical condition that suppressed their immune systems. No one could figure it out, but since this happened so far away, hardly anyone locally gave any importance. This mysterious disease started spreading. Most victims became very ill, and many had died. Worse yet, the malady appeared to be contagious.

Then it was rumored that a male flight attendant transmitted it in other cities through multi-partner sex at bathhouses, including a few cases here in L.A. If there was a factual basis to the claim that this man was a culprit or not, the fact remained. The ailment had reached the West Coast.

It was a good time to get out of Dodge. We went on the road and had some adventures. From Window Rock to Canyon De Chelly, we visited several sights, stopping at many trading posts. Along the way, Jim bought a lot of fiber. I purchased some Native American artifacts and bags of blue cornmeal to make into tortillas and tamales when we got home.

One of our stops was at a meeting of weavers. While Jim attended this, I hiked nearby, discovering a stream with an amazing waterfall that descended from some red rocks. The afternoon heat was so intense I took off my clothes and bathed in the creek. When I shared this experience, Jim snapped, "You visited one of the most sacred spots on the reservation."

"Really? My curiosity often leads me into places like this."

He warned, "Don't reveal to anyone that you were there, let alone bathed in the waters. It is strictly off-limits to non-Navajo."

"I didn't see any signs. What's the problem? I didn't hurt anyone."

"I don't want to ruffle any feathers. I like to keep a low profile."

"Sometimes you keep too low a profile. You only live once. When I was in the Peace Corps, I didn't meet that shaman I told you about by playing it safe. You need to take some risks to experience rewards."

"There are some adventures I'd rather do without."

When we returned to L.A., the press was full of warnings to limit one's sexual activities until the mystery disease was figured out. Most people in the gay community hoped this would just be a temporary glitch on their partying. Many couples like us returned to monogamy for the time being. Our life fell into a routine as we worked with Jonathan in the garden, grew vegetables, and grilled them on our patio, all activities I enjoyed immensely.

A few months later, I heard from my sister Leslie that she was unhappy with my dad's decision to exclude me. "I'm sorry you can't be with us anymore. I miss seeing you. Hey, I just moved out on my own. Would you and Jim like to come for dinner and meet my boyfriend Barry?"

Grateful she was reaching out, I replied, "I miss you too. I'll have to ask Jim if he's available. I've hated being away from the family, but I'm not gonna crawl back on my knees. I did nothing to deserve this."

"I don't blame you. If I were walking in your shoes, I don't know if I'd have the courage to stick up for myself like you've done." Then she added, "I can't say if Dad or Judy feel the same. When I bring up the matter, they won't discuss it. This whole thing makes me sick."

"I appreciate your considering my point of view. I've sometimes wondered what it's been like for you guys."

"To be honest, at first we tried to have a good time without you. But after a while, things became tense. You know how Dad complains about everything when he gets on his high horse. It's become so serious around the dinner table. I miss the way you lightened things up."

"Thanks, sis."

Despite her apology, there was no invitation for me, let alone Jim, to join the family at my father's house. During the holidays, I was still the odd man out. Jim's folks were located back in the Midwest, so it was a meager Christmas and no Chanukah.

The Gay Plague

The disease now had a name, AIDS, also called HIV. It caused one's immune system to fail by attacking the body's T-cells and appeared to be transmitted by sexual contact through sharing of bodily fluids like sperm and blood. Though there was no contagion by kissing or through the air or water, many people panicked. They avoided socializing with anyone they knew to be gay.

The CDC came out with a list of do's and don'ts for safe sex. Celibacy or monogamy was the best way of handling the situation. Using condoms and limiting physical contact to specific practices was the next best thing. All it took to get infected was one exposure to the wrong person doing the wrong thing. Some people immediately changed their behavior. Others only gradually weaned themselves off unprotected sex.

At the bathhouses, safe practices were slow to catch on. Those with many partners often were in denial as they used drugs to accompany their play. Not ones to take undue risks, Jim and I stopped all outside activity and practiced safe sex with each other from then on.

At that time, there were no reliable tests for exposure. One only learned about this when symptoms hit. By then, it was too late to do anything. A regular bathhouse patron, Leo was one of the first men I knew to manifest symptoms of this dreaded disease.

Deaths in The Family

A national recession pushed AIDS to the bottom of priorities. While scientists at the CDC worked to cope with the retrovirus, Washington refused to get involved. President Reagan thought the gay lifestyle was decadent. Though the CDC tried to convince federal officials that HIV didn't care if one was gay or straight, they had similar views. It was not until this condition had spread to the mainstream population later in the '80s that any government help to combat the epidemic became available.

In the meantime, I had my hands full of illness and death, not from AIDS, but family members who succumbed to other diseases. My Aunt Ellen, a lifelong smoker, contracted lung cancer and followed my mom to her final resting place.

Meanwhile, Uncle Ernie and Aunt Zelda moved to California. Zelda had a reoccurrence of a cancer that had plagued her years before and wanted to spend what appeared to be her final days in a warmer climate. After a brave fight, she was gone as well. I helped Uncle Ernie with the funeral held at the graveside without any rabbi present. It was the first time I'd seen my immediate family in over three years. There was hardly a word uttered between us during the entire ceremony.

I read a few passages from "The Prophet" by Kahlil Gibran and then spoke. "Zelda was a special person who inspired me to be my best. She listened to my dreams and encouraged me to pursue them with imagination, soul, and *chutzpah*, a wonderful combination. The way she expressed her enthusiasm for life, it's no wonder she raised such a wonderful family. She will be sorely missed by all of us."

I had everyone in tears. Though Ernie and his daughters hugged me warmly, Irv, Judy, and Leslie kept their distance. Physical affection was not part of the Freberg repertoire. My father was more touched by the ceremony than he revealed there. Afterwards, I received a phone call from him. "I appreciate the kind words you said about Zelda."

Surprised, I replied, "Thanks, Dad. She was special to me."

"I also want to offer you an apology."

"Really? For what?"

"I've begun to realize that many of my views are old school."

"I never thought I'd ever hear you say that."

"It's hard to admit this. While I still don't approve of your lifestyle, society's opinions about gay people have changed."

"That's true."

"Son, I come from a different generation where homos were considered to be deviants. I'll try to accept your situation as best as I can. All I ask from you is to honor my feelings and not flaunt it in front of me."

Realizing the gravity of his words, I softened. "Gosh, I don't know what to say. I need some time to think about this."

He responded in kind, "I understand."

"Thanks. I appreciate your effort to reach out to me."

I hung up the phone, feeling a burden taken off my shoulders. I realized it must have taken a lot for my dad to admit the error of his ways, yet the road between us had been closed for so long it still had a lot of potholes.

Farewell To A Patriarch

A few months later, on my father's seventy-fifth birthday, I decided to help him celebrate the milestone. Nervously, I called him. "Dad?"

"Yes, son."

"Saturday's your birthday. Can I take you out for dinner?"

"Sure, that would be nice."

"Where would you like to go?"

"Lately, I've been wanting some good Mexican food."

"I know just the place. You've been there, the one downtown with the great margaritas and the colorful waitresses."

"You mean the restaurant that Leo once took us to?"

"Yes. Do you think you might enjoy going there again?"

"Of course. I still remember those wonderful green corn tamales. Will it be just you and me or…."

I couldn't believe my ears. Convinced that my dad's apology was for real, I said, "You know, Jim might like to join us. It's up to you."

"Bring him along. I've never really had a chance to talk with him."

"Fine. I'll make reservations. You can meet us in the lobby."

We three met as planned. Though encouraged, I still had my doubts. Jim was his usual reserved self. We were seated at an elegant table next to a splashing fountain. After a hearty meal accompanied by live mariachis and cocktails, my dad opened up. "Jim, I've gone to so many doctors to treat my back. What do you chiropractors do that's different?"

"We treat the whole body, not just symptoms. By getting into balance, you start healing on your own and don't need as many drugs."

My father cracked one of his typical remarks, "Now you tell me. I've got enough medications at home to open my own pharmacy."

This caused Jim to reply, "Maybe it's time to clean out your medicine chest. You might even save yourself some money this way."

My dad joked, "Hey, now you're talking my language."

After sharing a good laugh, he chirped, "This was a great margarita."

"I'm glad you're enjoying it. Want another?"

"I'd love one, but it's a long drive home. I'd better not."

As I'd prearranged, several waitresses arrived at the table with three cups of flan with lighted candles in them and sang "Happy Birthday." After dessert and opening presents, my dad excused himself. "Thanks for the meal and the gifts. But if you boys don't mind, I need to go home. I just don't seem to have the energy that I used to."

As he slowly walked out of the restaurant, I had no way of knowing that this would be the last time I'd see him alive. A couple of weeks later while attending a health fair with Jim, I got an emergency message to say that my dad had suffered a heart attack and died instantly. I had another funeral, eulogy, and grieving process to go through.

At the memorial service, only Judy, Leslie, Barry, an ailing Leo, and Uncle Ernie attended. Jim wasn't able to take off work. A few of my dad's business associates sent sympathy cards. I gave another eulogy, but not with the passion I'd expressed at my mom's and Aunt Zelda's rites. The passing of a severe patriarch didn't inspire as much emotion.

"For someone who never finished high school, Irv accomplished what he set out to do in his life, to achieve financial security for his family. He was challenging to live with, yet at times he could be very charming. I'll never forget the vacations he took us on and the restaurants we stopped at, how he taught me to take the check up to the cashier with a twenty-dollar bill and return with the change. Although he rarely praised us for our abilities, I know deep inside he was proud of us. As we lay his body to rest, let's be grateful for all he provided."

At the age of forty, I suddenly became the eldest in my family. Appointed executor of my father's affairs, I cleaned up a house long neglected, got it ready for sale, and tried to console two emotional sisters who didn't trust me to do a good job. I did this work alone, embittered by all the bureaucracy I needed to muddle through. Dealing with a lot of unresolved guilt, my relationship with Jim went into a tailspin. When I tried to share issues that came up for me, there was hardly any support. His reclusive personality became painfully even more distant.

During this time, Jim focused all his energies on Jonathan, which only added to my discomfort. I confessed this to one of my friends, and she said it seemed to be a case of unrequited love. Her analysis may have been subject to interpretation, but it rang true. When I needed Jim the most, he simply was not there for me.

I wondered if he'd ever been into the relationship as much as I was. His lack of sexual commitment before we were under the gun of HIV should have been a red flag. We'd latched onto each other on the rebound. When recovering from the vibrant Leo, I may have gone too far to the other side of the emotional pendulum.

That summer when Jim went to see his relatives in the Midwest, he took Jonathan along with him, leaving me behind. When I protested, there was no offer to make a separate trip, even a weekend, for the two of us. After he got back, I confronted him. "We never spend quality time together anymore. I can't tell you how unimportant you've made me feel in your life. What do you have to say about this?"

In his customary style, Jim was non-responsive. Frustrated by this stonewalling, I shouted angrily, "I can't take your silent treatment anymore. Either we go in for counseling together or I'm moving out."

Once again, he said nothing. He walked out of the room, leaving me exasperated. This was the straw that broke the camel's back. Like crossroads I'd come to before, it was time to make a change.

The Track Club, The HIV Test, & The Gay Olympics

Packing my things into boxes, I moved to a rental farther east in the Alhambra area. Here I regrouped and licked my wounds. After my father's estate was settled, I took the lion's share of my inheritance and bought a modest Craftsman-style home nearby. A relatively peaceful, solitary existence waited for me there.

The media was full of bad news about HIV. Most people came down with opportunistic infections that went on to kill them. There was no treatment and no cure. It was like in the dark days of the Middle Ages.

I continued attending track club meetings. Besides getting needed exercise, I enjoyed the camaraderie. Not one of the speedy members of the group, I did my best to keep up with them and ran many 5K and 10K races. I had a collection of T-shirts given to participants as souvenirs. For the first time in my life, I felt like an athlete.

AIDS was sometimes discussed, but most members wanted to get their minds off it. Early to bed and early to rise, unlike the night owls about town, our conversations were a mix of concerns about running and men. One of my buddies urged, "Train harder. The next 10K race is a month away. Aren't you trying to set another personal record?"

I replied, "I can't seem to break an 8-minute mile like you guys."

The man teased, "Stay behind one of those hunks with muscles under his tank top and shorts. That'll give you the motivation."

"I know. How do you think I got my last P. R.?"

The track club had potlucks at a member's house after a practice. Though most in the group looked straight, the way we served gourmet quiches and splashy fruit salads, it was obvious one was in gay company.

One day, I went to see Leo, who by now had progressed to ARC (AIDS Related Complex). This meant fairly low T-cells and minor symptoms. Though he had a little fever and weight loss, he wasn't that sick. Rather than try to support his health, he rebelled against his condition.

On one visit, I advised, "I'm sorry you don't feel well. Don't you think you should cut down on all the crap you put into your body? How will you get better if you don't take care of yourself?"

He shot back, "If I want to drink and get stoned, it's my business. I know these cigarettes will give me cancer someday, but I don't care. I won't live long enough to get it anyway."

"The way you're going, you're probably right."

Leo's future looked bleak. He'd moved out of our former Silverlake home and into his shop to save money. His negative attitude prevented anyone from assisting him through this.

Meanwhile, AIDS spread to intravenous drug users, infecting their partners who had no idea they were at risk. A test to screen for the virus finally arrived. The gay press encouraged us all to take it, but most refused, not wanting to know they had a fatal time bomb inside them.

At the same time, AZT, a powerful but toxic drug, appeared. It reduced HIV's insatiable appetite. There were some good results, but the side effects were debilitating. Leo was put on a high dose and improved. The nausea and dizziness it caused seemed better than wasting away.

After a fling with a track club buddy ended, I entered a period of celibacy. People were afraid. Dating was a minefield I didn't want to negotiate. Overcoming my reluctance, I put a personal ad in a gay rag. A nice fellow named Dan responded and we went out for coffee. There was a mutual attraction, but the guy was very fearful. He wouldn't consider going out again until I took an HIV test. Dan had tested inconclusive, then negative. I agreed to find out my status.

Taking a trip to the gay center in Hollywood, I had my blood drawn and was told to come back later to get my results. When it was time to return a week later, I chickened out and waited a month before trying again. Then I went to a clinic farther away where I felt less conspicuous. At this place, it took two weeks before my results would be available. I put Dan off with excuses, saying I needed more time.

Meanwhile, the track club had scheduled an outing up in San Francisco so we could run in the Gay Olympics. Gay athletes from across the U.S. and around the world participated. This was a good way to get HIV off my mind. A group of us drove up together and had a wonderful time racing, watching events, and partying afterwards.

One night after a spirited evening with my fellow jocks, I walked past a park that was known to be cruisy. It had been a while since I'd trolled for sex, but far from home with no one watching, I succumbed to the temptation. I walked along the parking lot filled with cars, many with men inside them looking for a connection. Then I saw a red sports car that flashed its headlights briefly on and off. Going over to check this out, a handsome man in his early forties beckoned me to get inside.

He drove over the Golden Gate Bridge to his place in Marin County, parking under a grove of large eucalyptus trees. We entered a nicely furnished home with organic art on the walls and scented candles flickering. Now if he'd asked, "Would you like to see my etchings?" we might have talked about modern art for a while. But instead, he led me straight into a bedroom filled with more artwork.

After our hot session of protected sex was over, the man started to open up. "This painting was given to me by a well-known recording star. We had a brief affair. When we broke up, he said I could keep it."

I gushed, "I'm impressed. Do you have any other celebrity art?"

Suddenly, instead of responding to my query, the man suggested we get dressed, led me to the car, and drove back to the park where we'd met. I returned to my running buddies with mixed feelings. This wasn't worth any bragging rights. To the guys in the track club, it probably would have been just another tacky story out of so many in the naked city.

Back at the events, it was a proud feeling to be part of a large group of gay people dedicated to improving our athletic abilities. The only downer was when the man who'd created the organization, a champion Olympic athlete himself, revealed at the closing ceremonies that he'd been diagnosed with AIDS. There was a moment of silence for the many people who had fallen to the disease and those still struggling with it. This was a bittersweet end to a celebration of gay spirit.

On the way home, our group stopped at a Bakersfield coffee shop, much like one my family would have eaten at years previously. We were all wearing Gay Olympics T-shirts. This was redneck territory, and the proprietors whisked us to a booth in a back corner. As we were making our way there, I overheard a surprised customer sitting at the counter say, "Gay Olympics? What will they think of next?"

Support Groups, Dr. Roth, & The Will To Live

After experiencing a week of roller coaster emotions, I knew when I got back home I'd have to face the music. Anxiously, I drove to the testing location, hoping I'd found out about the disease in time to prevent exposure. Leo already was sick. Besides spilled spaghetti sauce, we may have shared viruses back then. I waited patiently at the center. When my name was called, a volunteer said a doctor would be out to speak with me. I could tell that the news would not be good. It wasn't. I was HIV positive.

The doctor rested a hand on my shoulder. He ran through some information, trying to bolster my spirits. "I know this is upsetting, but AIDS is an unpredictable disease. There is a lot we don't know about it. Some people may take years before they come down with symptoms. There's even a chance you won't get sick at all."

Surprised to hear this, I replied, "That's not what I've read."

"You know how the media sensationalizes everything. If you take good care of yourself, you can at least slow down its progression."

He handed me some paperwork to read on how to boost my immune system, how the virus is transmitted, and how to practice safe sex. I barely heard what the man was saying. I didn't read the printed matter, just wanting to go somewhere and have a good cry.

I took myself out to a Chinese restaurant and the kind of meal I used to share with Gracie back in my Valley days - chop suey, egg rolls, butterfly shrimp, and the works. My life was irrevocably changed. There was no use fighting the truth. I had to roll with it.

The next afternoon I called Dan to tell him the news. This kind man was saddened to hear the results. That night, he took me out to a gay Mexican restaurant for dinner. He asked, "You want another drink to chase down those enchiladas? It's on me."

I answered, "No thanks. One is just fine. I don't drink much. A hangover is not what I need. I feel bad enough as it is."

"Maybe if we stay for the drag show, it'll help to cheer you up."

"Frankly, I don't think I would enjoy that right now. Let me finish up my plate and then you can drive me home. Okay?"

"Sure."

At the end of the evening, Dan said he'd have to think about seeing me again. The next time we spoke, he'd decided he couldn't risk being with an HIV-infected person. The irony is that a year later, he came down with symptoms and was told that he'd received a false negative test result. But this was way after the fact. This was the first of countless times that I was turned down by prospective partners afraid to get involved with me because of my health status.

One of the first things I did was to search for a support group. I knew the value of sharing experiences with others in the same boat. Also, I wanted to find an HIV-positive partner. I was let down on both counts.

The encounter groups were divided into symptomatic and asymptomatic. I chose a group from the latter category. At my first meeting, there were a dozen men my age sitting in a circle sharing their battles, mostly defeats, with this disease. It was more of a complaint than a support session. Ever since my camping days with Lewis and Winston, I'd learned to keep my drama queen in check. I was now in a room full of unbridled whiners. They'd resigned themselves to their imminent demise, playing up the dramatics of "my woe is bigger than yours."

One of the members shared, "I've had a miserable week. I came down with a bad cold and couldn't tell if my fever was a night sweat or not. The next morning I lost one of my earrings. It's so hard to find things when my dementia sets in."

Another participant darted back, "Darling, you can't possibly have dementia already. You're just a dizzy queen like the rest of us."

The first guy responded cattily, "That's easy for you to say, honey. You went to pieces last week because you lost another pound. I knew you'd get it back with a hot fudge at Baskin Robbins and you did."

Someone else volunteered, "If you think things are bad for you, I lost my crystal connection. Now I can't even get a hard-on anymore without it."

Another dude suggested, "Can't you just use poppers?"

A guy in the back of the room shared, "My boyfriend won't have sex with me anymore because he thinks the spot on my leg is Kaposi's Sarcoma. He won't believe me when I tell him it's only a birthmark."

Someone else came up with a logical response, "Just share your birthmark with somebody else. That'll make him jealous."

Another guy said, "Yesterday I went to Vegas and blew my disability check. Now I've got nothing to live on for another week."

"Poor dear. There's always the food bank."

"But that doesn't pay my rent."

I remembered the exotic diseases I pretended to have when I was a child. This was the real thing, yet nobody in the room was on their deathbed. The role of Camille dying of consumption might come soon enough, but why hasten its appearance. There was too much life to be lived before its arrival. When it came time for my share, I introduced myself. "I'm Sam. This is my first time here. I just got my test results last week."

The queenie guy greeted me, "Poor darling. Welcome to our sinking ship. There's always room for one more."

I continued, "Don't throw me a life preserver just yet. I've read that 5% of us may not get sick. I hope to be one of them."

The member with the acid tongue advised me. "Hey, Pollyana, get real. Don't believe a word of that bullshit. Take off those rose-colored glasses, honey, and join the pity party with the rest of us."

That turned out to be the most comforting remark uttered. I resolved to seek out support group number two, still hoping to find someone to go out with for dinner and a movie. The next group was much the same. I would have been sympathetic for anyone who was actually sick, but I had the feeling that for most of these guys, this was a dress rehearsal. There was no one with whom I wanted to spend a weekend night, let alone five minutes.

After visiting several groups, I couldn't bear all the whining and complaining. Finally, I found a meeting of asymptomatic men that had a more positive if not the most realistic attitude. Their focus was on what I would call cures du jour, miracle treatments reputed to boost the immune system. These "Hail Mary's" were at least going in the right direction. What I got from these sessions was a dose of reality. It was clear I'd be in this position for a long haul, hopefully a very long haul.

The next item on my HIV agenda was to go to my doctor and get a physical. A few years earlier, Dr. Roth had been recommended to me by one of my music students. Though in family practice, this caring professional was familiar with AIDS in its many stages. He'd taken some blood work on me when we were concerned about the state of my immune system before screening was available. The last battery of tests done a year previously showed my numbers to be strong. Some new ones revealed a little decline, but Dr. Roth predicted that if it continued at this slow rate, I might have a few years before having to deal with any serious health challenges. Howlin' Wolf's blues song "Going Down Slowly" began playing in the back of my mind.

This was like when the judge had sentenced me to two years probation. It was a relief not to have to go to jail, but having to be on my best behavior was not conducive to a good night's sleep, even if I was now sleeping alone. I worked on tightening my health regimen. The track club helped to keep me in shape. If anyone was to make it onto a lifeboat out of the Titanic, it was going to be Sam Freberg.

Angela & Healing Hands

Mitigating my medical concerns was my inheritance, enough to live on for a few years. Many in my support groups partied, spending their funds while they still had time. Others lived on the dole, taking an easy way out. I didn't want to go down either of these paths. I enjoyed teaching, a reason to get up in the morning. Knowing too much play would drain my resources and too much work could tax my immune system, I took neither of these roads, but a middle one.

I planted a vegetable garden and baked my own bread like I'd done with Jim. Not pleased to hear that Jim had found a new boyfriend, I did my best to forget him. Meanwhile, I stayed in touch with Leo, whose shop no longer could afford to keep Beverly. She was eager to move on to other work anyway. I also maintained my friendship with her. Occasionally, we got together for lunch.

One afternoon, I turned on the television to watch a daytime talk show. A guest on the program was a woman named Angela, a New Age healer working with AIDS people. She encouraged us to deal with our condition and heal ourselves. Her premise was that if we admitted on some level that we helped to cause our disease, we also had the power to heal it. She held weekly meetings in West Hollywood to encourage AIDS patients to turn our lives around. I was inspired to check it out.

The night I attended my first meeting with Angela it was hard to find a parking place. It seemed there was a special event going on. Expecting to enter a classroom with thirty or so people, I was shocked to walk into a large auditorium with a few hundred participants. I thought, *When they were talking epidemic on the news, they weren't kidding.*

My smart aleck swagger was replaced by jaw-dropping awe. Not only were there rows of young men assembled waiting to hear her talk and ask questions, there were many emaciated guys in wheelchairs, the symptomatic ones I wanted to avoid. This was serious stuff, and suddenly I was frightened. If this was to be my future, I thought of leaving. If there was a high cliff nearby, I was ready to jump off.

I found an empty seat and listened to Angela speak about taking responsibility for one's condition. I soon learned that this remarkable woman had written several books and amassed quite a following. This meeting was much like being at an Advocate Experience weekend, but for the AIDS crowd. She began preaching her mantra of learning to create one's way back to health. "Your mind paves a path for your body to follow. No matter how dark things get, there's light at the end of the tunnel. Drop your past baggage and live in the present."

I had an epiphany. *That's just what Brian tried tell me years ago.* I realized that there was much to learn from her. I was not alone. The group inside was hanging on her every word.

After a short lecture, she opened the room to questions, many similar to the concerns I'd heard in my support groups. Some, however, were much more troubling. No matter how serious or dramatic the share, she had an amazing ability to let each person say whatever he or she needed to get off his or her chest before responding.

One fellow related, "My name is Anthony. I was diagnosed with the CMV virus. Does that mean I'm going to go blind from it? I'm afraid I won't be able to drive my car anymore. What can I do?"

When I'd hear people complain, I tried to block them out. Instead of interrupting, she waited for a pause before answering them. Seeing how accepting this amazing woman was inspired me to emulate her.

"I know you're feeling a lot of fear over this right now, but just because you have a microbe in your system doesn't mean that it will take over. The CMV virus is a living organism and responds to the environment it resides in. Focus on taking care of yourself, imagine your eyes possessing clear sight, and you may be surprised. Your mind is very powerful. Meditate on clearing this invader from your body."

The anxious guy wailed, "It's easy for you to say this because you don't have my disease. What makes you feel your approach works?"

"Honey, I know from experience. Several years ago, I was diagnosed with terminal cancer, but with the help of a few teachers and guides, I was able to turn my condition around without chemotherapy or radiation. The more you focus on your fears, the more you assist in manifesting their appearance. But if you stay calm, you can get past them. There is no guarantee, but when your brain is full of negativity, it blocks any good result. Now let's put Anthony in our healing circle tonight. May our thoughts and prayers help him drive away this threat to his eyesight. He truly deserves to have strong and clear vision."

I later learned that this was part of the beliefs stressed in her Church of Religious Science background. Her energy seemed similar to the shaman's field when he was casting his spells.

In addition to these talks, there were tables where volunteer massage therapists and energy practitioners gave healing sessions to anyone in need. I was too shy to go up to one these tables at first, but in later visits, I took advantage of some of this freely given work.

When the meeting was over, the large crowd filed out of the room. As I made my way back to my car, I could hear the words of a Peter Gabriel song run through my head "Don't give up, 'cause you have friends. Don't give up, you're not beaten yet. Don't give up."

Back home, I assimilated what I'd experienced. Knowing this was an opportunity to grow, I resolved to attend these meetings regularly. For several years, I hardly missed any. Through them I picked up a new set of friends, most of them HIV positive, many who'd progressed to AIDS. I learned not to be afraid of my condition.

I continued to gather meaning from all the sharing in the room. Sometimes there was laughter, sometimes tears. Angela used each person's story to create a teaching moment. Receiving treatments on the healing tables created an interest in me to study these techniques. A course taught by a volunteer healer was my first step in this direction.

I learned that Reiki is a traditional practice that originated in Japan. Although not an instant cure for any illness or condition, it does promote the body's natural healing abilities. This channeling of energy had been handed down from teacher to student in a manner similar to how Indian sitar music is taught, from guru to disciple. Having experienced this kind of instruction before, I was favorably disposed to this approach.

My Reiki teacher introduced the ritual, saying, "Before I initiate you into this sacred energy, tell me why you want to learn to use it."

I replied, "I want to learn how to heal others."

"That's admirable, but the first thing a practitioner needs to learn is how to heal oneself. After I transmit this energy to you, I'll show you some hand positions to direct it. Once we get a handle on this, we'll all go around the room practicing on each other."

An important thing I learned about doing energy work was that it takes two people, the giver and the receiver. One needs to be open to the energy in order to benefit from it. A disease like AIDS, with limited treatment options, had forced a large segment of the gay population to be willing to try this. Whenever I was given Reiki energy, I felt a sense of relaxation that helped my body run efficiently like a well-tuned engine. I was looking forward to being able to return my good fortune to others.

One of the issues raised at Angela's meetings was whether to take the drug AZT or fight the disease holistically, with strong opinions on both sides. The drug often made people so sick they felt like giving up. Treating the disease exclusively with alternative methods only slowed its progression. Even the man who initiated me into Reiki fell very ill a month later and had to be hospitalized. There was no certain path.

At one meeting, Angela introduced the group to Andrew, a psychologist who gave workshops to HIV patients who needed to come to grips with addictions to alcohol, drugs, and compulsive sex that were dragging them down. Many had risen above these behaviors only to fall into old patterns when faced with an AIDS diagnosis. In WeHo, compulsive sex was so prevalent it was not considered to be an addiction, but a way of life. Though my cruising episodes by then were few and far between, I still had urges. So I added these workshops to my calendar.

I was now commuting to town several times a week. I went to Angela's seminars, the addiction meeting, my "cure du jour" support group, and did volunteer work at an AIDS support house. The retrovirus had completely taken over my life. I really needed a break.

Healer By Default

One of the men in this workshop mentioned a sweat lodge given for recovering addicts. It was a traditional Native American ceremony to cleanse toxins out of one's body while offering prayers to the spirits and ancestors. This was held in the Valley not far from where I grew up.

A dozen participants greeted me there. Each of us was told to donate a contribution and a medicine gift like a packet of tobacco for the sweat leader. A potluck was held afterwards. I baked some bread for the occasion. Everyone pitched in to assist the short, overweight fellow that conducted the ritual, a reputed medicine man from a Colorado tribe who'd come a long way to share this ancient practice. I didn't know what a medicine man looked liked, but I took him at his word.

We all put blankets over a structure of tree branches and rope tied together and folded them into a dome. When this was done, we fashioned a door for an entrance. Inside the lodge, a hole was dug in the center to place heated rocks. A wood fire was lit to heat the rocks and a fire person designated to monitor it. Using a pair of deer antlers, he brought red-hot stones inside to the leader at the appointed moment.

We crawled into the lodge and seated ourselves around the center hole. Once all was in place, the leader recited incantations, pouring water over the hot rocks to create steam, causing everyone to sweat profusely. He sprinkled sage and cedar over the stones, giving the space a spellbinding fragrance. There were four rounds, each one more intense. Prayers were made to the ancestors, native songs were sung, drums played, and individual requests for help for oneself, family, or friends were made.

"I've been sober for two years, but when my buddies drink while watching sporting events it's difficult not to join them. I ask the spirits for help in maintaining my abstinence with so many temptations around me."

The group replied, "Ho."

"My husband fell off the path and I need support in keeping him from doing drugs the way he did before we met."

"Ho, all my ancestors."

"Even though I haven't used in several years, my mother still won't allow me go out at night alone. Help me to win back her trust."

"Ho, Great Spirit."

The final round completed, we crawled outside and recited traditional words of thanks. At the potluck, the leader invited us to his reservation to learn more about these practices. I was the only one who expressed a desire to go. The man wrote down a date, time, and a PO box to contact him. When I got home, I thanked my lucky stars for this opportunity. I wouldn't have to fly 4,000 miles to visit a shaman. An 800-mile drive would suffice.

After some correspondence, I packed my camping gear and started out. As I drove into Colorado, rain started to fall. When I got to the reservation, the ground was saturated. I tried to book a room at the motel, but there were no vacancies. I had to make the best of it.

It rained all night and water leaked into my tent. Thunder and lightning kept me up half the night. Despite this, I woke up early, got dressed, and prepared for an exciting day. When I arrived at the reservation cafe at the appointed time, the sweat leader, a.k.a. medicine man, wasn't there. I waited and waited. After an hour, I asked the cashier, "I had an appointment to see Manuel Williams here. Have you seen him?"

She laughed, "Manuel? What do you want with him?"

"He's a medicine man who said he's going to teach me everything."

"Honey, I'm afraid your friend is no medicine man. There are a lot of people who go around pretending they are, especially to outsiders. He lives with his mother and they're out of town for the weekend."

"He knew I was coming."

"Darlin', it looks like you're out of luck."

"But I drove 800 miles to get here. What am I going to do now?" I slumped down on a chair and burst out in tears.

The cashier tried to comfort me. "All is not lost. Tonight we're having a pow-wow and tomorrow there's a bear dance ceremony. It won't be the same as personal instruction, but you'll be able to get a feel of how we do things here. No need to go home empty handed."

Already on the reservation, I drove around the countryside. It was springtime and the green hills were covered with boulders full of *anasazi*, ancestor spirits. This reminded me of my Big Sur days. That night, I went to the community center. Tribe members of all ages were dressed in brightly colored outfits with bells and feathers, competing for prizes as they paraded around the room in front of the judges.

In the morning, I joined a crowd of spectators to watch the bear dance. I was mesmerized by the hypnotic movements and captivated by the pulsating drums and powerful energy. Of the many participants, only a few were still standing through sheer fortitude as they moved three steps forward and three steps back to imitate movements of the bear.

Suddenly, large thunderclouds formed and it started raining heavily. The crowd scampered as a voice came over the loudspeaker to say the dance was finished. The drummers grabbed their instruments and left. One of the warriors keeled over where I was standing. An elder cried, "Does anyone know CPR? The man has stopped breathing." Someone tried to revive him but was having a hard time. No medical doctor was there. An ambulance was summoned, but it would take fifteen minutes. I volunteered, "I'm trained in healing. Maybe I can help him breathe."

The elder replied, "We'd be grateful for anything you can do."

I summoned some Reiki energy, and after intoning a few sacred words I placed my hands on the dancer's chest. Within a few seconds, the man regained his breath and his trauma lessened. I could feel the energy circulating through both our bodies.

By the time the ambulance arrived, the dancer was awake and breathing deeply. The paramedics placed him on a gurney and took him to a hospital. The elder shook my hand and thanked me for my assistance. Everyone left for shelter and I was soon alone. Although unable to meet the supposed medicine man, in a small way I'd become one myself.

Act Up & Acupuncture Down

When I got back home, there was sad news. Two participants in Angela's workshop had died. My "cure du jour" support group also had lost a member. In addition, one of the fellows in my addiction workshop succumbed to a case of pneumonia that was treated too late.

Recently, with the help of AZT, Leo had been holding his own. But while working on a painting well into the wee hours for several nights, he came down with AIDS-related pneumonia. Fortunately, it was found early and he recovered. But in his weakened state, Leo had to give up his shop and move in with in his folks in Chino Hills.

I was angry. Gay people were dropping like flies and the government was doing nothing about it. If we were straight men, there would have been a full court press. But in Reagan's second term, all efforts were delayed. The FDA dragged its feet on new medications in the pipeline. As more of us came down with the disease, the lone AIDS treatment was at best only slightly effective.

In 1987, ACT UP, a militant group of gay men and supporters, was organized to protest this frustrating state of affairs. With their signature slogan "Silence = Death," they became a media-savvy outfit skilled at conveying their message to the public. At one of Angela's sessions, a member from the group stood up and said, "We're having a demonstration next Saturday to protest budget cuts to our health clinic and need some volunteers to join us." I offered my assistance.

By the end of the '80s, the situation improved only slightly. Every new treatment failed to deliver in clinical trials. Meanwhile, my blood tests showed more slippage. I needed to intervene. Trying AZT briefly, I found the nausea and diarrhea intolerable. Though Western medicine wanted me to strike pre-emptively, my body told me otherwise.

I turned to a Chinese doctor of oriental medicine who had success with AIDS patients using acupuncture and herbal treatments to retard the retrovirus. This practitioner was located in my old stomping grounds in Venice. Going there allowed me to reflect on how much had changed for me in the past decade. While waiting to be treated there, the party atmosphere of the '70s was a distant memory.

At my first session, my new health practitioner told me, "Let me see your tongue again. Just as I thought! Your spleen is yang deficient, your pulse is weak, and your system is dry and overheated."

He then inserted a dozen or so needles in meridians of my autonomic nervous system. Any points that were evaluated as hyper, hypo, or blocked, areas where the "chi" or body energy was not flowing properly, were balanced. These sites were similar to the Reiki hand positions I'd studied. I came for treatments weekly and the procedures opened up a world of new tools, terms, and technology for me to explore.

After each session, the doctor wrote me a prescription adjusted by his observations for herbs to make into a tea. Living close to Chinatown, I found an herbalist there to fill them. At a little store lined with bins containing leaves, seeds, and dried flowers, I gave the elderly man in the shop my weekly recipe, enjoying watching him use antique scales and an abacus to figure the price. These formulations weren't covered by my insurance like doctor visits, but they were nowhere as taxing as the virus would be if left unchecked.

Within a few weeks, my body was invigorated. Further blood tests confirmed that my downward spiral of T-cells had been halted. After a year of treatment, my immune system was back in a normal range. All this was without a single side effect. Also during this period, I attended Reiki circles where practitioners exchanged healing energies. My health stayed intact unlike so many others around me.

So Many Memorial Services, So Little Time

In the early '90s, the first President Bush occupied the White House. He was more pragmatic than his predecessor when it came to social issues. We ACT UP people didn't get all we wanted out of the federal officials, but at least we were listened to. Some funds became available for new medicines and preventative information.

Meanwhile, the audience at Angela's workshops thinned out. Besides pneumonia and a form of skin cancer called Kaposi's Sarcoma, many participants had fungal infections that became nails in their coffins. I went to countless memorial services at auditoriums, churches, synagogues, and cemeteries, often contributing to the chorus of eulogies for a departed member. As soon as I stopped grieving over a friend, it was time to start the process all over again.

Occasionally, I visited Leo at his folks' house. He'd greet me with a coffee cup in one hand, a cigarette in the other, and a joint rolled up in his back pocket. "My parents keep nagging me to go to church. They've been on my case to attend an AIDS support group there."

"I wouldn't let anyone push me to go to temple. What do you say?"

"I went to a meeting last week and it wasn't that bad. They told us we're all sinners, but we'll be forgiven if we repent."

"You're just ill, not a sinner. If I were in your shoes, I'd try a holistic Hail Mary with acupuncture instead of all that religious stuff. It's been working pretty well for me."

"Your doctor is too far away and too expensive."

"Screw the costs. Don't you want to stay alive for the cure?"

"By the time they find something for this disease, I'll be long gone. Or I'll develop lung cancer. Everyone in my support group has accepted the fact that we won't be around much longer."

On one visit, I brought Beverly along. She hadn't seen Leo in a while and took time off work at a downtown charity. The family greeted us with a special dinner cooked by Nina. Wine glasses were raised to Leo's health as if he were well. Though Nina appealed to him with a hearty *"Mangia, mangia,"* he hardly touched his plate.

A couple of months later, Leo passed. Beverly and I attended the memorial service. The priest described what an angel he was, not mentioning anything about his being gay or his nefarious activities. By no means a choirboy, Leo's robes were cut from an entirely different cloth. The suited-and-tied man displayed in the open casket was a stranger to us both.

People gave speeches in his memory. When it was my turn to speak, I said, "Leo was a very caring person. When he and I lived in Silverlake together, he brought total strangers who were destitute to our home. In the true spirit of Christ, he fed and clothed these lost souls before taking them back to their shabby residences." Leo's large extended family was deeply moved. I left out the part that this was usually after a wild night of poppers, drugs, and hot sex.

Not a word was said about AIDS. Leo's parents told everyone that his death was caused by a terminal lung infection from his long history of chain smoking. On the way back home, Bev and I shared our disappointment that the family was so deep in denial.

By that time, the NAMES project, a traveling exhibition of quilts memorializing people who'd died of AIDS, had begun. Beverly, with her home economics skills, convinced his mom to make a quilt for Leo with her. The design was traditional Italian. I would have preferred an angel vs devil theme, but remembering him was the important thing.

Lanie, Hubby, & Baby

During this time, a good friend of mine had a sad turn of events. She'd been one of Leo's art store clients, a brassy woman who worked in the film industry named Lanie. Like him, she was a vivacious Italian who loved people, food, and partying. She used to invite us to her house for gatherings filled with fun and laughter.

Her crowd was usually a mix of straight and gay people, and she hosted potlucks serving savory dips, fanciful salads, spicy casseroles, and decadent desserts. We played games like charades and sang campy songs like "My Boyfriend's Back" and "Chapel Of Love". To say this was a lively group would be an understatement.

At one festive gathering when Lanie crowed, "Anyone want seconds on apple pie?" I joked, "Only if it's from the Big Apple."

"Honey, I'm from the Big Apple. You got a problem with that?"

Someone else remarked, "You New Yorkers are all alike. All you want to do is party."

She retorted, "Like I said. You got a problem with that?"

A handsome hunk seductively teased, "Only if I don't get a scoop of Butter Pecan on my pie."

The vamp in Lanie sassed, "Hey, baby, I'll butter your pecan any day if you sample my pie."

He returned her playfulness. "Maybe I'll have to try a slice."

In her best Mae West impersonation, she chimed, "I don't have any problem with that."

A few years later, she married a wonderful man named Giovanni. Leo and I attended the wedding separately. By that time, we were no longer an item. Not long afterwards, the newlyweds had a baby. When the child arrived, since I'd distanced myself from her social circle, I sent them a card and my best wishes.

Shortly after her infant's first birthday, she called to tell me that the little girl was very sick. After coming down with several infections, the doctors discovered she had AIDS. Further tests revealed both parents were also HIV positive. Giovanni had lived in Greenwich Village before the epidemic, straddling a bisexual tightrope. Lanie had dated many gay guys in her wilder days. The couple was relieved to have found each other and felt that their monogamous relationship was all the protection they needed. Sadly, they were wrong.

When I paid her a visit, we embraced and cried together. Her living room, a prior site of outrageous movie posters, was now filled with colorful plastic toys, baby photos, and other toddler paraphernalia. I tried to offer Lanie and her spouse some Reiki energy, but they were not receptive. I told them of my Chinese acupuncturist and how well I was doing. They had no interest. They'd hired the best doctors and trusted Western medicine implicitly, figuring the more money they threw at this, the better the results would be.

The infant died first, and Giovanni not long afterwards. I went to both funerals, but declined the opportunity to give any eulogies. My oratory skills by then were spent. After a short period of mourning, Lanie joined a heterosexual AIDS support group and made an attempt at hosting festivities like the ones she'd thrown before.

The last time I saw her was at an event where she was laughing at everything in her inimitable way. She was bombed as she called out to me, "You gotta meet my new boyfriend, Marcus. He's a surfer dude from my group. Isn't he a hunk?"

Marcus was a tall guy with bloodshot eyes and long blond hair in a ponytail. I extended my hand, "Glad to meet you, Marcus."

Shaking it, he said, "You want a hit of this joint? It's good stuff."

I responded, "Thanks, but no thanks."

The hostess with the mostest whined, "Don't be such a party pooper." She sang wildly, "It's my party and I'll smoke if I want to, drink if I want to, and screw if I want to."

Lanie seemed to want to go down with the Titanic. A few months later, an iceberg came to her rescue. She passed on, most likely eager to join her afflicted family. I went to the funeral, but had to leave the reception early. My grief was more than I could handle.

CHAPTER 9
GOING DOWN SLOWLY

Recession, 976 Lines, & Donald-Bob

On Election Day in 1992, I joined some buddies from Angela's workshop to watch Bill Clinton defeat George H. W. Bush for the presidency. With a new gay-friendly chief executive on the horizon, we looked forward to effective medicines and additional funding. However, the nation's financial situation was challenging. Unemployment had risen and several of my students had to quit their music lessons. This forced me to have to refinance my house just to stay afloat.

I signed up for AIDS services such as dental work and joined an HIV food bank to help make ends meet. Though the groceries were free, much of the white bread, white sugar, and canned goods weren't as nutritious as I was used to. I accepted what was offered and gave away to others what I couldn't bring myself to consume. Despite the best efforts of my acupuncturist, my T-cells started falling again. The medical community had discovered that whatever one threw at HIV, the microbe had an ability to mutate around any treatment.

Attendance at Angela's workshops continued to decline. One week, she announced she was leaving. The robes of a saint can only be worn for so long before burnout occurs. She passed the baton to Andrew, the addiction seminar leader.

AIDS kept spreading, often from people who refused to get tested and felt that by not knowing their status they didn't have to disclose anything. Because dating was so risky, a new venue, 976 phone fantasy lines, became popular. They were an easy means to avoid exposure and keep from getting involved with a partner who might become ill. Once I found them, my sexual compulsion became active again. Rather than seek a personal encounter, I revisited these lines at $2 a pop, draining my finances.

I got tired of this solitary existence and responded to some personal ads with phone numbers posted there. One ad led me to a man who said his name was Bob. This fellow was looking for (sigh!) a steady boyfriend. He was passive and wanted an aggressive partner. Though a switch hitter, I was anxious to connect with someone and played along.

We met for dinner and liked each other. At the end of the date, I nervously disclosed my HIV status. This had so often been a deal breaker I steeled myself for rejection.   Much to my surprise, Bob did not dismiss me, saying he needed time to think about it. A week later, when he called me back, Bob said his real name was Donald. Using a false name was common on the phone lines. Then he added, "If we use condoms, I'm OK with seeing you."

I replied, "I was sure you'd turn me away like others have done."

"I thought of that, but there are so many people still doing unsafe sex. Since you've been honest, I actually feel safer with you."

Grateful for this acceptance, I responded, "You're a decent man for giving me a chance. Don't worry, I'll play very safe."

This was the start of a successful relationship, at least for a while. Donald had a good paying job at the Port of Los Angeles. He liked to go out for breakfast, lunch, and dinner. I kept up with these culinary excursions, even though it was an expense I could not afford. We spent weekends at each other's residences for several months.

In addition to dining out, we took several car trips. One favorite spot was Laughlin, a Nevada gambling center where he introduced me to the excitement of playing slot machines. As a child, I'd watched my parents gamble in Las Vegas. As an adult, I'd drop a few dollars here and there. It was $20 frittered away on entertainment and nothing more.

Donald liked to spend hours at a time, hypnotized by the spinning wheels, flashing lights, jangling coins, and mechanical music, bells, and whistles. I'd play alongside him, then take a walk outside to stare at the Colorado River. I longed to be out in nature instead. Sharing this with him led us to plan a camping trip together. We drove to Zion National Park in Utah where we had a great time. Back home, Donald mingled easily with my friends. We seemed to be getting along just fine.

But two things spoiled this. My new squeeze was limited in his choice of sexual activity, leaving me wanting to experience other sides of my nature, especially on the weekdays when we were not able to see each other. This was exacerbated by the easy availability of dial-a-trick on the 976 lines. Even more upsetting to me was that Donald was still very secretive about his sexual preference. This came to the fore when he asked me, "Want to join me on a trip to see my Mom?"

"I'd love to meet your mother and tell her how special you are to me."

"Wait. She doesn't know about me, let alone us. In fact, we'll have to sleep in separate bedrooms. I don't want to take any chances."

"But the way we act, we're an open book. Mothers can tell."

"It's separate rooms. There's nothing more to discuss."

Donald hated disagreements. While I saw the world in varying shades of gray and would have worked to find a compromise, he was strictly black and white. A few nights before we were leaving, he ended the relationship. This came out of the blue with no opportunity to make sense of things. I was badly hurt. Rather than going back to playing on the phone, I camouflaged my disappointment by driving out to the casinos, especially the Indian gambling houses in California, closer to home. At the time, this seemed to be a harmless diversion.

Before our breakup, we'd bought plane tickets for a European vacation. It was too late to back out and get a refund, so I traveled solo on a tight budget. I took advantage of my single status to do as I pleased. Instead of visiting popular tourist spots and waiting in long lines as Donald wished, I enjoyed staying in small-town hotels, ate at tiny cafes, picnicked in the countryside, and went to folk concerts in village parks. Even though this stretched my finances, I realized this might be my only chance to do so.

Financial Stress & A New Profession

When I got back to the States, I was exhausted and came down with one bad cold after another. The high I'd experienced in Europe turned into a state of depression. When I visited Dr. Roth, the news was even more upsetting. My T-cells had fallen to a dangerously low range.

To add insult to injury, I received a letter from my insurance company announcing that the terms of the policy I'd bought well before I knew about my HIV condition were changed. They formed a new subdivision offering the same coverage at the same price, but everyone had to update their health records, disclosing any pre-existing conditions. Those who refused to do so could stay in the old company, but their rates would double. In six months, they doubled again.

My dwindling income was no match for these big expenses. Disclosing my health status meant immediate cancellation. Since no other company would take me, I was trapped. Without this coverage I couldn't afford my acupuncture treatments. I ran up my credit cards, borrowing from one card to pay off another. By the end of the year, I was deep in debt, feeling it was better to be alive and a debtor than pushing up daisies with a good credit score. I began searching for new sources of revenue. A friend who taught massage workshops suggested that I learn to become a masseur. I enrolled and soon was schooled in various techniques.

I bought a massage table and hung up a shingle, but my remote house attracted few customers. So I put ads in several papers, both gay and straight, receiving enough responses to start a home-based business, traveling to wherever my skills were needed. This included nice houses, modest apartments, and plush commercial establishments.

This work put me in a tricky position, a "healer" aka borderline sexual partner on the sly. Not one to work in the prostitution industry and aware of my HIV condition, I knew that with my addiction propensities and potential legal issues, this could be very slippery territory. So I walked a fine line dodging erotic requests both overt and covert.

A typical night might be getting a phone call from an executive from out of town staying at a fancy hotel. "Am I speaking to Sam?"

"Yes. How can I help you?"

"I read your ad and need assistance unwinding from a stressful day. Are you available tonight?"

"Yes, I am."

"Great. Do you have a table?"

"Sure."

"Terrific. You know where the hotel is?"

"I work there often."

"I'm in room 843. Can you be here at 10:30?"

"Of course."

These hotel gigs paid well. As a hospitality committee of one, I carried my massage table, freshly laundered sheets, and soothing oils to the customer's suite, returning to my car with a nice sum. I learned to do a balancing act to satisfy my customers' needs both safely and legally.

A frustrating aspect of my massage career was, though I took further courses at an oriental massage school and was certified, the city of Los Angeles wouldn't give me a license because I was HIV positive. Even after the school wrote a letter to request permission for me to work exclusively with AIDS patients, the authorities refused to grant this. An irony was that undercover officers only called on and supervised licensed masseurs and establishments. So like others in my situation, I worked under the radar and away from any law enforcement scrutiny.

Being a Reiki practitioner, I'd also been trained in healing with my hands. Emphasizing therapy, not recreation, I had no trouble turning away clients with dubious requests. Attentive to each customer's needs, I gained insights into their behaviors. Through this work, I began to come to terms with my own sexuality and how to practice detachment. Making myself available 24/7, I worked off my debt in two years.

My Massage Table Leads To Love & Friendship

Although some sexual offers were temptations difficult to refuse, I occasionally gave out my private telephone number to a massage client I found appealing, in case he wanted to meet outside of business. This practice of discrete invitation led to a surprising result.

One of the customers that took me up on this was a gracious, tall, lanky, kinky-haired Creole guy from Louisiana with a romantic flair named Lionel. This attractive man showed up at my door with a bouquet of flowers and a box of See's candies. I couldn't believe my eyes. It was as if Linda Kleinman, my high school not-to-be-sweetheart, had sent her brother over. Martha and the Vandellas' song "Heat Wave" started playing in my mind.

Once my HIV disclosure was accepted, we began a hot affair as we shared a love of spicy food, sex, and local travel. Yet both of us had intimacy issues. Whenever I tried to get too close to him, he retreated to his condo near Koreatown. Although our sexual chemistry was steamy within our safe confines, we were gun-shy. We saw each other intermittently for years, but never made a firm commitment. After a long time of doing without, though limited, this affection was welcome.

My massage table opened up other doors. Another client became a good friend. Porter was a balding, overweight, married fellow in his fifties with a serious case of diabetes. He needed treatment on his swollen feet that had neuropathy. A bit feminine, Porter had a campy sense of humor. If you didn't know he was married, you'd think he was gay. Often, he'd stay after a session, and the two of us enjoyed each other's company.

When I found out that he worked as a nurse, I was curious. "How long have you been in the profession?"

"Long enough to know better."

"Don't people tease you about being in a female occupation?"

"Of course they do. My wife is also a nurse. She's so butch you wouldn't believe it. We're always looked at with suspicion."

"Why?"

"People see me decorating the house while she repairs the car."

"So?"

"We're from Minnesota and we never really fit in there."

"You don't like tuna casseroles and Jello served with Cool Whip?"

"Don't like Miracle Whip or Velveeta either. Because we lived in St. Paul doesn't mean we eat lutefisk."

"What's that?"

"You Jews eat gefilte fish?"

"Sometimes we do."

"Lutefisk is even worse."

Porter's wife, Nancy, was an AIDS nurse. As we two men shared stories, he mentioned a case of hers where a woman, her husband, and their baby had all died of AIDS. It dawned on me that he must have been talking about my friend Lanie. He was. This amazing coincidence served to deepen our relationship. It wasn't long before I had two new friends, and the three of us began to socialize regularly.

At this point, Beverly reentered my life. The charitable organization where she'd been working needed massage volunteers. Knowing that I'd been trained professionally, she called to ask if I could help out. Unfortunately, my unlicensed status prevented me from participating. However, this renewed contact wasn't lost as we began hanging out again, often sharing lunches at ethnic cafes.

One time when Nancy came over to pick up Porter after a massage, I arranged for Beverly to arrive at the same time. Hearing her talk about working with the homeless, the couple became interested in her. The four of us started meeting for coffee and conversation.

During my prior relationship with Jim, Beverly had befriended him. After he and I broke up, she maintained this friendship. Jim went with a new boyfriend for a while, but now he was once again single. She suggested we get back in touch. At first, the energy between us was lukewarm, but we still had much in common and rekindled our bond, albeit platonically. The seeds of a new social circle had been planted.

Beverly's Cul-De-Sac Wedding

At one of our get-togethers, Beverly had some good news to share. She'd been dating an intriguing man who worked at her charitable organization. After a few months, he'd asked her to marry him. She accepted. We bombarded her with questions about her new partner.

Niles was an ex-pat Brit of English and French heritage who'd moved to the U.S. to escape conflicts that had erupted in his household. His mother, Julia, descended from one of Stratford-On-Avon's noblest families, had outraged her blue-blooded relatives when she married a commoner named Maurice Cul-De-Sac. Hailing from the Normandy area. Maurice was a handsome, dark-haired Frenchman with a wonderful sense of humor. However, his coarse plebian mannerisms irritated and alienated her parents. After a few years of marriage and the birth of their two children, his uncouth behavior started grating on Julia's nerves as well. Realizing that she'd made a poor choice and knowing that divorce was socially unacceptable, she started having serial affairs on the side.

Needless to say, the Cul-De-Sac household was filled with angst. Niles couldn't wait to leave the family nest. Once he graduated from school, he immigrated to Los Angeles where he rebelled against his semi-snooty upbringing by getting a job helping the homeless. He raised funds from the charity's wealthy patrons and redistributed them to bums on the street that stood in line for financial assistance. Beverly was smitten with his genteel manners and street smarts. When she discovered his street last name, she felt this would be a marriage made in heaven.

She proudly displayed the elegant ring Niles had given her. We could hardly wait to meet her new catch and help her plan the wedding. She wanted a street affair, a block party in front of her parents' mansion in Angelino Heights. We suggested a menu of street cuisine and a list of songs to be played by a band of street musicians including songs such as "Dancing In The Street" and "On the Street Where You Live."

Unfortunately, this matrimonial ceremony was not to be. When Bev introduced Niles to us, though charming on a superficial level, he seemed ill at ease. Porter and Nancy saw red flags. They warned that she should wed a Thoroughfare, not a Cul-De-Sac. Jim wondered if Niles' conflicted lineage would make him constantly at war with himself.

Then out of the blue, he told Beverly that he'd quit his job and was going back to England. In tears, she asked him why. He replied, "I've had it with these low-life people. I'm returning to work with my mum and her Tory party politicians. No more common man missions for me."

Beverly was crestfallen. Not only had Niles left her, he'd become an enemy to street people. I tried to comfort her, having had my share of romantic abandonment. After a period of gloom, Bev returned to her cheerful self. It wasn't long before we were regaling others again with our silly word play.

Uncle Ernie's Farewell

Later that year, I got a call from one of my East Coast cousins. She'd flown to L.A. to visit her father, whose heart had been failing him. Before anyone else could get there, Uncle Ernie passed peacefully in his sleep. I asked how I could support her. She requested that I set up a funeral service at the family gravesite where Irv, Sheila, and Zelda were buried.

With my sisters and several East Coast relatives present, I gave a eulogy inspired by gratitude for my supportive uncle. "Ernie was one of the most caring people I've ever met. Not only was he a devoted husband who helped raise two beautiful daughters, he was a rock of support helping me navigate the turbulence in my family. His words of encouragement saw me through some tough times. He will be missed by all of us that had the good fortune to know him."

T-Cell Rites & Return To Cruising

The following year, my insurance company doubled the cost of my policy again. Fed up with this practice, I sought an alternative. I applied for a state health insurance plan for high-risk individuals. My application was accepted, but the policy did not cover acupuncture and I had to stop treatments. This approach wasn't working well anyway.

My blood count continued slipping. Things looked bleak. Although a couple of new medications were in the pipeline, they also had toxic side effects. I wanted to be around if a cure was found, but began to doubt my ability to do so. At a lunch with Beverly, I confided, "My test showed I lost thirty T-cells."

"Sorry to hear that." What does it mean?"

"I'm now vulnerable to fevers, night sweats, and fungal infections."

"How awful."

"They haven't yet manifested themselves, but they're waiting in the wings. I feel like having an R.I.P. ceremony for each departed cell."

"Great idea. Why don't we see if we can give them all names starting with the letter 'T'. I'll start. How about Terry?"

"OK, let's call one Thelma."

"Tom."

"Timothy."

We soon bid farewells to Thad, Tina, Tony, Trent and so on. This lifted both our spirits. Next month, when a test showed an increased count, we also named the new arrivals with T names. In future tests, when I gained or lost more, we made additional names. Trying to keep from repeating any, we resorted to appellations like Tim Jr. and Thaddeus III.

During this unsettling time, Lionel would appear suddenly and retreat just as quickly. Seeing him off and on only whetted my sexual appetite and helped to make my addictive longings resurface. When Lionel was gone for a while, I began cruising again. Tired of dealing with my HIV status, I traveled out of town where I could do this anonymously. Rationalizing this bad behavior by sticking to strict safe practices, I visited truck stops and rest stops during this downward spiral. These escapes were a smokescreen camouflaging my unhappy state of mind.

Felipe & La Vida Loca

What helped to put a stop to this self-destructive pattern was when I received a response from a long-forgotten personal ad. Felipe, a Hispanic fellow who lived nearby, had written. This bisexual dude had broken up with a girlfriend and was looking for a friend with benefits. Not quite looking for a lover, but in my position at the time I felt I couldn't be too choosy.

Although he acted macho, Felipe swung whichever way the wind blew. He still lived with his family in the barrio, so the two of us had to get together in what was called a "down low" situation. "Third Rate Romance, Low Rent Rendezvous" was right up our alley.

Felipe enjoyed talking about cars, sports, and rock music. I related to all three. Instead of the dinner and movie routine with Leo, or organic tea and oranges with Jim, a typical evening with Felipe was foreplay, *antojitos* at a *taqueria*, a *mercadito* stop for *paletas* (Mexican popsicles), then home to finish what we'd started earlier.

Sometimes to enhance this, Felipe tried to turn me onto pot. "Dude, take a hit of this. My cousin got it from Michoacan."

"Sorry guy, I don't do that anymore."

A refusal like this only made him press harder. "It'll make getting it on so much hotter. Don't be such a wuss."

I was resolute. "It may work for you, but I'm not going there."

I did not want to tax my body any farther than necessary. The more Felipe urged me to live *La Vida Loca*, the more I wished for *La Vida No Tan Loca*, pleading I could not keep up with him. Ironically, a few years earlier, this was exactly what I would have been begging for.

Felipe wasn't interested in a monogamous relationship and often slipped out of sight. So I continued to see Lionel. This alternation of sexual partners sometimes worked out serendipitously. Occasionally, they came uncomfortably close to bumping heads. But with some deft maneuvering and a little luck, the two never did meet.

For the present, my sexual needs were taken care of. Financially, I was at least treading water, maintaining enough students and clients to keep the wolf from my door. I'd call this a period of Jewish optimism. The only thing I'd complain about was I didn't have much to complain about. This was soon about to change.

AIDS Symptoms & The Welcome Wagon

There were new HIV meds on the horizon, but I was not interested in drug trials. I preferred that they work out the bugs first. So I tried to hold my health and energy together the best I could.

While the retrovirus made assaults on my immune system, terrorists attacked New York City's World Trade Center. Not a large disaster, it portended worse things. Soon a similar eruption disturbed my well-being. After a feverish night, I woke up to see white powdery stuff on my tongue. My first opportunistic infection had arrived.

Seeing this, Dr. Roth said, "You've got thrush, a candida infection. Your T-cells are in the range that makes you susceptible to this."

Filled with concern, I inquired, "How serious is it, Doctor?"

"By itself, it's not too bad. I'll prescribe you some medication. However, you're liable to come down with any of several fungal infections now. I'm sorry to say your last blood test showed that you've officially progressed to AIDS. I know you don't want to take AZT, but at least we need to give you some pneumonia prophylaxis."

"I understand."

"Also, I encourage you to try Zerit. It's like AZT, but not as toxic."

"I'll check into it. Let me get a second opinion first."

"Whatever you say. Now, I don't mean to frighten you, but don't you think it's time to draw up a will and a power of attorney?"

"What?"

"Do you have your affairs in order?"

"Not yet." I wasn't ready for this. My emotions went into an uproar. I didn't want to face what seemed to be inevitable. At that time, I'd begun going on the Internet regularly. Researching Zerit, I found that the drug often caused people to come down with neuropathy, the diabetes symptom my friend Porter suffered from.

In the mid '90s, a new class of HIV fighters called protease inhibitors was showing promising results, but it caused a lot of physical discomfort. I was not willing to be a guinea pig and turned to an alternative HIV center instead where volunteer acupuncturists worked. This helped to slow the progression of the disease, but it seemed to be a band-aid at best. I tried to buy whatever time I could.

One day, I discovered a bad skin infection. Calling Dr. Roth, I found that my beloved doctor was no longer covered on the state insurance program. Not able to afford him, I went to an HMO clinic that I was eligible for instead. There I was told this rash was cellulitus, a condition needing to be treated with intravenous drugs immediately.

A PICC line was inserted into my wrist. I was taught how to self-administer these vitally needed medications at home. This was not pleasant, but the protocol worked and I soon got better. Even with my new acupuncture treatments, I had to keep fending off a series of infections and fevers, none life threatening, but upsetting nonetheless.

I kept these conditions secret from Felipe and Lionel, making excuses not to see them until I got better. I'd learned not to be a wimp. This stoicism was put to the test. With a daily self-dose of Reiki energy and a new healing circle, I was able to keep my disease from taking over.

Just when I began to steer an even keel again, I got a disturbing phone call from a city social worker.

"Am I speaking to Sam Freberg?"

"Yes. What about? Who are you?"

"I'm calling from County Services about your medical condition. We need to schedule an appointment for a home visit."

"Sorry, I don't want any services right now. Leave me alone."

"I have some important information that might be helpful to you."

The next week, comfortably seated in my living room, she asked, "Are you aware that you have officially progressed to AIDS?"

"Yes. So what? Big deal!"

"Here are some pamphlets you might want to read."

"I'm already familiar with most of this. I've worked in the HIV community for years."

"Good for you. There are some updates and changes with which you may want to familiarize yourself."

I listened to her spiel, relieved when she finally left. That night, I had another bad dream. I was on the Jerry Springer show, a Jewish holiday program combined with Ralph Edward's "This Is Your Life." Jerry and Ralph wore yamulkes and Hebraic side braids on their temples. People in my past made comments on how I disappointed them.

The studio personnel sat me on a stool, wearing a dunce cap, while each person unloaded their grievances. After a complaint, a random member of the studio audience was asked to press one of 5 buttons in front of them. Forgiven – 0 points; venial status – 1 point; mortal status – 2 points; cardinal status – 3 points; inquisition status – 5 points.

If I escaped with less than 10 points by the end of the show, I'd be awarded an all-expense-paid weekend in Miami Beach. If I received between 10 and 50 points, I could beg for forgiveness by phoning a friend, social worker, rabbi, or priest. If I had more than 50 points, I'd be voted off the planet by being burned at the stake.

The first complainer was my mom. "Sam has one eyebrow." 1 point. Then Judy entered. "My brother is a big crybaby." 2 points. Leslie came onstage and said, "Sam used to fake coming down with yellow fever." 1 point. "And he pretended to give it to me." 2 more points. My dad entered carrying a sock and groaned, "This piece of *schmutz* contains some of my son's bodily fluids." A loud cardinal buzzer was heard. 3 more points. Cries of "Sam, Sam, Sam," reverberated.

Reggie added, "Sam doesn't know how to fish." 1 point. Charlie taunted, "Sam is a queer." 3 points. Cherie grumbled, "He's a very poor kisser." 3 more points. Carol wailed, "I was a jilted bride that Sam left at the altar." The women in the audience sounded a loud chorus of boos. The point total jumped. I could kiss Miami goodbye.

Grievances then came faster. Brian chastised me for living in the past. 3 points. Leo wearing a priest's robe excommunicated me for leaving my clothes around the house. 3 points. A vice squad member shouted that I'd propositioned him. 5 points. The public defender said I was an unrepentant criminal. 5 points. The total was teetering toward disaster.

Mrs. B., Uncle Ernie, and Beverly tried to ring some forgiveness bells, protesting that I was a good person. But it was too late. What put me over the edge was when Miss Stewart, cackling like a witch, revealed that I'd skipped the fifth grade and had to go back to elementary school and take it again. The Inquisition buzzers sounded.

Some stagehands brought in a stake, tied me to it with a rope, and Richard Pryor entered with a box of matches. He mooned me sassily and lit a match. "This white boy can kiss my fat black ass." Jim Morrison and the Doors started performing "C'mon Baby, Light My Fire." The stake was ignited, and the flames roared up around me as I screamed, "Enough already. Just let me die."

Just before I woke up with a night sweat, Mrs. B. paid me another visit, saying, "Honey, you need help. It's time for you to see a therapist again." The next morning, I thumbed desperately through the pamphlets that the County woman had given me and searched for one.

Dr. Brenner & The First of 12 Steps

Calling a few names on the list, I found a professional, Dr. Russel Brenner, in my area. At our first session, this helpful man encouraged me to express how I felt about my health status. "I've heard enough about your abusive parents. We've all had problems with our upbringing. I need you to speak in present tense."

"Sorry, once I get started talking about them, it's hard to stop."

"I understand. You talk so much about guilt and shame. How has being diagnosed with HIV impacted this?"

"I'm afraid to tell anyone these days, especially someone I want to have sex with. I purposely try to avoid bringing it up."

"Isn't that immoral, not to mention illegal?"

"But I do things safely."

"You don't give your partner any say in this?"

"If they ask me, I tell them the truth. But if they don't want to bring it up, why should I?"

"Maybe that's why you're so fond of anonymous encounters." My face turned red and tears welled in my eyes. "Am I right?"

I blurted, "Yes, I've driven long distances so I won't be recognized. All those truck drivers want is a quick one anyway."

"No wonder you're unhappy. What does quick sex do for you?"

I confessed, "Nothing. Absolutely nothing." I hesitated and then added, "In fact, it makes me feel worse."

"And the risks you take? Getting beaten up? You're setting yourself up for entrapment. You could get arrested."

"I've been there." Hesitatingly, I admitted, "Look, I'm at my wit's end. Sometimes when my partners are unavailable and I'm horny, I don't know what to do or where to go."

Dr. Brenner scribbled on a piece of paper and gave it to me "Here's a phone number for Sexual Compulsives Anonymous, a 12-step group for people in your situation. This could be a way out of your dilemma."

After putting this suggestion off for a while, I finally relented. I had no idea how much these meetings would help me.

Walking into my first SCA group, I was a bundle of nerves. A dozen men were seated facing each other in a circle around a large table. Feeling vulnerable, I tried not to look anyone in the eye. As everyone went around the room, reading a paragraph each from a program pamphlet, the structure made me feel a little more at ease.

With my multi-addicted history, I had no problem relating to the behavioral characteristics described in the book. I saw how much I was torn between following along with the text and wanting to cruise the other men in the room, most of whom were gay. At once, I knew this was the right place for me to be. When it was time for individual sharing, I heard horror stories worse than mine.

One member shared, "I had twenty-five days of abstinence, but it's back to day one for me. I know I should go home after work, but I can't keep from going to the park and cruising in my car."

Another said, "I have forty-two days of sobriety but still get urges. My boyfriend can tell I visit the bars by smelling the cigarette smoke on my clothes. When I say I only stopped for a drink, he doesn't believe me."

A third revealed, "I have two years on the program without anonymous sex. But this gorgeous sixteen-year old moved in down the street. I can't keep my hands off her when she comes on to me. I'm so afraid I'll get arrested for having sex with a minor. That's statutory rape."

The next guy shared, "It's day one again. I got caught in a cruisy public restroom and was thrown in jail for a second time. My attorney is trying to keep me from being registered as a sex offender."

Still another member revealed, "I've been abstinent for five years. I want to thank you for your stories because they help me not to slip back into my old behaviors. You remind me of what waits for me if I do."

These scary confessions brought back memories of my arrest in Griffith Park. I thought back to the dark days where I'd once been. It was a whole new experience to be with other men, especially the gay men who were encouraging each other not to be cavalier about sex.

I didn't share about myself that evening, but at my next meeting I opened up. "Hi, My name is Sam F." The group responded with the obligatory "Hello, Sam."

I continued, "I've been abstinent for two months, but I still have desires to travel out of town and seek anonymous encounters like I did for many years. I appreciate the group's support for helping to keep me from slipping back into this destructive pattern."

The room filled with applause. When the meeting ended, a few members welcomed me to the group, offering words of encouragement. Others were ashamed of themselves, retreating immediately. Not my first rodeo when it came to addiction workshops, this was my first exposure to an official 12-step venue. It would become a new way of life for me from then on. Soon I was going to as many recovery groups as I used to attend AIDS workshops.

I worked all 12 steps of recovery, earned my 180-day sobriety chip, and celebrated my one-year birthday. I became secretary of my group, and helped other sex addicts to stay on track. Yet, without this distraction in my life, I was like a dry drunk. Drinking had never been a problem for me, but I still had a hole in my soul. This was a classic example of Jewish pessimism. When nothing bad was going on, it only meant things could soon get worse.

Chapter 10
COMING CLEAN

Farewell To Cruising & Hello to Casinos

Even though I'd stopped cruising, my mind was still troubled. Dr. Brenner warned that I was susceptible to a relapse or transference to another compulsive behavior like alcohol or drugs. The man was right. Not long afterwards, I replaced my prior need for random sexual activity by patronizing casinos with a similar intensity.

For a while I was a lightweight gambler, not winning or losing much or playing for any length of time. But after I got a taste of the adrenaline rush I experienced feeding coins into slot machines with Donald, I began gambling more frequently. This became a convenient way to get disease and financial worries off my mind. I gradually upped the ante until I'd spend every dollar I made that week. After one long frustrating night, I expressed my concern to Dr. Brenner.

"You warned me about transferring my sexual jones to another activity."

"What's your problem now?"

"Well, it's not that bad yet, but I'm afraid that..." I hesitated.

"Out with it. You've been to enough 12-step meetings to know that until you admit a problem, there's no way to deal with it. "

"Well, it's just a few dollars here and there."

"Stop beating around the bush. What are you trying to tell me?"

"I lost eighty dollars gambling at an Indian casino."

"You spent enough to pay for the therapy that others contribute to make available for you. That's unfair. And considering your financial state, it doesn't make any sense."

"I know it's crazy. I hardly had the money to put enough gas in my tank to drive home afterwards. I just couldn't stop myself."

"And whose fault was that? Don't tell me it's your folks again."

"They weren't the best role models. They used to leave us kids in front of the casinos in Vegas where we could watch them gamble from outside. I couldn't wait to grow up and be a big shot like them."

"Did they drive you to the casino?"

"Of course not."

"And Mr. Big Shot, were you acting like an adult last night?"

"I can't believe at my age I'm still like an out-of-control child."

"Point well taken. We all make mistakes. Now, where did you go last time when you hit bottom?

"Do they have 12-step groups for gambling?"

"Sure. You wouldn't believe how many recovery groups there are, meetings for everything from overspending to overeating. There are even workaholic groups for Type A people who are so driven that they never slow down and enjoy their lives."

"That's me sometimes. It seems I'm on a treadmill running away from myself. I get so lonely, I just want to get lost in a crowd."

"Does that help?"

"It doesn't. I'm just another basket case in a roomful of losers."

"Like the way you felt cruising at closing time in a gay bar?"

"Oh my God, you're right."

I tried to take this advice to heart, but I wasn't ready to give up my new escape. What probably had driven me over the line between recreation and addiction was the night I won my first jackpot. The casinos have billboards with the slogan "We want you to win." Losing may create a gambling addict. Winning exacerbates this. There are few more intense highs than when flashing lights go off and you win a pile of money without having had to earn it. This is much like listening to Queen singing "We Are The Champions Of The World."

Despite my best efforts to leave earlier, I'd stay at the casinos until the employees began serving free coffee and donuts in the morning to keep me feeding currency into the slots. My eyes would be as glazed as the pastries I'd consume. After a binge while hanging out with strangers in the night, I'd fight my way home through morning rush hour traffic while cursing myself for not being able to say "No." As one of my recovery buddies often said, "One bet was too many and a million never enough."

I began attending Gambler's Anonymous meetings to learn to control this habit, thinking that it would be an easy fix like taking a college course.

But similar to how alcoholics have to learn to stop entirely, so do problem gamblers. Few ever want to do this. I was no exception. I became dependent on my recovery groups to help me stay on the wagon. If compulsive sex was difficult for me to give up, this was even harder. I prayed to my Higher Power to get this monkey off my back.

Willa Mae & the Extended Family

As the twentieth century neared its end, protease inhibitors showed promising results. I held out until more data was in. During Bill Clinton's second term, the country prospered again. With the economy booming, I picked up some new students and set up a few workshops. When real estate prices escalated, I took out a home equity loan and suddenly had a new source of funds. This provided an opportunity to make a few improvements in my life. But I had to be vigilant. It also enabled me to keep feeding my gambling habit.

During the previous decade, my sisters had moved out of state, Leslie to Texas, and Judy to Hawaii. With a need for family-like ties, I reached out to my circle of friends. I invited them over for potluck dinners and parties. A new addition to this group was Willa Mae, a woman I met at a sweat lodge, another activity I'd resumed.

Willa Mae was from Council Bluffs, Iowa, the "sin city" across the Missouri river from Omaha, Nebraska. A jolly Midwestern lady, she was earthy and in her early forties, a recovering Catholic with a fetish for votive candles and a devilish sense of humor. I liked her outrageous jokes and she salted them with enough foul language and pearls of wisdom to be fascinating.

On one occasion, Willa Mae approached me in a feisty mood, "Let's go to Home Depot and hang out in the power tool department again. Remember, last time when we had those contractors splitting a gut over our conversation about getting nailed?"

I replied, "You mean, getting screwed?"

"Nailed, screwed? Talk softly, but carry a heavy tool belt."

"We were almost chased out of the store for suggesting that one shouldn't wear a big tool belt unless one had a big tool to go with it."

"That plumber down the aisle sure thought we were funny."

Her interest in Native American culture and paganism added much to my new social circle. She and Beverly became pals, donning leopard-skin clothing and lighting Our Lady of Guadalupe candles together.

Willa Mae and I had established our bond on a day when we were both asked to help out a friend who needed to gather willow branches to build a structure for a sweat lodge he was hosting. We followed him to a dry creek where its riparian environment had many trees. After a few hours of painstaking work, we arrived back at his ranch.

A dozen participants were waiting for us, gathered for our monthly ceremony. Blankets were laid over the top of the lodge and an entrance flap created. Ribbons that had been cut up with prayers attached were hung from the poles inside. A Lakota medicine man from South Dakota, who was brought in for the occasion, led the sweat with appropriate chants, hot rocks, and herb-scented steam. During each of four rounds, everyone had a chance to ask the spirits for guidance. This ritual had a more authentic vibe than the one I'd visited a few years previously.

"*Wakan Tonka*, Great Spirit, bless all who have come to worship with us. We look to you for guidance. *Tunkasila*. Grandfather, support us."

One of the men in the group asked, "May the Great Spirit help my family understand how difficult it has been to stay on the right path since I lost my job. May they teach us patience and forgiveness."

"Ho."

A woman near him prayed, "May Grandmother Earth assist me in convincing my son to avoid the bad crowd he's fallen into."

Willa Mae chanted, "May the sprits lead us to take better care of Mother Earth, our precious home."

"Ho. *Tunkasila*."

I intoned, "May the Blessed Ones help us all to maintain our health and give me the strength to rebuild my immune system."

"Ho. *Wakan Tonka*, the Great One."

These prayers, like many others made that day, were only partially answered, as is the case with spiritual work. That is why it is said that these rites are practiced; they must be repeated to be effective. After the sweat, our group celebrated with a tasty potluck.

This inspired me to start a similar tradition at home. My L.A. potlucks became events built on themes like nationalities and meals created on occasions like Halloween or President's Day. Beverly and Selma baked and decorated cakes for each occasion. Willa Mae was a fan of the marshmallow candy Peeps, and she fashioned desserts with titles like "Peeps Crossing The Delaware." Other memorable ones included cakes decorated like Mount Rushmore or strewn with roads to imaginary lands. Prizes were awarded for the most creative dishes.

I also returned to my Jewish roots and began hosting Passover seders. The breaking of matzoh, the brisket, and unleavened honey cake helped cement the good feelings of the group, not to mention the traditional glasses of wine. If one didn't have a good time, it was his or her fault.

Naomi, Casey, Honesty, & Martha

At one of my seders Beverly brought her friend Naomi along, a vibrant lady who added further dimension to the group. Like me, she was a "recovering Jew" who liked to fuse spiritual practices from outside sources with the religion of her birth. Though a few years older than me, she had a young energy about her that was contagious. Naomi and her husband Casey were retired university professors. They were also established authors and had run a theater together.

This fun pair introduced new topics to our conversations. Whenever there was a holiday dinner, they explained the origins of how that day came to be special with tidbits of information. For example, at a feminist theme potluck, they enlightened everyone with tales of Seneca Falls, the birthplace of the women's movement.

A cultural icon often discussed in the group was Diogenes, the iconoclastic Greek philosopher who believed that virtue was better revealed in action than in dogma. Taken with this role model, I joked, "Look guys, I just bought a lantern. I'm going out on the streets to look for an honest man. Have you seen any lately?"

Casey teased me cynically. "You better put on some hiking boots. These days, it may take you a while to find one."

Beverly kidded me. "And what streets are you going to visit? Better stay out of those dark alleyways. They could get you in trouble."

I replied, "You never know where you could pick up some honesty. You might find it in unexpected places."

Willa Mae chimed, "I've been looking for a man to make an honest woman out of me for a long time."

Naomi was not to be outdone. "You know what they say in 12-step programs. You have to learn to be honest, open, and willing."

Willa Mae shot back, "For the right guy, I'll be especially willing."

I chuckled, "Let's go search together. Maybe we can find an honest man at Home Depot. I've always had a thing for contractors."

Beverly teased, "I don't have a clue what you all are talking about, but I'll put on an orange apron and join in anyway."

The group roared with laughter as dessert was served. It was a hazelnut torte that Selma had baked with a presidential frosting made out of pork barrel spending sweetened with a few choice political spoils.

Another friend of Beverly's joined these festivities. Martha was a lively overweight black woman with an outrageous sense of humor. She worked at the same charitable organization as Beverly and had entertaining stories about the characters that hung around there. At work, Martha supervised the soup kitchen menus. She also volunteered to do research for these meals by patronizing the all-you-can-eat buffets around town like Po' Folks. Not only did this woman like to eat, she could also cook up a storm. Every dish she brought to a potluck was swimming in country gravy. She was as saucy as her dishes.

Martha and I bonded over health concerns. Martha had diabetes and coped with weak spells much like my bouts with opportunistic infections. We'd often consult with each other over the phone, sharing symptoms and our attempts to stem our various bodily discomforts.

Hawaii, Judy, Bad Lungs, & Buddhist Monk

As I expanded this social circle, my gambling activity slowed. Slips became fewer and fewer. Despite this improvement, my health continued to decline. I stubbornly refused drug therapy, still trying to defeat my disease holistically. I didn't know even if I took any of the new medications, how much longer I had to live.

I decided to visit my sister Judy in Hawaii. We'd experienced some misunderstandings and it was part of my recovery to make amends. I also wanted to see the area again while I still was able to.

Living simply, I was not a fan of my sister's values. She'd run a very successful business, but her affluence did not seem to bring her joy. She often ranted about how people should lead their lives. Our recent phone conversations were frosty. She was preoccupied with re-fighting prior battles in the old Freberg family, complaining about having been shortchanged and continuing to ask me for confirmation. I requested several times not to talk about this. As one of my 12-step buddies had once quoted, "You can't make forward progress by looking through the rearview mirror."

I flew into the Honolulu airport, the same place I'd visited in the Peace Corps. A smaller plane flew me to the Big Island where Judy lived. From the minute she greeted me, I regretted the decision to visit her, not to mention take on the expense. When we walked into her house, she showed me the guest room. "Look, I've got this space all decorated for you with family photos."

"You shouldn't have."

"It took me a while, but I thought you'd like it."

"To be honest, sis, I really don't want to look at these. How many times do I have to tell you I'm not interested in old family issues?"

"Here's all of us eating with chopsticks in a Chinese restaurant."

"That's where Dad belted me for trying to order shark-fin soup."

"And here's where we went to Tijuana."

"That's where Mom and Dad fought over too much spending on *chatckhes*."

"And this is when..."

"Isn't it time to move on from the past? If you don't mind, I'm going to sleep in the living room. I don't want to be surrounded by it."

"After all the work I did?"

"I never asked you to do this."

Judy stormed out of the room in a huff. Knowing things could get uncomfortable with her, I had the presence of mind to reserve a rent-a-car for a solo drive around the island. Before I left, she gave me a list of things to see, right out of my mom's "honey-do" tradition. Some of the items I had little interest in, but one thing intrigued me, a Buddhist monastery on the island's southern tip. Since it rented out rooms, I planned to visit the place and stay there overnight.

Just as I was getting ready to embark, I caught a bad cold. It went immediately to my lungs and I had trouble breathing. I had a high fever, felt dizzy and weak, and feared the worst, the dreaded AIDS pneumonia. When I asked Judy to take me to a doctor, she refused.

"You're probably making this up, like you did with all those silly diseases you pretended to have when we were young."

"No, sis, I'm really sick and this is very frightening. I've got to get medical help right away."

"Sorry, I'm late for a pedicure," she said as she bolted out the door.

Cursing her selfishness, I got on the phone and discovered that my HMO had a branch nearby. Barely able to drive myself to its acute care clinic, I was looked at right away. The doctor ordered some immediate X-rays. Fortunately, it was just bronchitis. With the help of a short course of antibiotics, I recovered quickly.

After a few days, no thanks to Judy, I was able to resume my plans. I visited the island's various regions and microclimates. This included lava deserts in the west, the northern area that reminded me of the Oregon coastline, the east shore with its rugged rock formations and amazing waterfalls, the lush, tropical city of Hilo, and the molten lava rivers descending from the still active volcano Mount Kilauea.

After a few days of freelancing, I reached the southern coast and pulled up to the monastery. It was lushly landscaped with tall palm trees and an amazing plethora of tropical flowers, a veritable Shangri-La. Large peacocks strutted freely over the grounds. I'd brought my own food and bedding and slept in a cot in an empty room the monks let me occupy for a nominal charge. The large kitchen was available for guests to make our own meals, vegetarian preferred. I felt right at home.

The next morning, I rose early and went to a *zazen* meditation service. I was the only one in the ashram when a bald monk in an orange robe entered, banged a gong, and started chanting. Suddenly the man stopped, walked out of the room, and came back with a glass of water and a few pills. He placed the pills in his mouth, sipped some water, looked at me, put the glass down, and continued the meditation.

After the service, I was struck by what I'd witnessed, taking this as a personal message. Still anxious over my lung infection, I was meditating whether to begin AIDS medication, having been on the fence for so long. I interpreted this as a signal to start doing so.

Before I left, Judy had written down a checklist of personal recommendations for my trip. When I returned, she went over this to see what I'd done and didn't do.

She began, "Did you visit the antique store with the great curios?"

"It was lovely, but a little high end for me."

"How about that hippie village where everything is based on marijuana and made from hemp?"

"I'm not into that scene anymore."

"Too bad. What about that Buddhist monastery?"

"That was a great suggestion. The grounds were gorgeous, the accommodations a real change of pace, and the price perfect for my budget. If I resided on this island, I'd be a frequent visitor."

"And how did you like the Flamingo Hotel?"

"I didn't stay there. It was too expensive, not really my style."

"You should have. They've got a great ocean view."

"Driving around the island, I saw my fill of ocean."

"I went to a lot of trouble to make that list and you hardly followed it."

"C'mon sis. Lighten up. I didn't travel all this way to argue."

"It makes me mad when you don't listen to me."

"I do listen. Just because I hear you doesn't mean I have to agree."

"You never agree."

"Sis, I'm a grown man and agree when I feel like it."

Although the experience at the Buddhist monastery helped me to handle Judy more diplomatically, I could hardly wait for my return flight.

Time For A Cocktail, Time For A Sponsor

Relieved to be back home and away from my sister, I went to my HMO and requested to start AIDS medication. This began a phase of testing which of the protease inhibitors I could stomach. Each of the choices got me so sick and feverish, I didn't want to continue. I was ready to make peace with the Almighty and do what many others had done, party their way out like my friend Lanie. Or maybe I'd escape to a tropical island and live out my final days in solitude.

I called some friends in the HIV medical community for advice and got a referral to an official at the CDC. A local grapevine mentioned that taking smaller dosages had helped some patients in a similar situation. The CDC fellow said that although this approach was not recommended, it might be worth a try.

I tried this scaled down version of what was called a drug cocktail. While not without a few side effects, they were manageable. In time, these abated and I started to get better. My doctors said that this treatment was not a cure and warned me to keep all sexual activity safe since it didn't prevent transmission. This was the best information the medical community had at its disposal at the time, though it was shown years later not necessarily to be the case.

Occasionally, I slipped back into gambling, especially during times of duress. On Election Day in 2000, after casting my vote for Al Gore, I drove out to an Indian gambling establishment. When I heard on the casino television that Gore was declared the winner, I took out a twenty-dollar bill and popped it into a slot machine to see if I could cap the victory with a jackpot. While I lost this and several other Andrew Jacksons, Gore fell behind George W. Bush. I returned home, broke and discouraged. While they were counting chads in Florida, I recalibrated my sobriety. Once more, I swore I'd never again waste my reserves so foolishly. Of all my addictions, gambling was the hardest to give up.

I went to my GA meeting and confessed yet another mea culpa. Afterwards, a nice fellow named Darryl with several years of abstinence came over to support me. "I see the trouble you're having stopping. Whenever you have an urge, call me first."

"Thanks, I can't seem to do this by myself. When I'm in that mind set, I don't want to talk to anyone."

"Most of us can't. That's why we're here for each other. Addiction is a disease of isolation. Remember, you're not in this alone."

The next time I had an urge to gamble, not only did I call Darryl, I asked him to be my sponsor. He agreed, and we worked on my recovery regularly through the years. Our relationship became a sanctuary and a lifeline during this stressful time.

Letting The Tears Roll

My immune system soon strengthened, and my health status was once again listed as asymptomatic. With less tension to deal with, my gambling urges decreased to where I usually could stop myself. When I felt slippery, I called Darryl, who helped to talk me past this.

Maintaining part-time relationships with both Lionel and Felipe, I had little interest in a full-time boyfriend. Sex was now shared for its own sake, rather than being used as a drug to cover up a sense of inadequacy. Acquiring more self-confidence on this bumpy road of recovery, I experienced increasing periods of serenity.

One spring weekend when I was camping by myself in the desert, I took along a CD of Native American flute music by Carlos Nakai to help me get to sleep. Its soothing sounds led me into a dream where I saw myself walking on land that I owned. Remarkably, upon awaking I noticed that I'd parked under a realty sign with land for sale. *What an amazing coincidence*, I thought, *or was it?*

After obtaining some information about the parcel, it was too large and its price was too high. So I asked the realtor, "Do you have anything smaller and less expensive?"

The man replied, "If you go a little farther out in the desert, you'll find some properties in your price range. Look them up on our website. I'm sure you'll find something there that could meet your needs."

On my next trip, I discovered some medium-sized lots with nice views and a fair amount of space around them. I started mulling over which one might be right for me. At the end of summer in 2001, while I was searching for property on September 11th, I heard on my car radio that the Twin Towers in Lower Manhattan had been attacked. The buildings were in imminent danger of collapse, the work of terrorists. The Pentagon in Washington D.C. was also hit.

I went to a cafe where a TV set was tuned to CNN. I witnessed people trapped and dying in the resulting inferno and collapse. It was horrible to see all the death and destruction. I thought of my AIDS buddies, many who in their own ways had tried to escape an oncoming disaster. This tragedy motivated me to release years of accumulated grief. I buried my face in my hands and let the tears roll. Flooded with survivor's guilt, I wondered *Why am I still alive and not them?*

This experience was a turning point. The fact that I survived this long became a call to return what others had given to me. In order to do this effectively, I needed to put a complete stop to my self-destructive habits and stay true to my Higher Being.

A few months after 9/11, I resumed my search for land. I found an appealing site, a place where I might eventually want to retire. I was astonished to be even thinking about retirement. It had been fifteen years since I was diagnosed with HIV. The only investments people were making then were for cemetery plots. The offer I put on the parcel was accepted. How many of my friends had fantasized about doing this? Being a landowner made me feel connected to the earth.

The Longhouse & The Potlatch

At a healing circle when the practitioners were discussing techniques, I mentioned my sweat lodge and Bear Dance experiences. A healer shared,

"Many Native Americans are into powerful stuff. When I visited a tribe in British Columbia, I couldn't believe how advanced their energy fields were. You could learn some valuable lessons from them."

This suggestion resonated in my imagination. A few months later I booked a flight north, rented a car, and packed some camping gear. On the night of the summer solstice, I settled in a campsite north of Seattle. The next day, I boarded a ferry to Vancouver Island and drove to an Indian Cultural Centre run by a tribe of salmon hunters and thunderbird worshipers. There I enjoyed watching the native artisans demonstrate the craft of making totem poles and a variety of masks.

As fascinating as this was, I wanted to see an authentic village. Asking one of the craftspeople about this, I received an unexpected reply. "You won't find any near here because most of us have blended into the general population. But if you drive to the northern tip of our island, you'll find the community you're looking for."

I was about to inquire how to get there when the man was called away. I returned to my vehicle and pulled out a map. An Indian reservation, or reserve as it was called, was located several hundred miles north. This would consume all of the time I'd allocated for my trip. Remembering how my junket to Colorado opened up unanticipated doors, I decided to change my plans and go.

After a long day's drive, I reached this northern region. At midnight twilight, I found a campground and settled in for a short night. The next day, I took a ferry to where a small museum decorated in the style of a longhouse displayed many artifacts. Brightly colored wooden statues filled the room along with stuffed birds, fish, and other wildlife.

I was fascinated by the tribe's potlatch tradition and the Christian missionaries' attempts to abolish it. It was common for families to hold parties where they gave away many of their possessions. This redistribution of wealth retained all sacred objects within the village. When well-meaning government officials, in an effort to preserve these artifacts, took them away to museums, the spiritual force they contained was broken. The villagers suffered decades of poverty and decay. Some concerned Canadians put an end to this practice. It was only when these possessions were returned that the tribe came back to life again.

Touched by this story, I wandered around the reserve lost in thought. Coming upon a large building that looked like a gymnasium, I entered its only open door and saw bleachers on both sides of the room with many large statues and murals in the front. Two women were busy cleaning. One of them called out, "You have to leave. We're going to lunch and no visitors are allowed here unsupervised."

I replied, "Is there any way I can return later?"

"We'll be back in an hour and you can look around while we finish setting up for tonight's ceremony. But leave your camera outside. No photographs can be taken here without the chief's permission."

When I returned, the women were so busy cleaning they didn't see me come in. The place was truly mystical. Two huge thick totem poles were flanked by massive artwork portraying eagles, thunderbirds, sharks, whales, frogs, wolves, bears, and a two-headed sea serpent. In the center was a large bark-covered chair, perhaps a throne. There was enough seating in the bleachers for several hundred people.

The women raked the earthen floor in a pattern similar to what tribes trace around a fire pit next to a sweat lodge. This physical presence was made even more striking by a powerful energy field. I felt a surge. Every cell in my body underwent a sense of renewal. I sensed that this was the real longhouse, not the tourist replica I'd visited originally. When the women finished, they noticed me. Again, I had to exit.

Returning to my car, I was overwhelmed by what I'd seen. The energy in the room lived up to what my fellow Reiki worker had promised. Recalling the shaman ritual in the South Pacific, I wanted to return later that night and sneak in on the tribal ceremony, but I had to drive back to Seattle to make my flight home.

Suddenly, I had an epiphany. So many different practices summoned a similar divine source, be it Japanese Reiki, South Pacific shamanism, Lakota sweat lodges, bear dances, or meditation mantras. On the journey home, I carried the images I'd observed in the longhouse with me. When I reflected on the potlatch, I realized that the natives had shown me something valuable. Why hold on to one's possessions with such a tight fist? My parents' parsimony had not brought them very much happiness. Neither had Aunt Ellen's or Judy's affluence.

Hadn't the universe always somehow managed to take care of me? Managing what I possessed like Ebenezer Scrooge only served to squeeze the life out of whatever I had. It was time for me to lighten up and not take myself, my work, my health, economic status, or anything else, even my addictions, so seriously.

I'd lost my parents and relatives, outgrown teachers, lovers, and friends, and survived it. Choosing neither high road nor low road, somewhere in the middle I'd done all right. Brian and Baba Ram Dass said to *Be Here Now*. I was finally beginning to understand.

New Home With A New Horizon

A few days after I returned home, I drove out to visit my newly purchased piece of the desert. Sitting on a blanket alongside my vehicle, I contemplated building a new home on this new horizon. While staring at the mountains in the distance, I went over my options. Drawing on my home equity I could afford to construct a modest house, somewhat smaller than my current residence.

I sketched several designs for this new homestead. At a 12-step group in the area, I met a general contractor named Jesse whom I liked and trusted. After reviewing what I had in mind, this knowledgeable builder gave me an estimate and time frame. He recommended keeping the project simple, emphasizing quality over quantity. Recalling the cheap monstrosity that my family once had bought in the suburbs, I saw the wisdom in his advice.

It was in the middle of George W. Bush's second term. Another friend of mine, a financial planner, warned me that the economy was poised to take a dive. If I wanted to build, it would be wise to get started sooner rather than later. Real estate prices had already started falling. If this trend continued, I might even have to sell my L.A. home in order to afford to live in the new place. So I borrowed against my equity and told Jesse to begin construction.

We assembled a crew, a pad was cleared, the foundation poured, and the structure was framed. Everything cost more than planned and the process took longer than expected. Spring turned into fall, and fall into winter. Bad weather caused delays, not to mention the frustrations of getting various permits and inspections. As I'd learned to do in other areas of my life, I stayed the course. A year after the initial groundbreaking, the house was ready for me to move in.

Since the new home had less room than the one in L.A., the spirit of the potlatch led me to give away many of my belongings. This was a liberating experience. After all the work I endured building and moving, I was eager to take a well-deserved breather. But this feeling of relief was short-lived. When I invited my financial friend to the new residence, he advised, "Sell your old house right away if you want to get your money out of it. The economy is getting even worse."

I didn't want to hear this. "But I'm so exhausted."

"You could lose your investment. Real estate prices are plunging."

Late that spring, I placed my house on the market. After two price reductions, I finally found a buyer. Escrow closed a few days before Lehman Brothers folded as the nation headed into The Great Recession.

Same-Sex Marriage Rumblings

Soon after I moved into my new place, Obama was elected President. When I went to cast my vote, I discovered that I was one of the few Democrats in this Republican district, another case of being the odd man out. I didn't let that get in the way of making new friends in the area. Meanwhile, I'd kept tabs with my L.A. social group. I invited a few of them to visit me in the desert. That Christmas, we celebrated chestnuts roasting on an open fire with cactus and mistletoe.

Settling into my custom-built environs, I realized that I was a lucky man. I loved my new surroundings and felt blessed to have made so many improvements in my life. The only thing missing was someone special to share it with. As often as I invited Lionel and Felipe over to visit me (separately, of course), I could not persuade either one to share more than an occasional overnight in my modest castle. Lionel was intimacy adverse. Felipe had family concerns to consider, and he was not really "out" with his activities.

Picking up a copy of a local rag, I perused the personal ads. Gay people were few and far between out in these hinterlands and most were already coupled. Internet inquiries requested disease-free partners, which put me out of the picture. The few times I ventured out to meet someone new went nowhere. It seemed I was better off alternating my part-timers than putting my hat in the ring again.

A rapidly growing issue in the gay community in the early twenty-first century was same-sex marriage. Some states had passed laws making it legal while others reacted to this by legislating bans against the practice. It was becoming a contentious civil rights struggle that was gathering steam. To me, the rights and privileges of civil unions seemed enough. But a few of my friends who were actively working to stop California's Proposition 8 to outlaw gay marriages convinced me to participate in some rallies and phone banks. There I befriended two men whose wedding vows were in danger of becoming annulled by this initiative.

Like many of my fellow activists, I was disappointed when the initiative passed. However, everyone knew that this fight was far from over. Even without a strong desire to find myself a husband, I was buoyed by the knowledge that tying the knot legally was becoming a potential choice for us. What a change in concerns from merely the right to assemble in a bar or march in a parade on a city street. Gay Liberation had come a long way since Richard Pryor had mooned the crowd at the Hollywood Bowl. And with my health still in decent shape, who knew what the future would hold for me. My self-confidence had risen to the point I could even envision myself as marriage material.

Sad Passings & A Tearful Housewarming

I was in the middle of planning a large housewarming celebration when I received dose after dose of sad news. Porter's wife Nancy was diagnosed with advanced cancer and only had a few weeks to live. Martha was hospitalized after a bad fall in her apartment. Then Jim unexplainably lost over thirty pounds and seemed to be seriously ill. Putting my plans on hold, I traveled to L.A. to see them.

Nancy passed much sooner than the doctors had predicted. Having been an AIDS nurse, she knew what wasting away was all about and did not want to prolong her or anybody else's agony. I went to the reception after her funeral and met many of the couple's family members. When it came to eulogies, I was silent, respectfully blessing the room with as much healing energy as I could.

Martha was in a hospital room connected to oxygen tubes because she had trouble breathing. When I arrived at her bedside, Beverly had just left after spending several hours comforting her friend. Seeing Martha in such a weakened state, I asked through my tears, "How are you feeling, girlfriend?"

She replied, "It's so nice of you to visit me. You know the saying 'It only hurts when I laugh?' Please don't crack too many jokes."

"I'm so sorry."

"Don't worry, I've got enough drugs in me right now, I don't feel much pain. I brought this on myself. You and everyone else said I should have gone to OA or Weight Watchers."

"I won't 'should' on you like that anymore."

"Thanks." She smiled at me, and then changed the subject. "You know this hospital food is such crap. When I get outta this place I'm gonna make up for this, even if it's my last supper."

"I know you. Anything worth eating is better with gravy on it."

"You got that right. You can inscribe it on my tombstone, darlin'."

"Hey, you're going to get better. When you get out, me and Bev will take you to a Chinese buffet. That's a little bit healthier."

"Sam, you're such a sweet man."

Martha never made it out of the hospital. Her big heart gave out a few nights later. Beverly and I had yet another funeral and reception to attend a week later.

Jim did not fare any better. In our last conversation, I asked him, "What's wrong? Jonathan told me you've been losing a lot of weight."

"I'm not sure. My systems are starting to break down."

"So what does your doctor say?"

"I don't trust Western medicine."

"But at least get your symptoms diagnosed. You can always decide how to treat them afterwards, either with meds or holistically. That's how I handled my disease."

"I'll get around to it." Deflecting this, Jim commented, "You asked me what trees you could plant on your property. How about a desert olive? They don't bear fruit, but they are very attractive and need little care in a dry area like yours."

I liked this. "I'll plant one near my patio and name it Jim."

"Don't be silly. I don't want a tree named after me."

"Too bad, guy. It's a done deal."

A few days later, I got a call from Jonathan saying that I needed to come to L.A. immediately. Jim had been diagnosed with the type of pneumonia that AIDS patients often come down with and was in grave condition. I couldn't make sense of this because not long after we broke up Jim had tested HIV negative. What he did later, I knew little about.

Several close friends were in the hospital waiting room when a code blue call came over the loudspeaker. That night Jim passed, not from lung failure as expected, but like Martha, from a heart condition. In his case, nobody had any clue about this beforehand.

Instead of the housewarming, I hosted a memorial ceremony on my property for these three departed friends. Over a dozen of my extended family members made the trek out to the desert for the wake. Jonathan carried a vase with him that contained Jim's ashes, depositing some into the soil next to the olive tree that I'd planted in his honor. A desert Aleppo pine tree was planted in memoriam for Nancy and a palo verde tree was dedicated to Martha.

I had no need to give any eulogies. The whole day had been one. The group's shared meal afterwards was not full of outrageous laughter like ones in the past, but the tears shed and warm embraces given that day were every bit as special.

Chapter 11
PASSING THE TORCH

AAA Arrives

At this point in my recollections, I was interrupted again. It was a man from Triple A calling to say he'd be there in a few minutes. I took this time to orient myself. Gratefully, I got out of my truck, gave the driver my membership card, and soon the tire was changed.

I called Darryl right away. "I'm finally good to go."

"I'm so glad to hear this. How far away are you?"

"I don't know, about twenty minutes."

"Looks like you'll just make it. Drive safely."

After I hung up, I drove the rest of the way inspired with what I'd revisited. I couldn't wait to share some of these insights.

The Newcomer

I walked into the meeting where a seat near the front was reserved for me. The group was in the middle of going around the room reciting portions of the program book. Once this was completed, I was going to be introduced to the crowd of about thirty members.

Before my name could be announced, a bedraggled, dark-haired man in his late forties nervously entered. The guy looked like he hadn't slept much in a couple of days and seemed to be at the end of his rope. He hesitantly took a seat in the back of the room, hunched over a table, put his head in his hands, and started sobbing.

The meeting leader, sensing that this arrival was a newcomer, interrupted the proceedings and asked, "Is this your first time at GA?" The troubled fellow shyly nodded yes. A customary chorus of "welcomes" followed. The leader gave me an envelope of literature and meeting schedules to hand the visitor. The mixed emotions of gratitude and fear on the man's face reminded me of how upset and confused I'd been at my initial meeting.

The leader addressed the newcomer, "We're glad to see you. Would you like to introduce yourself to the group?

He responded, "My name is Julian D. I'm a recovering alcoholic and drug addict, and I think I'm a compulsive gambler as well."

The room reverberated with "Hi, Julian."

The leader continued, "Julian, to help you determine if you are in the right place, I'm going to ask you a list of questions from one of the booklets on the table in front of you on the table. Open up to page 167. A simple 'yes' or 'no' will do." After Julian answered affirmatively to almost every question, the leader added, "You answered yes to sixteen out of twenty questions that the program describes as characteristics of a compulsive gambler."

Julian muttered, "I was afraid of that."

"We encourage you to keep your copy and read through the entire book later. For now, we invite you to share what brought you here."

After gathering his thoughts, Julian spoke. "I've suspected for a while that I have a gambling problem, but I'm not ready to say much about it yet. Though I've experienced sobriety in other programs, this gambling thing is more powerful than my other addictions. I've run out of money. My partner is about to leave me. I could lose my home and may even have to live out in the street. I really need some help."

The leader reassured him, "We've all been in your shoes. We'll support you the best we can. Hope and recovery is here if you seek it. Now, let's continue. Next on our agenda is our featured speaker, Sam F."

Coming Full Circle

So taken with Julian's share, I forgot my nervousness as I walked up to the front. In the past, I might have been upset at having being upstaged by all this drama, but I took the man's grim reminder of my darker days to heighten the emotion of my presentation.

I began, "I am Sam F., compulsive gambler."

"Hi, Sam," they roared back.

"I haven't placed a bet in eight years and ten days." Applause resonated through the room.

"Julian, I also welcome you to our group. I remember my first meeting. Your words remind me how hopeless my life seemed when I entered the program. I hope you hear something that inspires you to want to come back and work on your recovery with us.

"Thank you for giving me the opportunity to speak today. I want to apologize for being late. Despite leaving early, I had car trouble and had to wait for assistance. As you can see, I barely made it. Since we're a little short on time, I'll make this presentation briefer than I intended.

"Like many of us, I grew up in a dysfunctional family. With poor role models, though I had a good education and work skills, I couldn't hold onto money, jobs, or relationships, always finding ways to sabotage any success or happiness that came into my path. I used compulsive sex, drugs, and gambling to cover up feelings of inferiority and run away from myself. About the only thing I didn't abuse was alcohol, but you gotta leave something for later, right?"

There were a few giggles in the room.

"Seriously, after hitting several bottoms, I made my way through a series of 12-step programs. While achieving progress in one area, I'd find somewhere else to act out. In desperation, I sought my sponsor Darryl, who helped me climb out of the depths I'd fallen into. With his encouragement, I've worked the steps of recovery, gradually turning my life over to my Higher Power. I still have my challenges. Even today when my car broke down, I had thoughts of taking out my frustration in a casino instead of coming here. But I know better than to make a bad thing worse. I'm still a work in progress, but my worst days today are better than my best days when I was using."

I continued speaking for a few more minutes, referring to several of the program's helpful slogans and sage words of advice that assisted me in turning my life around. After receiving a stirring ovation, I expressed my gratitude to the group. Before closing the meeting, everyone stood up, held hands, and repeated, "God grant me the serenity to accept the things I cannot change, the courage to change the things I can, and the wisdom to know the difference."

Outside the meeting, I went over to the newcomer and offered my support, handing him my phone number. Julian looked back with a sense of relief and said that he'd be in touch.

On the drive home, I reflected on how much my life had changed. The affectionate hugs I received from group members accompanied me back to my residence. Before I arrived, I stopped at a nursery and bought another tree to add to the grove I'd already planted on my property. I was looking forward to watching them all grow, finally able to enjoy reaping what I'd sowed in my long, and now fruitful, life.

A few days later, Julian called me. We got together at a local Starbuck's. With all the lessons I'd learned, we had much to share. This began a mutually beneficial, sponsor-sponsee relationship. I'd come full circle. Now it was my turn to pass on the torch.

Not long after this, Beverly drove out to my house for a visit. It had been over two years since the service for our departed friends. I revealed plans to dedicate more trees to others as they passed on as well, a veritable memorial grove.

Beverly joked, "And where is my tree, dear?'

"I'm not ready to say goodbye to anyone as special as you. But here's one I dedicated to my folks and one I planted in honor of Leo."

"I loved Leo. He was the one who brought us together. You and I have been friends for over 25 years now, longer than many marriages."

"That's right."

I went inside to get a bottle of wine and two glasses to commemorate our friendship. We clinked our glasses and toasted.

"To us."

"To us."

Beverly became introspective. "Sam, you've dedicated trees to so many people. Which one is your tree?"

"They're all my trees, each one of them. The way I see it, every tree rooted in Planet Earth is mine and I am theirs."

After Beverly left, I looked out on the horizon and observed an eagle soaring above. I called Reyna to accompany me on a walk in my beloved desert. Feeling the warm wind blowing on my face, I gazed serenely at the silhouettes of the nearby mountains. Since I'd revisited my life that day when my car broke down on the highway, I'd been living with an increasing sense of acceptance. Every good, bad, ugly, and stunningly beautiful moment of my life, seasoned with a sea of salty tears and the sweet laughter-filled times with my many friends and lovers, added up to such an incredible adventure.

In the distance, I saw the beaming face of my mentor, Mrs. B. She crowed enthusiastically, "I'm proud of you, Sam. You took the longer road." I immediately felt every cell in my body fill with joy.

Going back to my living room, I mentally updated the message in the photo above my fireplace mantle *[SEX - Cool! DRUGS - Used To Be Cool! ROCK 'N ROLL - Still Cool! FREEDOM - Even Better!]*. Whether the personal waters of Jordan I'd crossed were dry washes, rippling streams, raging rivers, or walks on the beach or in the desert with my Higher Power, I embraced them all. With shamanic chants and sweat lodge drums reverberating within me, I heeded the words of Baba Ram Dass and the late Dr. Martin Luther King, "Free at last, one blissful day at a time."

ABOUT THE AUTHOR

[DAVID] CAT COHEN is an active author member of the **Palm Springs Writers Guild**. Among his eight self-published books on food, travel, home construction, and music is the gourmet cookbook **Chicken Soups From Around The World**, the adventurous off-the-beaten-track **Road Stories Southwest** and **Road Poems U.S.A.,** the narrative of how he designed and built his home in **My Desert Blog Cabin**, and the instructional **Writing And Marketing Songs For An Original Act.**

Cat has been a longtime **ASCAP** songwriter with pop, R&B, jazz and blues songs cut by recording artists Cheryl Lynn, Syreeta, Freddie Hubbard, and Bo Diddley. He's also has had his work featured in the **HBO** movie **The Rat Pack** and the **Universal** feature film **Undercover Brother**. He's written several musicals including the anti-drug **The Not So Great Escape**, commissioned by **Opera Pacific** and performed in schools throughout Southern California. An album of his tunes **Songs Of Survival and Sweet Surrender** is available at CD Baby.

Currently, Cat performs as a pop music therapist in hospitals, senior homes, and rehab centers, a **One-Man-Orchestra** on his synthesizer helping to bring healing through American and International songs as well as some of his own. He lives in the high desert between Palm Springs and Joshua Tree, CA.